# Fountain of Dreams

# Fountain of Dreams

## Josie Litton

**WHEELER**
CHIVERS

This Large Print book is published by Wheeler Publishing,
Waterville, Maine USA and by BBC Audiobooks, Ltd,
Bath, England.

Published in 2003 in the U.S. by arrangement with
Bantam Books, an imprint of the Bantam Dell Publishing Group, a
division of Random House, Inc.

Published in 2003 in the U.K. by arrangement with the author.

U.S.  Hardcover 1-58724-484-5   (Romance)
U.K.  Hardcover 0-7540-7734-9   (Chivers Large Print)

The text of this Large Print edition is unabridged.
Other aspects of the book may vary from the original edition.

Set in 16 pt. Plantin by Myrna S. Raven.

Printed in the United States on permanent paper.

**British Library Cataloguing-in-Publication Data available**

**Library of Congress Cataloging-in-Publication Data**

Litton, Josie.
    Fountain of dreams / Josie Litton.
      p. cm.
    ISBN 1-58724-484-5 (lg. print : hc : alk. paper)
    1. Sabotage — Fiction.   2. Large type books.   I. Title.
PS3612.I885F68 2003
   813'.6—dc21                            2003053495

*For my family with
thanks for love, patience, and just
the right amount of teasing.*

*And for my readers, many
of whom have become friends.
Thank you all for your support
and encouragement.*

# Chapter One

*London, Spring 1837*

Lights shining in the high windows of the mansion's ground floor appeared and disappeared among the leafy branches of trees that swayed in the steady breeze off the river. The hour was shortly before midnight. In the walled park surrounding the house, an owl swept soundlessly from its perch. Wings barely moving, it soared over the open ground before descending rapidly to pluck a hapless mouse.

The man waiting in the dark shadows of the bushes saw the catch and smiled faintly. He, too, would hunt soon. Several hours before, he had gotten close enough to the house to confirm that the family was at dinner. He watched them briefly through one of the windows — Prince Alexandros; his wife, Princess Joanna; their nephew, Prince Andreas; and their daughter, Princess Amelia, were all relaxed and in good humor. They had no inkling that their privileged world was about to be shattered.

He had withdrawn to wait and now stirred a little, flexing muscles that would otherwise cramp as he remained concealed behind the thick bushes just inside the high stone walls. The night was cool and damp, but he scarcely noticed. He had known far worse.

He was a tall man, lean and very fit. For this night's work, he was dressed in the garb of a London office worker, a respectable man who earned his portion in a counting house, perhaps, or as a solicitor's secretary. A man neither poor enough nor rich enough to attract attention. His dark trousers and jacket, of plain but sturdy wool, made him all but invisible in the shadows. He had turned up the jacket collar for further concealment and pulled the brim of his felt hat down close to eyes that some had likened to the color of steel.

He was without weapons, although, to be fair, he would still have the advantage against most armed opponents. If the guards found him, he wanted to appear a harmless drunk who had wandered where he should not. For that purpose, he had rubbed dirt on the jacket and trousers such as would result from an inebriated climb over a stone wall, and he carried a half-empty bottle of whiskey in the pocket of the jacket.

By the look of it, the ruse would not be necessary. While it might be true that there was no residence better guarded in all of London, the patrols were at regular intervals, therefore predictable. That was expected. The security around the manor was intended to insulate its inhabitants from the waves of popular unrest that roared through London periodically, not from a lone man intent on gaining access.

Gray eyes flickered in the darkness. He waited, patient and watchful. The lights were extinguished on the ground floor as other lights appeared on the floor above. The family retired early by the standards of society. They preferred one another's company to the customary round of balls, routs, masquerades, assemblies, and the like. According to his information, they had no social commitments on this night. That suited his purposes perfectly.

The patrol was good; he scarcely heard it coming even though he was expecting it. The three men passed within a dozen feet of him. They did not speak and their steps were almost entirely silent. They were, he knew, part of the military force that was among the most feared in all the world. The warriors of Akora, the Fortress Kingdom beyond the Pillars of Hercules, had maintained that mysterious land's freedom and sovereignty for centuries. Ancient, legendary, and only recently beginning to emerge into the modern world, Akora fascinated many, but not him. He cared nothing for the place and hoped most sincerely to have nothing to do with it.

The patrol passed by him. He took a breath, cleared his mind, and ran across the open space of lawn. In little more than a heartbeat, he reached the bushes beneath the ground-floor windows. Crouching there, he paused and listened intently.

No sound from the house or the surrounding

grounds suggested that his presence had been detected. Cautiously, he stood and looked into the now dark dining room. The servants had finished clearing the table and would be going to their own rest soon. Only the guards on patrol and on duty in the hall would be awake.

He moved again, around a corner to the back of the house, and looked up. Directly above him were the windows of what he had already confirmed was Princess Amelia's bedroom.

The patrol was returning. He pressed against the wall of the house, blending into the contours of stone and shadow, waiting.

When the patrol was gone, he took a length of black cloth from an inside pocket of his jacket, put it over his face, and tied it at the back of his head. Only his eyes remained visible.

He grasped the stones an arm's reach above him, his fingers digging into the mortar between them, and hoisted himself up smoothly and easily. His feet found the narrow indentation that was just deep enough for him to balance on. Steadied, he reached up again. Swiftly, silently he climbed the wall.

There was a stone balcony outside the princess's windows. He swung onto it, dropped, and listened again for any sound that would warn he was detected. When none came, he slowly eased the French doors open.

The room was dark, but he could make out the placement of the furniture, particularly the bed hung with gauzy curtains.

His quarry lay on her side. He could not make out her features, but he knew well enough what she looked like, having observed her for several days as she went about London. She was not precisely beautiful, but her face had a certain unique appeal and, so far as he had seen, there was nothing lacking in her figure. He had also noticed her to be an exuberant woman, confident and outgoing, given to frequent smiles and ready laughter. That seemed at odds with her reputation, namely that she was cold and proud, an unfeeling breaker of hearts, a spinster at twenty-five despite her family's wealth and power.

If the lady's unmarried state troubled her, there was no sign of it. Lost in sleep, she breathed slowly and deeply. For just an instant, he felt . . . not doubt precisely, never that. Just a twinge of regret that he hadn't been able to come up with a different plan.

But he wasn't a man to linger over his shortcomings. In a single movement, he brushed aside the curtains and seized hold of her. She woke instantly with a gasp that was smothered by the covers in which he quickly rolled her. Although she struggled fiercely, within seconds he had the gag in her mouth and a hood secured over her head.

Far from being cowed, her efforts to escape redoubled. She was surprisingly strong. No match for his strength, of course, but still she proved more than a handful.

He might have cautioned her to stop, but he could not risk her recognizing his voice. Instead, he tightened his grip warningly. But not, it seemed, quite enough. To his astonishment, his squirming, struggling captive got an arm loose and promptly landed a solid punch to his jaw.

Only a lifetime of self-discipline stopped him from cursing out loud. He wrapped her ever more tightly in the covers and moved quickly to the door.

The inside of the house was not patrolled. That, too, he had confirmed during his surveillance. The guards were stationed only in the central hall.

He avoided them by using the back stairs frequented by the servants. The going was difficult because the squirming bundle in his arms refused to desist. Trussed as securely as a Christmas goose, the princess continued to struggle. It was all he could do to keep hold of her without actually causing her harm.

He reached the ground-floor landing and paused. She could not escape him, of that he had no doubt. But neither did he underestimate his potential peril. If she managed to get out more than a muffled cry . . .

The Akorans would take him prisoner, but he doubted very much that they would turn him over to the British authorities. Everything he knew about them suggested they would handle the matter themselves in their own way, presuming they didn't just kill him outright.

She'd damn well better be worth all the trouble.

He opened the door and stepped outside. If his calculations were correct, he had not quite five minutes before the patrol passed again. Enough time to cross the lawn, get through the trees, and scale the wall.

Or it would be if Shadow was on post.

He was, as evidenced by the large shape concealed in the foliage of the upper branches of the trees, and by the rope tangling down the near side of the wall. With an inner sigh of relief, he dumped his unwilling burden into the sling at the end of the rope, secured her firmly, and tugged to signal Shadow. Immediately, the sling began to rise. He watched long enough to confirm that his captive was still struggling fiercely, before climbing the wall himself. Settled beside Shadow, who gave him a quick nod, he helped hoist the sling.

Scant seconds before the patrol was due to return, it was done. With his quarry slung over his shoulder and Shadow following close behind, he ran down the road and around a corner to a waiting carriage.

The wheels were turning even before the door was closed.

What in bloody hell? this couldn't be happening to her! She absolutely could not have

13

been taken from her well-protected home in the dead of night, snatched by some lout with hard hands, strong arms, and apparently no desire to live much longer.

Not a word, not a sound out of him, not even when she landed a punch that at the very least should have prompted a curse. And that, more than anything, worried her.

Either a mute had kidnapped her or her captor was a man of uncommon self-control who knew exactly what he was doing.

Heart hammering, Amelia struggled against her own terror. At all cost, she had to keep her mind clear. Better to concentrate on anger so great it pushed out fear. There were two men . . . she thought. There might be more, but there had to be at least two to have gotten her over the wall. Neither had spoken, and the hood drawn over her head assured she could see nothing.

What was their plan? Ransom? Something worse? Her parents had never mistaken ignorance for innocence. All their children, herself included, had a sensible appreciation of the world, both its glories and its dangers.

But so far, at least, she was unharmed. Even when she struck out at him, he did not retaliate beyond holding her more tightly. What did that mean?

Did it matter? Whoever they were, whatever their intent, they had to be mad. Her father, uncles, brothers, and cousins would never rest until she was both safe and avenged. If she could speak, she could try to convince him to stop now, before it was too late for him and anyone else involved, but the gag was tight around her mouth. She could breathe around it well enough, but could make only the most muffled sounds.

The hood over her head shut out all light, while the covers kept her tightly trussed. She could not see, speak, or move. So completely was she cut off from the world, that she could smell only the fabric close around her head and nothing else. But she could hear and feel.

The clatter of the horses' hooves rang sharply, telling her they were moving over cobblestone streets like those near her home. But in which direction? To the south lay the river and the docks. Did he intend to take a ship, to spirit her far away? Her dread took a further leap forward but she refused to give into it. If ransom was his goal, as she had to hope, it was unlikely he would remove her very far from London.

If not a ship, perhaps they were heading for one of the coaching roads that ran in all directions from the capital. The roads were much improved of late. Given good horses, great distances could be covered more quickly than ever before.

There was even the new railroad, in operation only a little more than a year, connecting London to Greenwich, but surely he would not use that. The railroad continued to attract great attention, and besides, it did not run at night.

Whatever his intent, each passing moment took her further from the hope of rescue.

For an appalling instant, tears threatened. She choked them back, but the tight, desperate sound penetrated the gag. She felt her captor stiffen, and on a sudden urge, coughed again.

His hand settled on the blankets near her face. Or at least she thought it did. It was damnably hard to tell.

What if she truly was choking? Why would he care unless he had some concern about keeping her alive? If he did, she might be able to use it to her advantage.

Gag be damned, she filled her lungs and summoned a desperate, hacking cough strong enough to convince anyone that she was in danger of expiring.

The blankets were loosened! She still couldn't see anything, but she could feel the cool night air. Another deep, prolonged cough set her throat to aching, but it didn't matter. She could move her arms and legs. Never mind that punch, he needed a good, swift kick.

She couldn't see to aim, but she hit some portion of him all the same. His chest . . . his thigh . . . whatever it was, it felt like steel. She almost feared that she had broken a toe, but it didn't matter. His hold on her loosened just enough. Her hand found the latch on the carriage door. She had it turned and the door opened, a rush of air heralding her success. In another moment, she would be out of the carriage. The fall would hurt, but anything was better than captivity. Even so, blinded by the hood, she hesitated the merest fraction of an instant.

Disbelief surged through him but did not dull the lightning-fast reflexes that had kept him alive through times far darker than these.

He had planned so carefully, thought out every step, considered every contingency. Or so he had believed. But he hadn't counted on a woman who didn't have the sense to know when she was bested.

Heedless for the moment of any consideration except preventing her escape, he gripped her firmly. Though she struggled still, he wound the blanket so tightly around her that finally she could not move at all. Any further sounds she made were too muffled for him to hear, which suited him perfectly.

They rode on through the night. Amelia did not try again to escape, but she remained stiff and unyielding against him. Another woman, caught in so desperate a situation, might have lapsed into exhausted sleep, but Amelia did not. Although he could not see her face, he knew by the feel of her in his arms that she remained entirely conscious. No doubt she was also deeply apprehensive. As there was no possibility of offering her any reassurance, he did not try. But he was relieved when, several hours outside of London, they at last reached their destination.

As Shadow took the carriage and horses around to the stables, he carried his unwilling guest into the small, ivy-draped house and through to a back bedroom. He stepped into the room, set her down on the far side of the bed, and withdrew quickly. As he was about to close the door, he looked back at her. The blanket had fallen away, leaving her in her sleep shift. The finely woven linen trimmed with lace did little to conceal her body. A body that was, he observed, at least as good as he had thought.

Her hands were on the hood covering her head. She was just about to snatch it off when he shut the door loudly enough for her to hear the solid *thud* that sealed her off from the world.

A room, not small, not large, lit by oil lamps. A narrow bed with a chest at its foot, a small table beside the bed, a larger table with a basin and ewer, both empty. There were two windows, heavily shuttered, and one door locked from the outside.

She could hardly have expected otherwise. Even so, a tremor ran through Amelia as she confronted the evidence that she truly was imprisoned. Sternly, she reminded herself that no good would come from cowardice. She was a princess of the royal house of Akora, and she

18

would damn well behave like one.

Her fingers tore at the gag, making quick work of it. Even more swiftly, she sought a means of escape. By her best estimate, it had been hours since she was taken. Morning would come soon, and when it did, her family would discover that she was missing. Her throat tightened at the thought of what they would think and, more importantly, fear. If only she could get free quickly, not only for her own sake but also to relieve their minds.

She was seeking a means of doing just that when the sound of a bolt being thrown back stopped her. Aware suddenly of her lack of proper clothing, she seized up the blanket and was winding it around herself when the door opened.

The man who stood in the doorway was immense. She was used to very tall men — her father, brothers, uncles, and male cousins were all six feet tall or better — but even by their standards, this man was a giant. Nor was he lacking in bulk. So broad were his shoulders and chest, that he seemed barely able to fit through the door. His hair and beard were both thick, black, and unkempt. He eyed her from beneath equally bushy black brows and spoke with an Irish lilt.

"I've brought food and water for ye, lass, an' a bit of advice to go with it. Mind your manners, try nothin' foolish an' no harm will come to ye."

Ignoring the warning, she faced him squarely. "You're mad or suicidal, perhaps both. Don't you realize what will happen to you when my family finds me?"

To her astonishment, the Irishman laughed. "They won't be findin' ye, least not till they're told where t'look." He stepped farther into the room, being careful to close the door behind him, and moved toward the table. Catching the direction of her gaze, he sighed. "Don't be thinkin' about gettin' past me, lass. That won't be happenin'. Best t'realize that ye're goin' to be here for awhile an' not be fussin' yerself about it."

"You can't seriously believe that I will just accept this?"

He shrugged massive shoulders, set down the tray he carried, and returned to the door. Amelia could not help but notice that he moved gracefully for a man of his size. No doubt he was correct, she couldn't have gotten past him. Nor was she inclined to try. There might well be other people in the house — the second man on the wall, for instance, and perhaps more — ready to respond if the Irish giant called an alarm. When she escaped — and she had to believe that she would — it would be without anyone knowing until she was much too far away for them to do anything about it.

"Whether ye accept it or not, lass, ye might as well get some sleep." He glanced around at the room. "I know this isn't what yer used to.

Best hope yer family pays up soon."

"You're holding me for ransom?" The small spurt of relief she felt faded quickly. He had allowed her to see his face. Why would he do that if he truly meant to release her when her family paid?

"Money makes the world go round, lass." He opened the door, stepped into what looked like a narrow corridor, and shut the door firmly behind him. She heard the bolt slide back into place.

Her shoulders almost slumped but she wouldn't let them. For the moment, at least, she was safe. However many more moments like that there might be, she intended to make good use of them.

But how?

The gray-eyed man grinned when the door he was watching bulged slightly. From the other side, he heard a muffled curse. The lady was more than he had expected, much more, but she was now snugly tucked away. For the first time in weeks, he allowed himself to relax, if only a little.

Soundlessly, he went down the corridor. Shadow followed him.

"That's one hell of a princess," Shadow said when they reached the parlor. His words held no hint of the Irish accent he had affected moments before. Instead, he spoke with the faint remnants of what had been a Kentucky twang before time and circumstance took both men far from that place.

"She is that." Because he trusted Shadow as he trusted no other, he added, "Put up more of a fight than I thought she would."

"Did she?" Shadow pulled off the heavy black wig and beard he had been wearing, and tossed them aside with evident relief. "Well, she's here now and that's what counts. How long do you figure it'll be before she gets that shutter off?"

"Morning, maybe? You drugged the food?"

Shadow nodded. "Just as you said. She ought to be dog-tired anyway."

"Once she wakes up, she's got to find her own way out. I tried not to be obvious."

"We'll see, then. What do you say to a drink?"

"Sounds good."

He was stretched out in front of the parlor fire, a welcome glass of bourbon in his hand, when the first drops of rain splashed against the windowpanes. He frowned; he had not calculated on the rain. Not that it was likely to matter. He doubted the purloined princess would stir before morning, and perhaps not until even later.

And then? . . . They would just have to see. So much rested on whether she behaved as he anticipated. If she did not . . .

He would have to start over. It would be unfortunate and difficult, but he would do so. His mission would be fulfilled, regardless of the cost.

However, it would all be so much easier if the lady played her part.

Her shoulder ached. Amelia rubbed it gingerly as she contemplated the unyielding door. She was wasting her strength. The door would not give. Another way out of the room would have to be found.

She ignored the food and water, being far too well trained to touch either. *In the hands of an enemy, neither drink nor eat. Any sustenance could contain poison or be drugged. Volunteer nothing. Seek every means of escape. Never give up hope.* All this she knew and more, she who had been born to privilege and protection. She knew because her parents understood the dangers of the world in which they lived, a world careening into a future unimaginable even a few decades ago, before the machines were invented that were changing everything, transforming the landscape, driving people from the farms and villages into the cities, clouding the skies — and yet also offering the hope of a better life, at least for some.

She knew also because she was a child of Akora, the Fortress Kingdom that had kept its freedom for more than three thousand years by never letting down its guard for an instant. It was the home she loved, for all that she yearned for some place unnamed, unknown, perhaps no more than a dream.

Turning away from the tray, Amelia gave her attention to the windows. She had examined them briefly and discovered that they were covered with heavy wooden shutters. Now she took a much closer look. One set of shutters seemed as immovable as the door. They must be latched very tightly from the outside. But the other . . .

A spurt of hope lit in her when the second set of shutters gave just slightly in response to her push. True, only a tiny crack opened between them, but it was enough for her to see an opportunity. If only she had some means of prying the shutters apart. Perhaps she could weaken the latch securing them, even break it apart.

She looked quickly around the room for something that might assist her, but nothing came to hand. Determined, she searched the drawers of the tables, looked under the bed, and finally pulled away the bed covers themselves. The bed was of wood, but the mattress she tugged aside was supported by thin metal slats. They were tightly wedged into the frame, but she managed to pull one loose.

Encouraged by her success, Amelia inserted one end of the slat into the crack between the shutters and pushed hard. At first nothing happened, but as she persevered, the crack widened slightly. She stopped and rested for a moment, then began again. Over and over she levered the slat into the crack, managing only to widen the space by an inch or two. Frustration filled her. Her hands ached, but far worse, she felt the first inklings of despair.

That would not do. Angrily brushing aside the dampness that had appeared on her cheeks, she redoubled her efforts. Long, seemingly fruitless minutes passed, but finally, just as she reached deep within herself for the very limits of her strength, there was a sudden, rending sound of metal coming apart.

For a scant moment she thought the slat had snapped, but quickly she saw that was not the case. Instead, the latch on the outside had torn away from the wood. It dangled from one of the now blessedly open shutters.

Cool night air revived her instantly. She dropped the slat, gathered the blanket more securely around her, and scrambled over the windowsill. From there, it was only a short drop to the ground.

The night was pitch-dark. At first she could scarcely see her hand in front of her face. But after a few minutes, the contours of a garden became evident. There was a wall, which made her throat tighten briefly. But almost directly in front of her she saw a gate.

Barefoot, the blanket fluttering behind her, Amelia ran toward it.

# Chapter Two

The road was dark and slippery in the rain, strewn with small stones that hurt her bare feet and added to her discomfort, but which did not dampen her determination.

Her breathing was labored and every muscle in her body hurt, but Amelia slogged on. Each moment was precious, for it took her farther from pursuit.

The carriage that brought her to the house had turned left just before coming to a halt. In the hope that London lay in that direction, she turned right the moment she was beyond the gate.

The full extent of her peril did not escape her. Besides the very real possibility that the Irish giant and whatever cohorts he had might realize she was gone and come after her, the prospects for a solitary woman — horseless, ill-clad, and without a penny — could prove grim indeed. She had to hope that she would find a decent coaching house or private residence where she could secure help.

But scarcely half an hour after making good her escape, she began to wonder if she had any hope of finding assistance. The road appeared to be more of a deserted back route than a major thoroughfare to and from London.

Slowed by darkness, rain, and her own condition, she had managed to cover well less than a mile, every step painfully gained, and had seen no sign of a house, barn, or any other indication of human habitation.

She shivered as the rain soaked through her blanket and shift. The night was not excessively cold, but wet as she was and exhausted, she soon became chilled. Walking would help to keep her warm, she reassured herself, and continued on.

A few more minutes passed in that unhappy state when it occurred to her that she might be headed in the wrong direction after all. Had the sky been clear, she would have been able to take her heading from the stars, for she knew them well. As it was, she had only memory to depend on, and the hope that she had not mistaken the carriage's final turn. The thought plagued her, feeding on her mounting discomfort until she stopped and looked back down the road along which she had come. There was nothing to be seen, not even a distant light from the house where she had been held. Nothing but the damn rain that sapped her strength, and . . .

What was that? Did her weary faculties deceive her or did she hear hoofbeats?

The Irishman! She scrambled quickly toward the side of the road and ducked down into the ditch that ran alongside it. A half-foot of cold, slimy water greeted her. She bit back a cry of dismay and went still as a horse emerged out of the gloom.

A horse and rider — a tall man to be sure, but not, she thought, as tall as the Irishman. An ally of his, then, perhaps searching for her in one direction while the Irishman went in the other?

That might well be, or the man might be an entirely innocent passerby and her only real hope of aid.

Even as her mind debated what to do, her body recognized her intolerable state. However great the risk, she could not let the chance of help go by. Rising up slightly, she kept herself braced to flee into the darkness at the first sign of danger.

"Here! Over here!"

For a heart-stopping moment, she thought the rider had not heard her, but an instant later, he drew rein and turned his mount toward the spot where she stood.

"What? . . ." His voice was deep and underscored by caution. "Who's there?"

"I am! I need help." She stood up straighter, clutching the blanket around her and wishing she could get a better look at him. As it was, he was only a large, dark shape atop a massive horse that pawed the ground and whinnied in its impatience to be gone.

He came closer, controlling his mount with ease. "What's happened to you, girl?" Surprise was evident in his tone, as was the fact that he was an American.

Trusting this was not how a pursuer would behave, she scrambled up onto the road. "I've fled from kidnappers and must return to London with all speed."

"Kidnappers?" He made no effort to mask his disbelief, nor could she truly blame him for doubting her. The claim sounded absurd even to her own ears.

The horse, which she could see now was blacker than the night itself, shied, but Amelia did not flinch. She had never met a horse she feared. "I am Princess Amelia of Akora. My family is in residence in London. If you would be so kind —"

"A princess, no less?" The man laughed softly. The sound shocked her, for it seemed starkly inappropriate to her circumstance. "This wouldn't be one of those Gypsy games I've heard of, to gull a poor traveler?"

"What? This is no game. I need help!"

"So you say." He scanned her from head to foot in a manner so thorough as to be insulting. She had to resist the urge to draw the blanket even more closely around herself, a gesture that would have been useless in any case.

Reluctantly, he said, "I suppose you're in a sorry enough state that I can't leave you here." He extended a hand. "Come on up, then; but I warn you, girl, if this is a trick, you'll regret it."

In all of Amelia's life, no one had ever questioned her honor. To find it doubted now, and by a rude American to boot, was just one more shock in what seemed to be an endless night of them.

When she did not respond immediately to his offer, he reached down, looped his arm around her waist, and lifted her onto the saddle in front of him with as much effort as he might afford thistledown. That was really quite astonishing, for she was no small woman. On the contrary, she stood inches taller than most females, and a lifetime of healthful activity had made her sleekly muscled. None of that seemed to matter to the man who settled her against him with disconcerting ease, not to mention intimacy.

At the touch of his broad chest against her back, Amelia jerked away. She might be soaked, exhausted, and in dire circumstances, but that was no excuse for personal weakness. To her surprise, not to say burgeoning ire, the American chuckled.

"Something wrong, *princess?*"

"Nothing, thank you." Her tone carried all the warmth of a frigid winter storm howling across the northern tundra. "If you would be so kind as to take me to the nearest inn —"

"I thought you said your family is in London."

"It is, but I would not wish to inconvenience you. No doubt I can find assistance elsewhere."

In truth, she had no such confidence, but she wasn't about to let him know that. The sooner she parted from her reluctant rescuer, the better.

"You're soaked through."

"How observant of you. It is, after all, raining."

"Why are you really out here? Running away from an unappreciative husband, perhaps?"

"I am not married, and I've already explained why I'm here."

"Right, you were kidnapped. That's a little hard to believe, *princess.*"

"Stop calling me that."

"But you said you're a princess . . . Annabelle, was it?"

Without thought, she twisted around in the saddle and glared at him. That was a mistake. The movement brought them into still closer contact. Even as her body absorbed the shock of his nearness, she found herself staring into features of such starkly masculine power that she momentarily forgot to breathe.

His face was lean and hard, shorn of any hint of softness. His eyes were a startling light gray set beneath dark brows. The hollows of his cheeks and his firm jaw were shadowed by a night's growth of beard. And his mouth . . .

She absolutely was not going to look at his mouth.

"My name is Amelia," she said as she hastily turned away.

"*Princess* Amelia?"

The weariness she had managed to hold at

bay until now descended on her suddenly. With a sigh, she said, "Look, it doesn't matter if you believe me or not. Just leave me at the nearest inn."

His arm tightened around her. He was silent for a moment before he said, "From Akora, you said? You sound English."

"I am English, at least partly. My mother is English born. My father holds estates here through his English grandfather, but he is also an Akoran prince."

"Hence you are a princess?"

"That's usually how it works."

As they spoke, he held the reins with one hand and with the other pulled off his cloak. Gruffly, he wrapped it around her. When she protested, he said, "Whoever you are, if you get much wetter, you'll likely take ill."

"I am never ill." All the same, she was glad of the cloak. It was warm, dry, and smelled faintly of good cigars. The aroma reminded her of her father and uncles, and that thought, in turn, brought tears perilously close yet again. Abruptly, she sneezed.

The man muttered under his breath. "There's an inn about half an hour from here. We'll stop there."

She was too tired to ask him how he knew that or, indeed, why he was on the road in the midst of a rainy night. It was all she could do to hold herself erect as they cantered on and on, until finally, far down the road, she saw the lights of the inn.

They were almost in front of it when Amelia roused herself enough to realize what he had said. "Wait, we can't both stop here. If we're seen together in such circumstances —"

Without warning, he took hold of her chin between long, hard fingers and turned her head toward him. "Is that what this is about, *princess?* Some scheme to see me hog-tied?" He looked amused. "You've picked the wrong man. I have scant concern for society's sensibilities and less still for your reputation."

Dumbfounded, she stared at him. "You think this is a plot to trap you into marriage?" When he made no effort to deny it, she said, "You have it backward, sir. It is I who wish to preserve myself from unwanted matrimony, not that my family would ever countenance such a thing. Still, there is no point courting scandal." She took hold of his arm laying across her waist and tried to lift it. "I have imposed upon you long enough. Leave me."

The deep rumble of his chest was, she realized, a laugh. "Now," he said, "you sound like a princess."

"I am weary of your disparagement, sir. Let me down."

In response, he swung from the saddle with lithe grace and lifted her into his arms. She did not want to be there, most definitely not. But she was so snug, so comfortable and comforted all in one, that it was very difficult to protest.

He was carrying her around to the back and up an outside flight of stairs. "How do you know this place?" she asked.

"I live near here — some of the time, at least. I rent a manor not five miles from where I found you."

"Why?" she asked, bemused. It was all too much. Her usual good sense was fading. His arms were strong, his nearness reassuring. That was madness. He was a rude American. She needed to go home, back where she belonged.

"London is well enough," he said, "but I'm not used to being in a city all the time. It wears on me."

She thought of his slight accent and beyond that, the sense that he was a man well able to deal with challenges, and perhaps less adept with the rules and regulations of society. "Are you a frontiersman?"

He laughed again, a deep, rich sound. "Dare I guess? You favor the penny novels that champion the likes of Daniel Boone and Davy Crockett."

"I may have read one or two," she confessed, for indeed she had. "What harm in that?"

"None, I suppose, although I suspect both those good men would have cracked a rib laughing at the way they're portrayed. At any rate, I've spent my share of time in the wilderness. It has a certain appeal."

"But you are here now."

"I am," he allowed, and kicked open a door

leading to a snug, warm chamber. "Be sensible enough to stay here, princess, while I square matters with the innkeeper."

"Tell him I am your sister," she urged, even as she sank into the down bed, into blissful ease, all her muscles suddenly limp and her mind unable to recall precisely why she had resented him only moments ago.

She heard him laugh again as he left the room. When next she knew, it was morning.

It couldn't be. She could not possibly have slept through the night, knowing how concerned her family would be, how urgent the necessity of her immediate return to London, how precarious her circumstances.

And yet it seemed she had.

With a curse that would have done her brothers proud, Amelia sprang from the bed. She was almost at the door when it opened suddenly. A sturdy countrywoman, with iron-gray hair pulled back into a bun and no hint of softness on her features, entered and regarded her sternly.

"You're awake. Good. The gentleman said you might be."

Amelia scrambled to bring her mind to order, well aware of how very bad all this must look. "I must leave here. I must reach London."

"As you say, but first you need to wash" — assessing eyes ran over her — "and dress. I am Mistress Porter. My 'usband and I own this inn and we run it proper. Just as well you know that."

Before Amelia could reply, Mistress Porter stood aside to admit a girl carrying a bucket of steaming water. Tea followed; blessed, reviving tea that drove the cobwebs from Amelia's head and was followed, wonder of wonders, by the arrival of a dress.

Not any such dress as she would find in her own extensive wardrobe, but a quite respectable dress all the same, despite being a discouraging brown. With it came a pair of well-worn shoes, half-boots really, of the sort a sensible country girl might wear. They, too, were brown.

"My daughter's," Mistress Porter said. "The dress will be short on you and the shoes may pinch, but they will do all the same, I think."

"Thank you," Amelia said quite properly. She was glad of the dress and shoes both, and gladder still to be warm and dry. Small things she had rarely thought of before had assumed great importance in the past few hours.

Tentatively, she asked, "The gentleman —"

"Mister Wolfson is downstairs waiting for you."

"Mister Wolfson?"

"Did you not know his name?"

"I was in need of help —"

"So he told us. Go on with you, then. He's waiting."

Unspoken, but evident all the same, was the

admonishment that it would not do to delay a gentleman, particularly not one who paid the bills for a bedraggled stray such as herself. Suitably urged, Amelia descended to the inn's common room, all but empty at this hour when proper travelers had gone on about their business.

Only Mister Wolfson remained, waiting for her.

"You look better," he said when he turned from the polished oak bar he had been leaning against and saw her at the foot of the steps. He surveyed her frankly. She quelled her discomfort — if it was truly that and not something else quite untoward — and returned his scrutiny in good measure.

He was as she remembered, only more so: tall, hard-edged, with a sense of wildness about him despite garb that was well made, even elegant. His jacket and trousers looked to be of the finest wool and were superbly tailored to a body apparently without fault. He was dressed all in shades of black and gray except for the startling whiteness of his shirt. Such austerity favored him, for he was a man whose innate presence required no embellishment.

Her stomach felt most peculiar. It must be from the tea she had drunk so quickly.

"I did not intend to sleep," she said. And then, because she was a properly brought up princess, she added, "I have been given to understand that your name is Wolfson. Although that hardly constitutes a proper introduction, I am grateful for your help, Mister Wolfson, and I would be most remiss not to acknowledge it."

Narrow lines crinkled around his eyes. "I'll give you this much, princess, you sound the part. Shall we go, or do you want breakfast first?"

Ignoring his remark, she replied, "I'd like to go. My family will be frantic."

"To London, then." He moved away from the counter where he had stood, drinking coffee. "Shall I drop you at the first palace we come to?"

"If you wish."

"You disappoint me. I'm set on meeting this family of yours."

He still thought she was lying. So be it, she would relish his surprise when he discovered otherwise.

"To Mayfair, then," she said and gave him the direction.

At the early morning hour, the road to London was thronged with all manner of travelers. Coaches, carriages, wagons, and riders jockeyed for room with those on foot. All evidence of the previous night's rain had disappeared, but it wouldn't have mattered in any event. The inn was set at a crossroads, where the dirt road along which Amelia had plodded, met one of the newly paved roads leading into London.

"I see Mister McAdam has been by," she

said, to distract herself from her too-great awareness of the man whose lean, hard body was so very close to her own. But then, how else was she to feel when she was once again perched in front of him on the black horse?

"That Scotsman who's set on paving everything?"

"It's an improvement, don't you think?"

"So long as it doesn't go too far."

His caution reminded her of what she had wondered the night before, whether he might be one of the frontiersmen about whom she had read so much. They were said to feel too confined if they could see the smoke of a neighbor's fire even miles away. With hindsight, the thought seemed only a fancy of her weary mind, yet there was something about him . . .

"You didn't tell me," she said. "Where in America are you from?"

"Here and there."

"Here originally, then there, or the other way around?"

His arm tightened around her in a manner she found disconcertingly pleasant. "Are princesses trained to be persistent?"

"Certainly, and to make conversation under all sorts of circumstances, with all sorts of people. For instance, I might charmingly inquire as to whether it was not possible to secure another horse this morning."

"A horse for you?" The question seemed to surprise him. "I suppose it might have been, but this seemed . . . friendlier. Besides, princess, I had no notion you could ride."

She who had sat her first mount before she could scarcely walk, and who loved nothing better than to fly over the plains of Akora bareback on a spirited steed said only, "I manage not to disgrace myself."

"I'll have to remember that."

It was the first suggestion that there might be some contact between them after they reached London. The notion disconcerted her, not in the least because she realized she was not especially eager to part from the rude but oddly engaging Mister Wolfson.

Unwilling to pursue that particular thought, she said, "You were telling me about here and there."

"Was I?" He sounded amused, and looked it as well when she glanced over her shoulder at him. He had shaved, and his hair — dark and neatly trimmed — appeared freshly washed. In the depth of night, she had not been able to guess how old he was, but now she thought him to be perhaps thirty years of age. Not soft or easy years by the look of him. He was as far from the self-indulgent British nobles she encountered in London as it was possible to be. With a start, she realized that he reminded her of the men of Akora, known to the world for their skill as warriors. Known also to Akoran women for their skill in an entirely different activity.

Really, her mind had never been so wayward. It must be the result of being kidnapped. The man himself couldn't be the cause. She was quite immune to men, or so she had concluded after turning down so many of them. The man she wanted, indeed even longed for and on occasion went so far as to dream of, did not seem to exist.

"Perhaps I can guess your origins," Amelia suggested on a sudden impulse. She ignored his skeptical look and pondered a moment. "You are not from Boston or anywhere in that vicinity."

"That's right," he admitted. "How did you know?"

"I have met people from Boston. They have a distinctive accent, as do many of the people I have met from your American South. You aren't from there, either."

"How is it you've encountered so many Americans, princess?" The question was asked lightly enough, but there was a certain hardness behind it.

"My grandparents have been to America many times and have American friends who have visited us here in England."

"Your English grandparents?"

"No, they died long before I was born. I am speaking of my father's parents."

"But they would be Akoran, would they not?" he reminded her pointedly. "Don't Akorans prefer to remain snug in their Fortress Kingdom?"

If he thought to test her knowledge of Akora, he was in for quite a surprise. Enjoying herself, Amelia said, "That certainly is true of most Akorans, but there have always been those among us who go out into the world, to learn of it and acquire that which can be useful to us."

"I see . . . including to America?"

"Exactly. In fact, my cousin Andreas was there just this past year."

Was it her imagination, or did his arm tighten around her a fraction more?

"Was he? What did he think of it?"

"He found it fascinating. But we were speaking of your origins. Not New England, not the South . . . Can it be you are from the Western territories?"

A moment passed before he said, ruefully, "Bravo, princess, you've a good ear. I'm Kentucky born. Know where that is?"

"West of the great Mississippi. Is that where you live now?"

He was silent long enough for her to think he did not intend to answer. Finally, he said, "I haven't been back to Kentucky in a long time."

She turned slightly, looking at him. The sun was behind them, making it difficult for her to see his features. She was like everyone else in that she relied on the little clues people gave in the raising of a brow, the tightening of a mouth, a change in the intonation of a voice. Little clues about thought and emotion never put into words, yet eloquent all the same.

And she was like no one else, at least no one she had ever met. Her Aunt Kassandra had said that she could "see" in some way that others could not, but that wasn't quite right. Nor could she say that she felt other people's emotions. She did not, and for that she was sensibly grateful. There were stories in her family about women who could feel the emotions of others. Invariably, such women had faced great challenges. No, in her case she simply knew what was in the hearts of others. Not always, not invariably, but often enough for her to have come to accept her ability as a simple fact of her life. To date, it had neither benefited nor harmed her particularly, although she did give it some credit for her avoidance of matrimony.

Sitting there in the saddle, looking at the American, she knew his . . . sadness? Too strong a word. Regret? That was closer — regret for what was gone beyond the hope of recapturing. But there was more, she sensed, before she could pull away, for she truly had no wish to intrude on his privacy. Strength, intelligence, courage . . .

The sun moved behind a tree. She could see his face, see the concern in eyes that looked shot through with silver. "What's wrong?" he asked.

"Nothing . . . nothing at all. I'm merely anxious to reach London."

"Your wish is about to be granted, princess."

She turned and looked up the road, seeing off in the distance the spire of St. Paul's Cathedral rising over the city, and beyond it the great, twining ribbon of the Thames sparkling in the sunlight. Impatience filled her as the snarl of vehicles and horses grew ever denser, slowing their progress. Being taken from London in the dead of night when there was very little traffic took far less time than returning to it at the height of the midday crush. But at length she knew herself to be very close to home.

"Turn left up here," she said, all but bouncing in the saddle.

"All right, but look, princess, I'm not going to leave you until I'm sure you're in good hands —"

"That's very kind of you. Up there, right there."

She could see the high stone wall surrounding the house. The immense wrought-iron gates, fully twelve feet high, stood open. Between them ran a driveway that led to the house itself, beautiful and gracious, gleaming white in the sun. Above the portico, fluttering lightly in the breeze, hung the crimson banner emblazoned with the golden bull's horns, symbol of the royal house of Akora.

Just short of the gates, the horse stopped. Bewildered, Amelia asked, "Why are you — ?"

"Princess, these people aren't to be fooled with. From everything I've heard, they can be

44

downright dangerous. Before this goes any further, why don't you just tell me who you really are?" He took hold of her chin lightly, turning her head so that she was looking at him. "I won't take you back anywhere you don't want to be or turn you over to anyone who might hurt you. You don't have to worry about that. But I can't help you if you won't be honest with me."

Astonished to discover that even now he did not believe her, but also touched by his evident desire to keep her from harm, Amelia put her hand over his, gently releasing his fingers. "Mister Wolfson, if you will just bear with me for a few more minutes, I assure you that your doubts will be put to rest."

He gestured toward the mansion. "In there?"

Anticipating the reception they would both receive, she grinned. "Most definitely in there."

With obvious reluctance, he spurred the horse forward.

# Chapter Three

"Kyril!"

A foreign word, Akoran most likely, shouted by one of the guards, the first to see them as they came down the driveway.

In response, a man appeared at the entrance of the house. He was tall, dark-haired, very fit for all that he had left youth behind. There was a woman beside him, her honey-blonde hair lightened by silver and her face creased with concern.

"Melly!" The woman's joy and relief could not be surpassed. She ran past the man, down the few steps to the driveway, and straight at them.

"Melly! Thank God!"

Amelia slipped from the saddle and threw herself into her mother's arms. They hugged amid tears and laughter.

"I'm all right!" Amelia said. "Everything's fine. I'm so sorry you were worried." She turned toward the black horse and the man who sat astride him.

"Mister Wolfson, please, you must meet my parents." She held out a hand, beckoning to him.

He came down off the horse without taking his eyes from the small cluster of people gathering quickly around her. There was the woman, crying even as she smiled; the dark-haired man; and several others, who hurried from the house to join them.

"This is Mister Wolfson," Amelia said, drawing him into the circle that formed around her. "He rescued me."

"Hardly that —" he began, but his words were drowned by fervent thanks. He was carried along by them up the steps and into the house. The dark-haired man stepped in front of him, looking at him assessingly.

"I am Amelia's father," he said. "We are in your debt."

"Not at all, sir. I was glad to help."

"You must tell us all that happened."

"Yes, of course, but I regret there is little I can say. I came upon your daughter on a road several miles from a house I rent."

"Where?"

"Where, sir?"

"The house you rent, the road where you found her? Where are they?"

He told him, sketching the location quickly. Amelia's father, Prince of Akora, lord also of extensive holdings in England, nodded. "You will show us?"

"Yes, of course, if you wish."

"Alex," the honey-haired woman interrupted. She still held her daughter, her arm looped through Amelia's as though she could not bear to let her go. "Pray, do not interrogate him.

Mister Wolfson, we cannot thank you enough."

"It was my pleasure, ma'am."

Amelia laughed. "Mister Wolfson has been extraordinarily patient. He did not believe I was a princess."

"Why wouldn't he believe you?" her father asked, frowning.

"Now Alex," her mother remonstrated. "We don't need to discuss all this here in the hall. Mister Wolfson, do come inside. The very least we can do is to offer you tea."

"He prefers coffee, Mother," Amelia said.

"Is that true, Mister Wolfson?" Joanna asked.

"Actually it is, ma'am."

"Coffee it will be, then. Alex, I do realize you have a great many questions, as do I, but please, let them both catch their breaths first."

"As you say, dearest, but there may be very little time if we are to have a hope of catching the men responsible for this outrage."

In the drawing room, the proper introductions were seen to, however belatedly.

"I am Alex Darcourt," Amelia's father said, "Prince of Akora and Marquess of Boswick."

"Niels Wolfson, sir."

The two men shook hands. As they did, Alex asked, "American, Mister Wolfson?"

"From Kentucky," Amelia interjected.

Alex nodded. "This is my wife, Princess Joanna, and my nephew, Prince Andreas." He indicated a tall young man who stepped for-

48

ward to shake Niels's hand.

"Very glad to meet you," Andreas said. "We're extremely grateful."

"Forgive me," Niels replied with a rueful smile, "but I'm still coming to terms with the fact that Amelia really is a princess."

He supposed it was a measure of their unbridled relief that no one so much as raised an eyebrow at his inadvertent use of the princess's given name. He had not meant to do that; it had slipped out. It wasn't like him to make mistakes, even small ones. He needed to be a damn sight more careful.

The coffee arrived as Amelia was assuring her mother that she was entirely fine.

"Just a bit footsore," she admitted. "I'm so terribly sorry we didn't press on last night, but —"

"As it was pouring rain," Niels interjected, "and the princess was exhausted, I thought it best to put up at an inn."

"Very sensible of you, I'm sure," Joanna said.

"Which inn would that be?" Alex asked. He spoke mildly, but his eyes never left Niels.

"The Three Swans, sir. I stayed there myself when I first came down from London, looking for a country house. It struck me as clean and reputable."

"And discreet?" Alex asked.

"No, sir, so far as I observed, the inn does not attract clientele requiring discretion." More lightly, he added, "The innkeeper's wife is something of a Tartar. I don't think she'd permit it."

"There, you see," Joanna exclaimed. "Mister Wolfson did everything entirely properly. Amelia, dearest, tell us what happened."

She did, relating briefly how she had been taken from her room and driven out of London.

"There were at least two men, but I saw only one of them — an Irishman, extremely tall and burly with a great deal of black hair on his head and face."

"Two men, you say?" her father inquired.

Amelia nodded. "There had to be. I was hoisted over the wall. One man alone, however strong, could not have managed that, or at least not nearly so quickly."

Her father accepted the cup of tea his wife poured for him, but set it on the mantel. His face was grim. "When I think that someone came into this house, despite all our security, and took my daughter from beneath my own roof —"

"Don't think of it, darling," Joanna said, reaching out a hand to him. "At least not more than you have already done. Self-recrimination serves no good purpose. What matters is that no harm has come to Amelia."

"None has, Father," she hastened to assure him. "Truth be told, now that I look back on the experience, it was rather exhilarating."

"Amelia —" Her cousin Andreas eyed her

doubtfully. He was a tall, very fit young man, as all the Akorans seemed to be. Though he wore English garb and spoke the language without any trace of an accent, there was a hint of wildness about him that was out of keeping with the civilized surroundings of the drawing room. Under other circumstances, Niels might have thought him something of a kindred spirit. As it was, he merely regarded him carefully.

"Well, it was," Amelia said. She was sitting on the settee beside her mother, looking quite appealing despite the rigors of the past night and the drab brown dress she wore. Her hair tumbled over her shoulders. In the sunlight streaming through the tall windows, she seemed very young and without artifice.

"You can go off and have adventures whenever you like, any man can. But it's quite a different matter for a woman."

"You can hardly claim that your life has been circumscribed," Andreas said lightly.

"I suppose not," she admitted, "when compared to others. Even so —" Her gaze turned in Niels's direction. He saw suddenly a hint of wistfulness that surprised him.

Before he could contemplate it very long, her father said, "I doubt you would have found the experience so — exhilarating, did you say? — if Mister Wolfson had not come along when he did. How did you happen to be on the road at such an hour, Mister Wolfson?"

"I had difficulty sleeping," Niels replied

51

smoothly, "and decided to get an early start for London."

"In the dark and rain?" Alex inquired. He spoke courteously enough, but left no doubt that he was willing to press the matter to a satisfactory answer.

"The rain was a surprise," Niels admitted with a smile. "As for the dark, it was only an hour or so till dawn when I set out. My horse, Brutus, came with me from America. He's used to such journeys. In fact" — with a glance at Amelia — "I think he finds them exhilarating."

Andreas laughed. "Good man, and from the sound of him, a good horse. Uncle, shall we agree Mister Wolfson's presence was fortuitous and let it go at that?"

"I suppose," Alex said and then, rather more graciously, smiled. But the cold light of determination never left his eyes. "We should be going."

Andreas moved toward the door. "I'll have the horses brought round. Will you ride your Brutus again, Mister Wolfson, or do you prefer another mount?"

"Brutus will do fine, thank you."

Amelia rose and went to her father. "Is there any point in my asking to come along?"

Joanna began to object but her husband made that unnecessary. "No, there is not. Stay here with your mother. Let her have the comfort of your presence." He smiled and touched Amelia's cheek gently. "You have shown

52

courage, my daughter. Now demonstrate equally good sense."

Alex was at the door of the drawing room, Niels behind him, when Amelia asked, "If you find them, what will you do with them?"

He looked back over his shoulder at the two women — wife and daughter — sitting in the elegant room of the house whose walls should have offered all necessary protection from a turbulent world, but instead served as a reminder that enemies could be anywhere.

"Not what I would like to do," he said and went out swiftly.

"How I feared for you," Joanna said gently when they were left alone. "But you have always been my wild child, ever ready to face any challenge."

Beside the torment she knew her mother must have experienced at the discovery that she was missing, Amelia's own disappointment seemed small indeed. With all her heart, she said, "I am so sorry you were put through this."

Her mother looked away for a moment. When she turned back again, the sheen of tears was gone from her eyes. She rose, smiling, and walked briskly to her daughter.

"You must tell me all, but you should also bathe and rest."

"A bath sounds wonderful, the rest less so. I will be too agitated to sleep."

"Until your father returns?"

"Yes, of course."

"And Mister Wolfson?"

"Will Mister Wolfson be returning?"

"I think," Joanna said as she accompanied her daughter out of the drawing room and toward the steps, "that we are in Mister Wolfson's debt and it would be churlish of us not to extend to him the hand of friendship."

"Father seems suspicious of him."

"Dear child, your father is suspicious of any man who comes near you. You know that."

"Yes, well, some of them at least deserve suspicion. They wish only to marry an heiress, someone who can bring them wealth and power. Or they are drawn to the mystery of Akora, thinking us exotic and wanting something of that for themselves."

"Do not say none of them were drawn to you yourself, for that is untrue."

"Perhaps," Amelia acknowledged, "but never was I first with any of them. I suppose that is why, when all is said and done, I am as yet unwed."

Joanna, ever loyal and loving, nodded. "Understandably enough. I was little younger than you when I met your father. Until then, I had no thought for matrimony."

"But when you met Father, you knew at once?"

"Well, no, not really. I knew I was . . . drawn to him, but beyond that, nothing was clear until much later."

Amelia frowned. "Didn't you wed only a short time after meeting?"

"Several months afterward," Joanna corrected gently.

Her daughter laughed. "There are some who would think that not so very long."

"It seemed long," her mother said with a woman's frankness.

They had reached the door of Amelia's bedchamber. Her hand on the knob, Joanna added, "Your American is an impressive man."

"I agree, but he is not mine." Though the idea sent a shiver of pleasure through her.

Her mother smiled and stood aside for her daughter to enter. A black crow of a woman awaited them within the bedchamber. Despite her formidable appearance, the woman, Mulridge, was the dearly loved companion of Joanna's childhood, who had become every bit as dear to Amelia herself. Ageless and often seemingly emotionless, she allowed herself only a quick sniff before gathering Amelia to her scrawny bosom.

"About time," Mulridge said. "All well and good to come riding up on that brute of a horse, but let no one tell me you don't need a bit of looking after."

"Exactly what I thought," Joanna said. "But she would stay talking. Even tried to convince Alex to let her go along with the men."

"Fool's errand, that," Mulridge said. "Culprits will be long flown and the nest bare."

"Probably so," Amelia admitted as she reached behind to undo the drab brown dress. Grateful though she was for it, she would be glad to have it off.

Mulridge quickly grew impatient with her fumbling efforts, turned her around, and undid it herself. Ever tidy, she folded it away as Amelia considered how her mother had spoken of Niels Wolfson. Her American. It was a tantalizing thought.

"Are you suggesting that Mister Wolfson is mine for the asking?" she inquired when the notion would not leave her mind.

"No," Joanna said frankly. "Indeed, he is not. I suspect that is part of why you are drawn to him."

"Whatever makes you think that?"

"I have eyes," Joanna said flatly.

Wrapping herself in a robe, Amelia said, "I would not mistake gratitude for anything else."

"Neither would I," her mother replied, and shared a speaking look with Mulridge.

The men returned shortly before nightfall. They looked tired, but worse, they were clearly frustrated.

"The house was empty," Alex said with disgust. He, Andreas, and Niels were with the ladies in the drawing room. A late supper had been brought in for the men, but none showed any appetite. "Nothing was left to be found. Not a scrap of paper, an item of clothing, nothing that might point in a fruitful direction.

"We will make inquiries," Alex continued, "as to who owns it, who may have been renting it, or who was seen in the vicinity. But for now, we have nothing to go on."

"They planned well," Amelia said. She had been thinking things over when she should have been resting. Exhaustion hovered at the edges of her mind, but for the moment she held it in abeyance. "They must have known the layout of this house and the routine of the guards."

"That suggests they are professionals," Niels said.

"The routine of this house has been altered," her father said grimly. "From now on, the guards will patrol on a random basis and more guards will be stationed throughout the house."

"We cannot live as though under siege," Joanna said gently. "Yet such precautions do seem wise, at least until we understand the nature of the danger."

"If they are professionals," Niels said, "perhaps they've carried out successful kidnappings elsewhere."

"I have heard of none," Alex said, yet the idea clearly interested him.

"They could have been kept quiet by people not eager to have them known, lest other villains be inspired to do the same."

"There is sense to that." Alex rubbed the back of his neck. "I will pursue it in the morning. If such things have happened, we will learn of them."

"Royce may know," Joanna said, referring to her brother.

"Uncle Royce and Aunt Kassandra should be here shortly," Andreas said, looking to Amelia. "Word was sent to them as soon as we knew you were missing."

"I wish there was some way to tell them I am well."

"Unfortunately," her father said, "by the time any such news could reach Hawkforte, they will be here."

"Who else did you tell?" she asked a little ruefully.

"No one," Andreas replied. "The king here is old and will die soon. The heir to the throne is a woman, young and untried. It is not a time to reveal weaknesses."

Her sensitivities heightened by fatigue and irked by what she regarded as her cousin's tendency to underestimate the abilities of women, Amelia said, "It was not weakness that freed me from that house."

Andreas inclined his head with wry amusement. "I mean no insult, Melly. We saw the shutter and realized what you had done. I merely state what is known to us all. We live in precarious times. Wouldn't you agree, Mister Wolfson?"

"I have never known any other kind," Niels replied as he stood. "I'd best be on my way.

There are undoubtedly matters you wish to discuss alone." To Alex, he said, "I wish we had been more successful, sir, but if I can be of any further assistance, do not hesitate to call on me."

"You have our utmost gratitude, Mister Wolfson," Joanna said. Her husband nodded his agreement. "We will never forget what you have done."

"I'm glad I came along when I did."

He turned to Amelia. "I hope you'll be able to put all this behind you speedily."

"I shall do my best, Mister Wolfson, and I also thank you."

He lingered for just a moment, looking at her, then nodded and went quickly out into the hall. Andreas saw him to the door. "Do you plan on being in London very long?" the prince asked.

Accepting his cloak from a servant, Niels said, "That depends on whether there's much of interest for me here. If not, I may head for the Continent."

"What are your interests, Mister Wolfson?"

"I'm a . . . collector, I suppose you could say."

With a smile that deflected any further questions, Niels took his leave. Brutus awaited him, the horse looking far fresher than his master felt. It had been a damnably long few days. He needed a bath, a bourbon, and some sleep, not necessarily in that order.

Shadow was waiting for him when he reached

the London town house he had rented at the same time he arranged for the country houses. Not a Shadow Amelia would have recognized. Along with the black wig and beard, the ersatz Irishman had removed the heavily padded coat that added so much to his girth and the boots with their false soles that contributed inches to his height. He was restored to himself — a tall but not giant-sized man with blond hair and a ready grin.

"How goes it, brother?" he asked when Niels entered the house after settling Brutus in his stall. Tired though the man might be, the horse always came first.

"Better than it might have," Niels said, grimacing. "If I hadn't thought to check on her —"

"Our pretty bird would have been gone, leaving us with a heap of trouble."

Without warning, Niels slammed a fist into the heavy door. The resulting pain helped to divert him a little, but not much. "What the hell was she thinking, going off in the middle of the night, getting herself soaked? She could have gotten lost, taken ill, run into the wrong sort of person."

"A kidnapper, for instance?" his brother asked dryly. "She's tougher than we thought. Good for her. At least it ended well." He looked at Niels. "It did, didn't it?"

Niels shrugged off his cloak and the jacket underneath it. He dropped both on a nearby chair. "I suppose. I took her father and cousin out to the house. You did a good job cleaning it, by the way; there was nothing to be found. And I managed to get in a suggestion that the kidnappers might be professionals who had done this thing before."

"A fine decoy. Are they at all suspicious of you?"

"Of course. I'm a man, to start with, and I don't think you'll find anyone more protective of their women than the Akorans. But there's also the little matter of why I was out on that road before dawn and just happened to come across their princess."

"They'll make inquiries."

"And they'll find what we've arranged for them to find. After that . . ." He paused and ran a hand over his face tiredly. "We wait for them to take the bait."

"Rum job, this," Shadow said. "Be better if we could just kill him."

"We don't know that he's guilty. Besides, killing one man won't settle anything. If he's guilty, they're all guilty."

"And if they are?"

"Then it will be war," Niels said quietly. "Bloody, awful war."

He spoke with the certainty of a man who knew to the marrow of his bones exactly how terrible that would be.

And on that note, he went to bed.

# Chapter Four

"Mister Wolfson . . . Mister Niels Wolfson . . ." Royce Hawkforte, Earl of Hawkforte, husband to Princess Kassandra, sister to Princess Joanna, friend and brother-in-law to Prince Alexandros, and uncle to Prince Andreas and Princess Amelia — all of whom sat in the drawing room in the bright light of a new day, listening to him attentively — consulted his notes.

"Or I might say, the Wolf."

"The Wolf?" Alex raised his eyebrows.

"Apparently the name refers to his service to his country, but the precise circumstances are unclear."

"I see," Alex said. "What else have you learned?"

"At a young age, he drew the attention of General Andrew Jackson, then in retirement from the military but planning his political career. Wolfson became his aide and continued to serve Jackson throughout the eight years of Jackson's presidency."

"In what capacity?" Andreas asked.

Royce smiled ruefully. He was a big man, tall and lean with a thick mane of golden hair. The woman seated beside him — his wife, Kassandra — bore a very feminine resemblance to her brother, Alex. Her dark hair was arranged in a neat coil at the nape of her neck. The look she gave her husband was evocative of their years of loving devotion to each other.

"Let me guess," Kassandra said. "That is unclear."

"Exactly," Royce affirmed. "I can only say with certainty that Mister Wolfson — the Wolf — has a reputation for getting things done. What that means exactly, I cannot say."

"All right . . ." Alex said. "What is he getting done these days?"

"That is —"

"Unclear." Amelia finished her uncle's sentence with a note of exasperation. "Really, is this necessary? Mister Wolfson saved me from great difficulty, if not far worse. Is it right that we repay him by laying his life bare?"

"It probably would not be," her uncle allowed. "However, have no fear, we seem to have no capacity to do that. As you know, Jackson completed his second term as president last month and was succeeded by his former vice president, Martin Van Buren. It appears that Mister Wolfson found that an opportune time to retire from public service, but again, that is not entirely clear."

"It makes perfect sense," Amelia insisted. "After years of service to his country, he took the occasion of his president's retirement to pursue his own interests. Isn't that logical?"

"It could be," her father said tentatively.

"When did Mister Wolfson arrive in England?"

"A fortnight ago," Royce replied. "He has engaged a town house here in London and a country house. To date, he has not gone about much in society, but that is bound to change when his presence is discovered."

"Why is that?" Joanna asked.

"Mister Wolfson appears to be a man of means. Certainly, he spends generously enough. Of course, the precise source of those means is —"

"Unclear?" Andreas ventured with a grin. More seriously, he said, "He told me he is a collector."

"That appears to be true," Royce said. "Mister Wolfson collects weapons."

"Weapons?" Alex was impressed despite himself. "What sort of weapons?"

"A wide variety, I gather, but mostly medieval. It is said that he has quite an admirable array."

"Which he keeps where?" Joanna asked.

"He may indeed be from Kentucky originally, as he told Melly, but he is long removed from there. More recently he has bought land in the state of New York, a sizable estate on the banks of the Hudson River. However, he has spent little time there, being more often occupied in Washington."

"Is he married?" Kassandra inquired.

"No, but that is not for want of effort by the hostesses of Washington . . . or New York,

Boston, Philadelphia, and elsewhere. No doubt the same will occur here once his presence becomes known."

"No doubt," Joanna murmured. She looked to her sister-in-law. "I was thinking how nice it would be if we invited Mister Wolfson to the reception Thursday."

Kassandra's smile hinted that she had already come to the same conclusion. "Do you think he would enjoy meeting Princess Victoria?"

"If he is still working for his government, in whatever capacity, he would," Joanna said. "After all, she will be queen."

"And if he is simply a private citizen," Amelia rejoined, "as he appears to be, it will do him good to get out and about."

"He may not see it that way once he comes within the grasp of society," Kassandra said, "but I daresay he knows how to protect himself. Yes, I do think he would enjoy the occasion."

"Then we are agreed," Joanna declared.

At the tender age of twenty-five, Amelia had long since learned to trust her instincts. They prompted her to cast a cautious glance in the direction of her mother and aunt. Those two ladies presented looks of such studied innocence that she knew instantly what they were about.

Knew and could not find the heart to demur.

Mister Wolfson — the Wolf — had occupied her thoughts since their encounter on the country road. Rather more to the point, he had also occupied her dreams.

She could not remember the last time an actual living and breathing man had done that, as opposed to a mere figure of fantasy. Indeed, she had no reason to believe one ever had.

She was looking forward to the reception, prompted by curiosity about the Princess Victoria, of whom little was known because she had lived such a life of retirement under the strict control of her mother. Only recently, at the insistence of her uncle, King William, was she emerging into public life. Amelia was not alone in wanting to take her measure. Of course, now there was an additional reason to anticipate the event.

How unfortunate that it was several days off.

"I was thinking of going to Smithfield," Andreas said. He looked to Amelia. "Would you like to come along?"

Before she could reply, a pair of demons exploded into the drawing room.

To be fair, they were not actually demons, although they could give an excellent imitation of such creatures. They were, in fact, her brothers — Lucius, called Luc in England, and Marcus, known as Marc. They were dubbed, the "two horsemen of the apocalypse," and with excellent reason.

"Kidnapped!" Luc exclaimed. He was the elder at twenty-two and tended to take the lead, although it was Marc who needed the more careful watching. The younger by eighteen months, he had more imagination than Luc and was, therefore, more dangerous.

"You have all the luck, sis," Luc continued as he hurtled himself onto the nearest settee. "Bolkum told us all about it, 'cept he didn't know who did it. Any idea, sir?" He looked to their father, who was regarding the pair with his usual stern amusement.

"We're trying to determine that," Alex said. "Of course, we are all very grateful that your sister was returned to us safely."

"Heard an American was involved," Marc said. He slouched in his chair with deceptive ease, rather like a loitering panther. Like his brother, he was tall and muscular, but whereas Luc sported the honey-hued hair of their mother, Marc was as dark as Alex himself. Both had been at Hawkforte with Royce and Kassandra, and had returned with them to London when word came of Amelia's disappearance.

"We were just speaking of him," Royce said. "His name is Niels Wolfson."

"The Wolf," Luc said promptly.

The older men exchanged a glance. "How did you know that?" Alex asked.

Luc shrugged. "Gossip in the clubs. You say he rescued Melly?"

"Not entirely," his sister said tartly. Growing up in a family of males who tended to be domineering, she had long since learned to assert herself without hesitation. "However, he did help."

"What do you know of him?" Andreas asked. At twenty-three, he was only slightly older than the other two and had often been their partner in mischief and mayhem. But there was an air of much greater seriousness and purpose about him, perhaps the result of his position as the son of the ruler of Akora.

"He's dangerous," Marc said promptly.

"Killed a lot of people in the war," Luc offered.

"Which war?" Royce asked.

Luc shrugged. "Don't know. Aren't the Americans always at war with someone — the British, the Mexicans, the Indians?"

"It's been more than twenty years since they took the field against the British," Alex said. "However, no one can accuse them of dodging a fight."

"At any rate," Marc said, "he helped Melly get free and that's what counts."

"Precisely what I have been trying to tell them," she declared. "But they seem to think he needs to be investigated."

"Why's that?" Luc asked. His gaze narrowed and his manner turned abruptly serious.

"No particular reason," Alex replied. "We are merely being cautious."

"You think he had something to do with whoever took Melly," Marc said. He had a tendency to cut straight through to the heart of any matter.

"That's absurd," Amelia exclaimed. "Why on

earth would he go to all the trouble of kidnapping me, only to help me get free?"

"I don't know," her father acknowledged. "It may be that by entertaining such a thought, we do Mister Wolfson a disservice. However, I think it behooves us to approach all aspects of this matter with caution."

No one disagreed with this, but after a moment, Kassandra turned to her niece. Deliberately, she said, "What do you think of Mister Wolfson, dear?"

Amelia knew what she was asking and, indeed, what they were all waiting to hear. They had given her time to recover, to rest and regain her strength. No one had bombarded her with demands for anything other than the most basic and necessary information about what had happened to her. But now they wanted to know and she could not blame them.

The gifts that occurred among the women were spoken of rarely within the family. It was understood that Joanna had the ability to find that which was lost — for hadn't she found her own brother when Royce was trapped on Akora years before? And had there not been a time when Kassandra, like her own tragic namesake from ancient Troy, saw the hidden pathways of the future?

Now it was the turn of a new generation of women.

"Mister Wolfson . . ." Amelia said slowly, thinking back to those moments on the black horse in the predawn hour, "has regrets."

"About what?" her mother asked gently.

"I don't know, nor should I. He has a right to privacy. I will say I know nothing to his detriment."

Silence followed this declaration until Kassandra reached over, patted her goddaughter's hand, and said, "That is settled, then."

"Nothing is settled," Alex protested immediately.

As one, the women, including Amelia, groaned.

"Dear husband," Joanna said. "We know nothing to Mister Wolfson's discredit and we are more in his debt than we can ever hope to repay. However much about him may be 'unclear,' I see no reason not to proceed with a giving heart."

"Bravo, Mother," Amelia murmured.

"I perceive we are defied," Royce said with a grin.

Andreas stood. "Why do we maintain the fiction about Akora being a place where 'warriors rule and women serve,' when the ladies inevitably make up their minds for themselves?"

With no expectation of an answer, for truly no Akoran man had one, Andreas looked to Amelia. "Coming with us?"

She rose immediately and smoothed her skirts. "Of course. Are you of a mind to buy?"

"I might be."

"Best go with him, then," Luc said as he

stood to join them. "Heaven only knows what he'll come home with."

"Any room left in those stables of yours?" Marc inquired as he, too, readied himself to go.

"There's always room," Andreas allowed, a shade defensively. He was well-known for his rescuing of horses that were, speaking charitably, past their prime. His stables were vast, but most of their occupants were unridable. They spent their days munching oats, drowsing in the sun, and enjoying the indulgences afforded by their master's kind heart.

"Then let us not delay," Amelia declared. She bent to kiss her mother, smiled at the others, and only just avoided speeding from the drawing room with unseemly haste.

She loved them dearly, her parents, her uncle and aunt, all her vast family in England and Akora, truly she did. But there were times when she needed to breathe, to feel like herself alone, set apart from all the rest with her own life.

"Just give me a few minutes to change," she said as she hurried off to her room. Mulridge was already there and helped her into her favorite crimson habit. She was back downstairs, tucking her hair under a plumed hat, when Bolkum brought the horses round.

He was a short, very hairy personage with thick black brows and farseeing eyes. To Amelia's knowledge, he had been in service with her family for a very long time, although how long precisely she could not have said. Her mother adored him and so did she.

"Smithfield. Going alone, are you?" he inquired as they mounted.

"Just the four of us, Bolkum," Luc said. "Think that's adequate?"

"Ah, well, young sir, as to that, I daresay the three of you can see to the Princess Amelia's safety, not that she herself wouldn't give any rum sort a good run." He inclined his head to Amelia, who smiled from her perch in the saddle of her favorite grey.

"Your confidence is appreciated, Bolkum."

He grinned and let the leads go. They proceeded down the driveway and out through the iron gates, more heavily guarded than before, Amelia noted.

London was . . . London. Busy, exciting, a city she was divided between loving and loathing. There were times when she thought only of living on Akora, home of her heart. But there were other times . . . truth be told, many other times . . . when she yearned to know the whole wide world, not only England, but far beyond.

For the moment, the ancient market at Smithfield would have to do. The sprawl of London threatened to overwhelm the area soon, but for the moment the fields where horses and cattle had been traded since medieval times remained intact.

Amelia and the others reached there after

threading their way through the city's encroaching streets. She came through the last patch of newly minted buildings, their stone still raw in the sunlight, and breathed deeply.

The smell of hay, horseflesh, leather, and manure had always pleased her. Indeed, it was a source of amazement that there were people who found it unpleasant. However, even she was willing to admit that the "aroma" of Smithfield was pungent. Fortunately, the wind was blowing away from them, creating a far more tolerable atmosphere than was often the case.

"Looks to be a good turnout," Andreas said.

"So it appears," Amelia agreed.

The day being fair and there being no reason for haste, the party rode slowly around the edges of the crowd. Luc spotted a boy hawking meat pies and bought one for each of them. They ate in their saddles, washing the pies down with cool cider offered in stirrup cups.

They had finished and Amelia was brushing the last of the crumbs from her habit when she beheld, just ahead of her, a large black horse and atop it . . . Mister Niels Wolfson.

At once, she turned to her cousin, looking for an explanation. But Andreas merely smiled and urged his mount forward.

Niels watched the quartet come toward him with the same attention he would give to enemies deploying on a battlefield. Yet even as he did so, he knew that to think of the royal foursome in any such way might be entirely wrong.

From deep within, he mustered a smile. He had managed a few hours of sleep and felt passably good, well enough to respond with satisfaction when the note came from Prince Andreas, inviting him to join them at Smithfield. They had taken the bait more quickly than he had expected; all the more reason, he reminded himself, to be cautious of them.

Even more reason, were it needed, was provided by the Princess Amelia. His smile turned genuine as his eyes lit with blatantly male appreciation.

"What is it?" she asked, frowning slightly.

He hesitated, not looking for trouble. Her cousin and the two he knew to be her brothers were watching him closely. Even so, he said, "Just that you look very fine."

She tried very hard not to smile and, to his pleasure, lost. Even so, her tone was tart. "Is that a Kentucky compliment, Mister Wolfson? Or did you hone your charms in the drawing rooms of Washington?"

They moved fast, these Akorans. He affected puzzlement. "Who said anything about Washington, Princess?"

"You must forgive us," Andreas intervened smoothly. He took a moment to effect the appropriate introductions, then continued. "But it is our custom to know with whom we are dealing. Your name is recognized here."

"Well, now, that's too bad. I've never much liked people's notice."

"You prefer to work behind the scenes, Mister Wolfson," Luc suggested.

"I do."

"Our Uncle Royce has the same preference," Marc said. "Only a small number of people have any idea how much power he really has, and that suits him perfectly. I suspect you are the same, sir."

Uncle Royce . . . that would be the Earl of Hawkforte. There was great speculation in Washington about the earl's service to the crown. Niels's own guess that the man wielded enormous influence had just been borne out. So, too, had he just been warned — rather adroitly — that the power of the Akorans reached directly into the highest levels of the British government.

All things considered, he'd best watch his step.

"Here to buy, are you?" he asked Andreas cheerfully.

"Perhaps, and I would value your advice." He nodded toward Amelia and her brothers. "This lot thinks I've a poor eye for horseflesh."

They grinned at one another with what gave every appearance of being a family joke. Niels had no interest in it. He gave them a moment, then asked, "Any news on the kidnappers?"

"Afraid not," the older of the two brothers replied. "But it's only a matter of time. They can't hide forever."

"Perhaps they've gone back to Ireland."

"If they were from there to start with," the younger said. He grinned. "Faith and begorra, the lads could have come from anywhere."

His effort at an Irish accent was inexact, but Niels took the point all the same. The Akorans were not easily misled. They had not maintained their sovereignty — and the mystery surrounding them — for thousands of years by being either foolish or careless.

"You must forgive my family," Amelia said with some asperity. "They are inordinately suspicious."

"Nothing of the sort," Niels assured her. "It's a smart man who looks around corners."

"More Kentucky wisdom, Mister Wolfson?" Andreas asked.

Niels laughed. "More like Washington wisdom. That's a far rougher place than any wilderness I've seen."

Andreas nodded, clearly satisfied with the response and with the man himself. "I liked Washington, for all that the climate is atrocious."

"When were you there?" Niels asked politely.

"Last year. It was my first visit. I'd like to return someday."

"Did you stop in New York? I have to admit, it is my favorite city."

"I did, and your point is well-taken. Do you know, there are people who claim that someday New York will be bigger than London?"

"That's hard to imagine, but the city does

have a certain appeal. Did you happen to come across the Blue Book?"

Andreas laughed. "A copy was presented to me my first hour in the city."

"What is the Blue Book?" Amelia asked.

Her cousin hesitated. "It is . . . a guidebook to the city of New York."

"And its many attractions," Niels added.

"Doesn't sound like anything terribly interesting," Luc offered.

"That's because you haven't been to that very entertaining city," Andreas said.

Niels turned his horse, the better to see the son of the Akoran ruler. "Where else did you go?"

"Philadelphia — a lovely town — and Baltimore." He paused a moment. "I was there when that terrible tragedy occurred."

"You must be speaking of the *Defiant*," Niels said. "A horrible loss, not only of a ship but also of most of her seamen."

Andreas nodded. "I wonder, has anyone determined exactly what happened?"

"There was an investigation, of course. The explosion was ruled an accident."

"Accident? . . ." Amelia looked from one man to the other. "Forgive me, but may I ask what you are talking about? What was this *Defiant* and what happened to her?"

"The *Defiant* was an American warship," Niels said quietly. "She was in dock in Baltimore, taking on stores. Most of her seamen were on board when there was an explosion, followed by a fire. The *Defiant* sank, and fifty-nine of her men were killed."

"How dreadful!" Amelia exclaimed. She looked to her cousin in bewilderment. "You said nothing of this when you came back from America."

"I said nothing of it to you," Andreas corrected gently.

Here was something important — to Andreas and, she rather thought, to Mister Niels Wolfson. Quietly, she asked, "Will you not do so now?"

Her cousin hesitated. She saw his gaze turn inward to the landscape of memory.

"I was close enough to the harbor to hear the explosion. I, along with the men who were accompanying me, went directly to the docks in the hope that we could be of some help. A great many other people did the same thing, but tragically there was very little anyone could do. Men were taken from the water on fire. The luckier among them died quickly. Others took longer. Shall I go on?"

Softly, Amelia said, "No." She reached out, touching his hand gently. "I am sorry, Andreas. I should not have asked."

He took a breath, the tension easing from his broad shoulders. "Apparently, I was more affected than I realized." He turned to Niels, who was watching them both. "So you say it was an accident, Mister Wolfson?"

"Would there be any reason to think it was otherwise?"

"I suppose not," Andreas said. "Still, it's hard to accept that life can end so capriciously."

Amelia looked from one to the other of the men. In the back of her mind stirred the thought that something was not as it should be. The impression was elusive and it faded before she could consider it any further.

"Let us find a more cheerful pursuit," she said and turned her mount toward the paddocks.

They were soon enmeshed in discussion of the various horses on offer, with her brothers especially forceful in their opinions. Even as she contributed her own, she remained vividly aware of the man who had come so unexpectedly into the circle of her family. Mister Niels Wolfson — late of Washington, New York, and Baltimore, excellent judge of horseflesh, and congenial company on a spring day in London. He seemed all that was sociable and civilized.

Where, then, was the Wolf?

# Chapter Five

"How did it go?" Shadow asked when Niels returned to the London house. It was late afternoon. The city hung suspended in the interval between the homeward trudge of the working people and society's rush out into the evening's entertainments.

Sticking a foot in the bootjack by the front door, Niels said, "Well enough, I suppose." He thrust off one boot coated with the mud of Smithfield and went to work on the other. Never mind that the servants would clean up whatever he tracked in. A sensible man avoided making a mess . . . if he could.

"Prince Andreas acknowledges being in Baltimore when the *Defiant* was destroyed."

"He could hardly not," Shadow said. "There were numerous witnesses to his presence."

Niels set the second boot next to the first and entered the house. Shadow stood aside to let him do so, then followed him down the hallway to the parlor they were using as an office.

"However," Niels continued, "the prince displays no knowledge of how the explosion occurred."

"Did you expect him to?" Shadow asked.

"Not at all. I just didn't expect him to be quite so good a liar . . . if he *is* lying."

Shadow tossed himself down on the nearest couch and regarded his brother. "You know my views. The Akorans are guilty as hell and we ought to be at war with them."

Niels smiled wearily. It was a continuing argument between them, one that only time and truth would resolve. "Which is why I was entrusted with this little jaunt and you're just along to help with the lifting."

Shadow clipped the end of a cigar taken from a cedar box on the nearby table. "I tell you, brother, you can weigh the facts from here to Christmas and the results will come out the same."

"They're guilty?"

"Exactly. What I can't see is why we're wastin' time here instead of going straight for them."

"We are here," Niels said as much to remind himself, "at the behest of President Van Buren."

Reaching a taper into the fire, Shadow grimaced. "Who doesn't want a war."

"Can you blame him? With all trust gone in the banks and little left in the currency, he has more than enough to manage without courting war."

"Just as well our money's in gold," Shadow observed as he lit his cigar.

Niels nodded but returned to the topic at hand. "If it comes to war, Van Buren will stiffen his spine or have it stiffened for him. But we must be sure before we act."

"Who had a better motive than the Akorans? Jackson was fed up with them refusin' to open diplomatic relations and worried they were on the verge of grantin' Britain a naval base. He agreed with the idea of sendin' the *Defiant* to find out what was goin' on. It was a damn good plan, if I do say so myself."

"Considering that you came up with it and were scheduled to lead the mission, I can see how you'd think that way."

"You didn't object when you found out about it," Shadow reminded him.

"No, I didn't. All things considered, it *was* a good plan. Risky, but good. Unfortunately, the *Defiant* never got out of the harbor."

"Neither did fifty-nine men, many of whom I counted as my friends." Abruptly, Shadow rose and walked over to the windows. He stood looking out, but it was clear his thoughts were elsewhere, miles and months away. "Hell, Wolf, I would have died with them. There are still times when I think maybe I should have."

"Don't say that."

A hard laugh broke from the younger man. "It's god-awful funny. If I hadn't been heatin' up the sheets with Fleur, I'd have gotten back to the ship just in time to get blasted to kingdom come."

"Nice girl, Fleur, I always liked her."

"Yeah, I've got some idea of how much you *liked* her. Anyway, it's just not possible for the

Akorans to get away with what they did."

"Whoever did it," Niels said quietly, "will pay. I promise you that."

Indeed, he had sworn it in the agonizing hours while he waited to learn whether his brother was among the living or dead. The vow had burned within him every day since. He would not rest until it was fulfilled.

"The Akorans may have thought they had reason to destroy the *Defiant*," he suggested. "But would they really have done it while a prince of their royal house was in the same city?"

"I think they wanted us to know," Shadow said grimly. He turned back into the room. "They wanted it right in our face."

"Then they will discover they have made a terrible mistake," Niels said. From a set of brackets near the door, he took a sword and turned it over slowly in his hands. The weapon was almost two centuries old, but its blade still held a keen edge. It had been used, it was said, against the army of the Grand Vizier Kara Mustafa during the relief of Vienna from the Moslems in 1683.

Watching him, Shadow said, "You might want to glance at the mail." He nodded toward the small stack of letters on a nearby table.

Niels replaced the sword in its resting place. "Something from Washington?" He hoped not. Van Buren had sent him off with a minimum of instructions. Niels wanted it to stay that way.

Shadow grinned. "Much better." He made a

gesture like a man casting a line.

Niels sifted through the letters quickly. They were mostly from New York, updates from the brothers' broker and lawyer. The economic situation in general was dire, but not for him or for Shadow. On the contrary, for them opportunities abounded. They were considering the purchase of several companies that both agreed were ripe for the taking. However, that would have to wait.

There was another envelope, very heavy, its flap secured by a wax seal imprinted with the bull's head of Akora. His name and address were written in a feminine hand.

After scanning the note inside, Niels handed it to his brother. "Looks as though they really have taken the bait.

"A reception for Princess Victoria tomorrow evening," he continued. "I didn't know she was allowed out."

"She isn't very often," Shadow said. "It will be just as well to get a look at her. By all reports, good King William will be shufflin' off this mortal coil before long."

"That's too bad," Niels said sincerely. "He's been less objectionable than most of the Hanovers."

"You'll go, of course?"

"Wouldn't dream of disappointing the very gracious Princess Joanna."

Shadow handed the letter back. "What about Princess Amelia?"

"What about her?"

"Lots to be said for a spirited woman."

"Maybe, unless you're deterred by the thought of being on the opposite side in a war against her father, uncles, brothers, and cousins."

"There is that," Shadow acknowledged. He handed the letter back. "Van Buren won't give you much longer."

"I may not need it." Niels opened a drawer in the table. Inside it was a leather folder. He took it out, laid it on the table, and flipped it open.

A man stared back at him, or at least the drawing of a man.

A man only a handful of other men had seen, and none of them left alive. Dying men had described him, and a gifted artist had turned their gasped recollections into the sketch.

The man looked like an angel. His features, perfectly formed to convey an impression of both beauty and dignity, were topped by a head of curling hair said to be golden. In the drawing, he was smiling at the viewer as though inviting the intimacy of shared pleasures. But his eyes — deep-set and thickly fringed — were flat.

The man might exist . . . or he might not. If he did, he was a mass murderer.

The question was, was he Akoran?

In general, the Akorans were a dark-haired people whose appearance reflected their ancestors' origins in the ancient world of the Mediterranean. But it was known that from time to time outsiders reached the Fortress Kingdom. Tradition claimed they were killed by a people determined to exclude all *xenos* — strangers. But the evidence of recent years put the lie to that notion.

Not only had two members of the same English family — Royce and Joanna Hawkforte — journeyed to Akora and returned safely, but they had also married into the ruling Akoran family. Moreover, the wife of no less than the Vanax of Akora, as close to a king as they had, was partly of English origin, shipwrecked on Akora as a child, raised as an Akoran, to be sure, but still a *xenos*. And most definitely not killed. To the contrary, she reigned now as a queen reputed to be beloved by all.

The golden-haired man might, therefore, be Akoran or even more simply, he might be working for them. The challenge was to find him — and quickly.

Within the circle of the Akorans, welcomed into their home and invited to their entertainments, Niels would hunt the man. If he was to be found there, the Wolf would discover him.

The man would die, but his death would be only the beginning of what promised to be savage justice.

The anguished voices of the doomed would be stilled by nothing less.

And Amelia? He frowned at the sudden thought of her. He would be wise to think of her strictly as a means to an end. Certainly, it had not crossed his mind that she could be anything else.

Until she climbed out of that ditch, all wet and muddy, and announced that she was a princess.

"I'll do anything! scrub floors, peel potatoes . . . both honorable occupations and certainly far more useful." Desperate, Amelia looked to her mother.

Joanna, normally the most loving and indulgent of parents, merely smiled. "Really, Melly, you exaggerate. It's only a fitting, and the last one at that."

"For this gown. This despicable, much hated gown that I wish never to see again."

"It is lovely. You said so yourself."

"Five fittings ago. Back when I did not live in fear of the knock on the door and the dread news that Madame Duprès had arrived."

"Madame Duprès has been making clothes for Kassandra and myself for years —"

"And for years you have avoided most fittings by having servants take your place. Servants, I might add, you feel compelled to lavishly compensate for the ordeal."

"I am merely trying to make the most efficient use of my time," Joanna claimed with a straight face. "Besides, you know you could do the same if there happened to be someone here who was a close match for you. But there isn't."

"A few inches in height —"

"It isn't just that, dear. You have a lovely long waist and you're a bit more endowed in the bosom than are most women. Your figure is exquisite. It should not be a cause of complaint."

"It wouldn't be if men could manage to look me in the eye rather than believing that my voice emanates from somewhere south of there."

Joanna laughed and squeezed her daughter's hand lightly. "I did not notice Mister Wolfson having that difficulty, but then I perceive he is a man of considerable control."

"I suppose . . ." Certainly he had shown no lack of control in dealing with her. The man was nothing short of high-handed, yet oddly enough, she couldn't manage to mind. "Has he replied to your invitation?"

"To the reception? Yes, he did. His note arrived not an hour ago. He is looking forward to the occasion."

"I'm glad *he* is," Amelia murmured even as she struggled against the sudden spurt of excitement that almost, if not entirely, lifted her mood. "About the dress —"

"Melly, you are of the royal house of Akora, not to mention equally proud lineages here in England. Do not be undone by a French seamstress."

On that note, her mother sallied off, leaving her to the tender ministrations of the dragon of haute couture who arrived all too soon and stayed all too long.

But all things, even those of such cosmic tedium that they seemed to alter the very nature of time itself, eventually came to an end. Released, Amelia hurtled her pin-poked body down the back stairs, out the nearest door and into the garden where she stood, drawing in deep, restoring breaths of fresh air.

Or at least air as fresh as teeming London permitted. What *was* that smell?

"It's the river," Andreas said, coming round a corner of the house in time to see her wrinkled nose. "Too many people dumping too much into it."

"Hard to believe the same people are still drinking water from the Thames," the man with him said. He smiled as he spoke and inclined his head to Amelia without taking his gaze from her.

"Lord Hawley, I didn't realize you were here." Nor was she pleased to discover his presence. Hawley . . . disturbed her. When she looked at him, she saw a man of rare, even ruthless determination, nothing else. His deeper feelings, assuming he possessed them, were not known to her. She did not assume that this reflected badly on his character. However, she was never entirely comfortable in the presence of Lord Simon Hawley, for all that he was accounted a handsome and charming man.

He was also, she realized, a would-be suitor, although he had gone about it rather more cleverly than most. Hawley did not besiege her. He let her know his interest, made himself pleasant to her family, and steadily appeared more and more in her life.

The truth was, she was not entirely sure what to do about him.

"You look a bit harried, Princess," he said.

Princess. Hawley said it without hidden meaning, unlike Mister Niels Wolfson, who always managed to give her title an ironic twist.

"Are you acquainted with Madame Duprès, my lord?"

"Of course. All society knows her." His smile turned indulgent. "Surely it is not such a hardship to have beautiful gowns made by her?"

"I believe Melly would rather be put on the rack," Andreas said with a fond grin.

"It's just that clothes are so much more complicated these days," she said a bit defensively. She knew perfectly well that compared to the miserable existences of so many in the city all around her, her complaints were small indeed.

"Lord Hawley and I are off to ride at Rotten Row," Andreas said. "Care to come with us?"

"Thank you, but no." Much as she loved to ride, and would gladly have gone with Andreas alone, Lord Hawley's presence deterred her. Even so, she turned to him politely. "Will you be at the reception tomorrow evening, my lord?"

"I intend to be and I shall look forward to seeing your hard-won gown, Princess."

His bow was everything that etiquette could require and more. Yet Amelia frowned as she watched him go.

She forgot about Simon Hawley quickly enough as she threw herself into helping her mother with final preparations for the reception. Before she became a princess of Akora, Joanna had been Lady of Hawkforte, that most ancient and renowned manor. There she had honed the talent for organization that still astounded her daughter.

"It's a matter of motivation," Joanna replied when Amelia said as much. They were walking briskly — Joanna never actually ran — from the dairy, with its deep cooling well where milk and cream were kept, to the kitchens a short distance away. Their footsteps sounded on the flagstone floor of the basement and echoed hollowly down the long brick walls. "Before I married, I deplored society and wished to have very little to do with it. But afterward, I realized that my personal preferences could not be allowed to interfere with the need to assure good relations between Akora and Britain."

"You've done wonderfully well," Amelia said. "Relations have never been better."

"That is true so far as it goes."

"You refer to Lord Melbourne's desire for formal diplomatic relations?"

"Your father has done everything possible to explain to the Prime Minister that friendship is preferable to a more official relationship, which might well lead to certain pressure on the part of Great Britain for accommodations that Akora does not intend to give."

"The naval base?"

Joanna nodded. "The government here denies it, but there is little doubt that Britain wants such a base."

"And will continue to seek it in the new reign?"

"I expect so. Certainly there is no reason to believe Melbourne will change his mind."

Just outside the kitchens, Amelia stopped and looked at her mother. It was quiet in the basement. The sounds of the house were muted. Dust motes danced in the sunlight finding its way through the windows cut high in the walls just where they emerged above ground. The world itself seemed held at bay.

"It's so odd to think of a girl younger than myself on the throne."

"The general consensus is that Victoria will be guided — not to say controlled — by those around her, but I wonder if that is entirely true."

"How can it be otherwise? She has been virtually sequestered all her life. Why, she has never even been allowed to have a room of her own but must still share her mother's."

"It is not healthy, the way they have kept her," Joanna agreed. She stuck her head in the kitchens, had a quick word with Cook who was directing preparations with the steely assurance of a general in the midst of battle, and drew her daughter toward the stairs. As they climbed up to the ground floor of the house, Joanna said, "But when I met her last year, although our encounter was very brief, I had the impression of a strong will, perhaps even a stubborn one."

"She will need strength," Amelia said, "if she is to rule in her own right. A bit of stubbornness probably wouldn't go amiss, either."

"I rather thought you'd be sympathetic to that," Joanna teased. More seriously, she added, "There is some news about the house where you were held. It was leased by an Irishman who did not balk at paying a half-year's rent in advance when the owner required it."

"An Irishman who is not to be found now?" To her knowledge, no sign had been found of the men who had kidnapped her.

"Not so far," her mother confirmed. "Your father has men watching the ports, but as yet they have found nothing."

They reached the back hall. An Akoran guard, bare-chested, wearing a kilt with a sword strapped to his side, saw them and nodded cordially. There were guards everywhere now. Amelia tried not to mind, but their presence was a constant reminder of the strange event that had occurred in her life and for which there was as yet no explanation.

"Of course," Joanna said, "there is no reason to presume the man you spoke with actually was an Irishman. The accent could easily be faked and his appearance altered."

"I wondered about that," Amelia acknowledged. "When he allowed me to see him, I thought that meant he intended to kill me."

A harsh sound escaped Joanna. She pressed her lips together firmly and took a quick breath. "I hoped that possibility had not occurred to you."

Gently, Amelia said, "I am your daughter, Mother, yours and Father's. Between the pair of you, I'm fortunate enough to have inherited a full measure of courage and, I hope, good sense."

"We have tried to prepare you to live in this world," Joanna acknowledged. She managed a smile. "It has not always been easy. You will learn for yourself that the instinct to protect one's children can be quite fierce. When we found you were missing, my first thought was that you should have been on Akora. You would be safe there."

On impulse, Amelia put an arm around her mother's shoulders. Joanna always seemed so strong, even indomitable, but just then, she seemed to be the one who needed reassurance. "I love Akora, but I am not convinced that my life is there."

"I know," Joanna said softly. "Yet I am not certain it is here, either."

"I could simply go on as I have, living in both."

"You could," her mother said tentatively. Her voice changed in some indefinable way from mother to woman. One woman speaking to another, striving for clarity. "Or you could do as I did and leap."

"Leap?"

"When I leaped aboard your father's ship." Joanna's smile was purely feminine. "Leaped into a different life. It was a leap of faith . . . and hope."

"You must have known —"

"I knew nothing. My brother was missing after setting off for Akora, the Fortress Kingdom wreathed in such legend and mystery, not to say threat for what the Akorans were said to do with strangers. Your father was the only chance of finding him. A foreign prince, alien and distant, who had already told me not to trouble him."

"He did not!" She had not heard this.

"Oh, he did, quite unmistakably — at a party at Carlton House, of all places."

"What did you do?" Amelia asked, fascinated by this sudden glimpse into her parents' lives before they were her parents. Back in the distant age when they were simply a man and a woman, striving to find a common accord.

"I dogged him," Joanna said, and her smile was that of a much younger woman in the bloom of her confidence. "Did you know, there is an old Irish saying: A man chases a woman until he is caught. I suspect that came to apply to your father."

Amelia laughed. The very idea of her father
. . . Yet it was charming and, she suspected suddenly, just possibly true.

"The two of you have managed very well together."

"We have, to my great joy. I would that
someday you know the same."

It was as frank as her mother had ever been
with her. Amelia did not know how to reply.
How did she say that she longed for just that,
yet doubted it was possible for her? The men
she had met . . . They did not compare to what
she knew her mother and her aunts had found.
Such love came so rarely. Dare she hope for it?

Not with Hawley, she was quite certain of
that. Or with any of the other men she had met
except . . .

The Wolf?

Oh, no, definitely not! A bold American to
whom she owed a debt, to be sure, but even so,
not a man any sensible woman would think of
in terms of a future.

She was a sensible woman.

*Princess.*

That deep and drawling voice. That smile . . .
Those hands.

A man of control and she was woman enough
to sense what that could mean.

"I doubt I will ever marry," she said stiffly.

Her mother laughed. Joanna — late of
Hawkforte, now of Akora — Joanna who had

96

leaped, laughed and laughed. And hugged her daughter close, as all around them the preparations went on for the royal reception and whatever it might bring.

# Chapter Six

"How do I look?" Niels asked. He frowned at himself in the full-length mirror. He was freshly shaved, his dark hair brushed back from his high forehead. The evening's activities required formal dress. He had to hope he'd gotten it right.

"Like a popinjay," Shadow replied and grinned hugely. He was stretched out on the four-poster bed, arms folded beneath his head, a man at his leisure while his brother confronted demon fashion.

"Damn it," Niels snarled. "Don't help."

Shadow laughed, bounded from the bed, and went to stand beside his brother. He looked at Niels in the mirror. "You don't look bad," he conceded.

"I'd better not."

"Why the concern? You've survived Washington drawing rooms. Does it get tougher than that?"

"I suspect it does — here." The English had had centuries to perfect the sharp barbs of social censure. He didn't care, it didn't matter. Yet it did. Nothing could detract from the mission, not even his own vulnerabilities.

A Kentucky boy. Come to wealth, come to power. Come here.

"Seriously," Shadow said. "You're fine."

Niels nodded shortly and looked back in the mirror at the man reflected in it. He wore a double-breasted frock coat of the finest black wool paired with trousers of the same, a wide stock of white linen with a shirt of creamier hue, short boots and a cape, which he thought ridiculous but was called for all the same. Just as importantly, he did not wear stays, though they were affected by some who called themselves men, or a high upstanding collar to keep his neck rigidly straight, or bows on his boots. There were some things a man simply wouldn't do even for love of country.

"Where's your gun?" Shadow asked.

"Here," he replied, showing the discreet leather holster beneath his coat.

His brother nodded. "Knife?"

Niels lifted one trouser leg fractionally.

"All right, then," Shadow said. "Looks like you're set."

"Looks like."

"It's not so bad," Shadow said in an effort to buck him up. "You'll find the Angel, kill him, and we'll be homeward bound."

"To gather the fleet and go to war."

"Fine thing, war, when it's justified."

"Some say Akora is a paradise."

"They're men, same as we are, and every bit as dangerous."

Niels turned from the mirror, from the sight of the man he must be, and embraced his

99

brother. Hands on his shoulders, he said, "We'll find the truth and we'll abide by it. Understood?"

"Don't let the princess distract you."

"She won't."

"She's beautiful in her own way, and she has strength."

"For God's sake, she's a princess."

Shadow grinned, put his hands on his brother's and stepped back a pace. "Think that matters between the sheets?"

"Maybe not, but according to you, she's the enemy."

"Aye," Shadow said and his eyes turned grim. "I wish to hell she weren't."

So did Niels, but he wasn't about to say so — not even to himself.

"We do as we must," he said instead, and went from the room out into the night.

The house was ablaze. Lights burned in every window and in the torchères positioned at intervals all the way up the driveway. Niels left his carriage in the thronged street and proceeded on foot. So great was the press, he estimated he otherwise would be another half hour before disembarking. All London, or at least all of society, had turned out to see the royal Akorans welcome the royal Victoria.

All London except for the ailing king, who was not likely to be missed.

The night was warm for April and, mercifully, the smell of the river was held at bay by a breeze that bore the sweeter scents of farmland and orchards still to be found west of the city.

He climbed the steps beneath the bull's-head banner and entered the hall he already knew. There he paused, after handing his cape to a footman, and looked around.

The high, domed hall was filled with the sort of chatter produced by people too aware of themselves. Ever mindful of whatever might be of interest, of any tidbit or advantage to be found.

It would be, he decided right then, a long night.

There was a receiving line. He avoided it and strolled along the outer edge of the crowd instead, looking at faces, seeking.

The Angel. So they had dubbed him in the dark hours after the destruction of the *Defiant*. The man seen planting the explosives that destroyed a proud ship and the men who would have sailed on her.

He had to be Akoran, or working for them. Try though he did, Niels could find no other explanation. No one else had reason to sabotage the *Defiant*. No one else would have dared.

Would they?

He could not let his personal feelings interfere with justice for the men of the *Defiant* and protection of his country.

Find the Angel. Make war. Kill.

Find peace.

How many men, in how many ages, had contemplated the same path?

He would do as he must, but —

Amelia. *Princess.* She was standing in the receiving line beside her parents and she looked beautiful in a gown of ivory silk that left her shoulders bare, hugged her bosom, and fell in some sort of lacy skirt to her feet. Her hair was drawn high on the crown of her head, twined with flowers he could almost smell. Her skin looked like summer apricots, warm to the touch, sweet to the taste. She was laughing.

Sweet heaven, spare him from a warm, lovely woman who was supposed to be an enemy.

A waiter passed, bearing a silver tray. He accepted a flute of champagne, drank it without tasting, still looking at Amelia. She stood beside another woman, also young but very short, who looked . . . intent. As though the moment might be snatched from her and she was determined to hold on to it.

Victoria.

Not plain, exactly, not beautiful, either, but pleasing enough for all that there wasn't much of her. Compared to the overblown Hanover men, including her own father, she was sweetly ordinary. But there was something in the set of her shoulders, the tilt of her head, the suddenness with which she turned to Amelia and smiled.

A bird freed from a cage.

That was it, or close to. In the hills of Kentucky he had known an old man who raised hawks. The man was some relation to him, but in the convoluted family ties of the place, he hadn't known precisely how. The hawks were kept blind and hooded in a mews until they grew to know the bargain they must make with men if they were ever to regain the sky.

Victoria had the look of a peregrine the old man had treasured.

He would write of this to Washington, give his impressions to Van Buren, for whatever good they might do. But the British princess was really of very little interest just then. That would change the instant the old king breathed in his last breath.

Amelia turned to speak to her father. She was startlingly graceful and . . . vivid. Yes, that was the word. She seemed vividly alive, unfettered by the perpetual caution and calculation that made so many people appear too much like automated mannequins. His body, seemingly detached from his brain or any semblance of good sense, stirred.

He had been too long without a woman. That had to be it. The princess was appealing, but there were plenty of lovely women for the asking. Or if it came to it, the buying. He liked frank and simple relationships; they suited him.

Nothing would be simple with this princess.

She laughed again and he watched the slight flush of her skin down the slender line of her throat to the swell of her full breasts. Abruptly, he turned away, seeking something, anything that would tame his wayward passions.

There was music playing — Mozart, he thought, although he knew little of such things. The air smelled of perfume, good food, and wine. Everywhere he looked, he saw beauty.

Nothing was dirty or ragged, desperate or hopeless. All was comfort, loveliness, and security.

Damn them.

The screams of doomed men, the moans of the weak and weary, the muffled sobs of the boy he had been. It was suddenly all too close, too real —

"Mister Wolfson?"

A hand soft on his arm, a voice very near. He turned and found himself looking into hazel eyes.

"Princess." She had left the receiving line, left her family and her royal guest, and come to him.

A dangerous woman.

"Are you all right?"

"Of course, I'm just overcome by the glamour of it all."

She looked startled for a moment, then shook her head chidingly. "You are not. If anything, you disapprove of us."

"How could you know that?"

What had he said and why? Too much frankness and not enough tether on his tongue. Worse yet, they were being observed. Her father, in particular, leveled a hard, steady look in Niels's direction even as a flutter of interest ran through the guests standing nearest to them.

The princess herself took no apparent offense at his unintended admission, saying only, "You are a republican, are you not?"

He reined in his mind, directed it down safer channels. "In the sense of opposing monarchy? Yes, I am."

"Your president, Andrew Jackson, has strong feelings about that."

He heard her well enough, though he was preoccupied watching her mouth. It looked very ripe and soft.

"Van Buren is president now," he said absently.

She pressed the point. "But Jackson was *your* president, the man you served. You must have had a reason for doing so."

Had he? A reason other than the opportunity Jackson had offered him? He liked Jackson, usually, and agreed with him for the most part, although there were issues, especially regarding the currency, on which they had clashed.

"I thought Jackson the best choice for the times." Eager to move beyond the subject of American politics, which he thought no great credit to his country, he took refuge in courtesy. "Thank you for inviting me."

"It was my mother's doing, but I was glad of it."

Her honesty surprised him. Whereas candor

had stumbled from him, hers seemed clear and deliberate. "Why so?"

"These events can be dreadfully dull. People have a tendency to alternate between posturing and gawking. I can't see you doing either."

She looked at him with unabashed directness and the beginnings of a smile curling the corners of her too-tempting mouth. Her voice was soft, slightly husky, beguilingly female. The sort of voice a man wouldn't mind hearing moan his name in the dark of night.

"What do you make of Princess Victoria?" he asked, not because he cared, but because he damn well had to focus on something other than Amelia herself.

She glanced in the direction of the young woman who was the heir to the British throne. "I cannot claim to be well acquainted with her, but she seems intent on fulfilling her responsibilities."

"Intention may not be sufficient in this case, but never mind. Do you usually stay long in England?"

"We are commonly here about half the year." She glanced toward her parents, who were chatting with the young Victoria. Her voice dropped. "This year, we will be here longer. You understand, there is expectation of a change on the throne."

"So it seems. Akora is very close to the British crown."

"My Uncle Royce, the Earl of Hawkforte, is

very close," she corrected. "The formal relationship between Akora and Britain is no different from what exists between us and every other country." She tilted her head slightly, looking at him. "Your own has tried to establish diplomatic relations and has been rebuffed, just as all others have."

Genuinely, he said, "I have no interest in such matters." Truly, he did not. Akora could choose to have diplomatic relations with every country in the world or none at all, it mattered not to him. He only wanted justice, however that might come.

"You represent your country, do you not?"

"I assure you, Princess, I am no diplomat."

She started to smile again but caught herself. "Are you not, Mister Wolfson? Yet you have just replied to my question without actually answering it. That must be rated a diplomatic skill."

He leaned back a little, balanced on the balls of his feet, and regarded her as a man takes the sight on a target. "What is it you want to know, Princess?"

She parried. "What makes you think I want to know anything?"

"You're circling around something. I'd like to know what it is."

"Last year," she said, "no fewer than three American emissaries came to my father here in London, sent by President Jackson to persuade him to support diplomatic relations with the United States. None had any success." Her eyes held his. "I wonder if you are the fourth such emissary."

He let the silence hang between them as he studied her. She was, in addition to everything else, intelligent. That was a complication he could have done without.

Her family — and Amelia herself — did not simply accept his presence at face value. They were questioning, perhaps speculating about his motives for being in London. He needed to quash that and do it very quickly.

Quietly, he said, "I am the man on the road, Princess. The man in the dark and the rain. Isn't that enough?"

She had the grace to look abashed. "Forgive me, Mister Wolfson." Her voice sent an unwonted tremor through him. "I greatly appreciate your assistance. It is just that I am protective of my family and my country."

"Of course you are. As for forgiveness, you need not ask. However, if you would be inclined to make amends . . ." He moved a little closer, narrowing the distance between them. She was wearing a light, spicy perfume he found enticing.

But then he suspected she would draw him under any circumstances.

"How?" She dropped her eyes for a moment, then raised them to meet his. He took the full impact of that golden gaze and smiled.

"Dance with me," the Wolf said and held out his hand.

It was, Amelia decided around midnight, a marvelous evening. The stars were shining, the breeze held the river stink at bay, and the company could not be surpassed.

There were, she knew, one hundred and eleven guests, and she did her best to be mindful of them all. But for her there truly was only one — Niels Wolfson.

Whether from across the full width of the room or in his arms for a very proper waltz, he commanded her senses. The way the gaslight struck the rugged lines of his face and gleamed off his ebony hair . . . the impact when he smiled suddenly and looked directly at her . . . the deep, faintly amused timbre of his voice that seemed to caress her . . . the warmth of his strong hand on her waist, effortlessly commanding her movements . . .

She felt giddy and almost laughed out loud at the sensation. Twenty-five years old and never had she known anything remotely like this, though certainly she had longed for it. She who was accounted a spinster by some, called cold and unfeeling by those who did not know her, who had all but despaired of ever meeting a man who could move her so.

An American, with a life in America. Well, she would have to think about all that. But now there was only the moment — rare and lovely — and she intended to enjoy it fully.

"You look," Andreas said softly, "like the proverbial cat." He had come up beside her without her noticing, so preoccupied was she.

Turning to her cousin, she smiled. "The cat who has swallowed the cream?"

"Precisely."

She laughed and reached out a hand to him. "Didn't you tell me last month that I tended to be overly serious?"

"You had beaten me at chess — yet again."

Joanna laughed just then at something Niels said. The two stood nearby chatting.

"I have decided to be frivolous instead," Amelia declared, watching them. Her mother approved of Niels, she could tell. It was not a decisive factor, but it did matter.

Andreas looked at her steadily. "No, I don't think you have." He bent his head in Niels's direction. "Indeed, cousin, I suspect you are more serious than ever."

"And do you also think me foolish?" She valued Andreas's opinion as well as her mother's.

"No," he said, considering. "I don't." When she smiled, he cautioned, "But there is much yet to know of him."

"Perhaps, but I doubt he can account for his lineage back the ten or twenty generations you might find adequate."

"A man should know where he comes from."

"A man should know who he is," she countered.

Andreas, who loved her, relented just a little.

"That is true. At any rate, we all trust your judgement."

Because of who she was and what she could do — usually, not always. Her gift was far from infallible. She might be wrong in this case.

*The moment, seize the moment.* "Excuse me," she said and went from her cousin to the man who, seeing her approach, nodded courteously to her mother and met her halfway.

The music took them, whirling them round and round. She went with it willingly, went with him, his hand strong at her waist, guiding her, his eyes never leaving hers. Round and round, in a world where danger seemed but a distant memory of another time and another place.

And yet it lingered there at the edges just beyond her vision, a rank and shuffling presence that darkened the borders of her gilded land.

# Chapter Seven

"He was not there," Niels said. His words were heavy with frustration. He threw his cape on the nearest chair and headed for the array of crystal decanters on a table at the far side of the room.

Stretched out on the settee where he had been dozing, Shadow lifted his head. "No sign of him?"

"Not a glimmer." Niels poured hefty brandies for them both. He was in no mood to drink alone. "The Angel may not exist. Or he may not have anything to do with the Akorans. Or he may be on Akora right now and we are left with no way to find him."

Shadow drew himself upright and went to stand beside his brother. He accepted the snifter Niels handed him. "It's early days. He'll turn up."

Loosening his stock, Niels said, "He'd damn well better. This is more complicated than I thought."

Shadow watched him take a long swallow of the brandy and grinned. "The woman. Oh, I'm sorry, the princess."

Niels shot him a look that would have made a lesser man quake. "She's nothing to do with this."

Shadow was not discouraged. "Doesn't she? Then you paid her no mind at this grand event, barely spoke to her, and certainly wasted no time dancin' attendance on her?"

"We did dance . . ." Niels looked away. An unwilling smile softened his hard mouth.

"Oh, hell, I was kiddin', but you're not. This is bad!"

"A dance, that's all." The man called Wolf was, at heart, honest. "A few dances," he amended, but then added in his own defense, "She's just a woman."

"I've seen her. She's *just* nothin'."

"She's not beautiful."

"What does that mean? Some bandbox cutie, all blonde curls and poutin' lips? You've never liked that sort. You've always liked the ones with an edge; we both know that."

Niels finished his brandy in a single swallow. The fire burned him but it was damn expensive heat and he'd bear it. "She's a *princess,* Shadow. All her life she's been protected, indulged, catered to. You know me better than any man. How long do you think I could stand a woman like that?"

"Seventy . . . eighty years, at the most."

"I'm serious!"

"So am I, brother. I just wish like hell she wasn't Akoran."

But she was, and the grim reality of that kept Niels awake long after his body demanded sleep. He lay on his back and listened to the creak of wheels and the clop of hooves steadily increasing on the street beyond the garden of the house. The voices of the hired cook and a fishmonger, chatting at the back door, floated up the stairwell. The laundress arrived and was ushered in with robust feminine laughter. Two lorry drivers nearly came to blows amid the encouragement of a quickly gathered crowd.

The city that some called the capital of the world — to the vast chagrin of Parisians — was well into a new day when Niels gave up finally and swung his legs over the edge of the bed. If he wasn't going to sleep — and clearly he wasn't — he might as well get on with it.

There were ways to find a man in London, apart from infiltrating the Akorans' social circle. Sharp eyes and ears were always available for the right price. He was going over the various possibilities when Shadow knocked at the door.

"Good," his brother said, "you're awake. I let you sleep as long as I could but —"

"Sleep is a faithless drudge. What is that?" Niels wiped the lather from his cheek as he indicated the letter Shadow held.

"A note from Benjamin Sherensky. He has learned of your presence in London, welcomes you, and invites you to do him the honor of callin'."

"Does he? I'm surprised he's waited this long."

"He's been out of the country, so I hear."

"Acquiring, no doubt. Perhaps he's found something of interest."

"Whether he has or not, you'll have to go."

"That's true," Niels agreed as he glanced in the mirror to fasten his collar studs. "Sherensky is the foremost dealer of antique weapons in England. Some of my best pieces come from him."

Shadow nodded. "It would look odd if you didn't find time for him."

Resigned to the need to make at least a gesture in the direction of the consuming interest that supposedly had brought him to England, Niels left the house a short time later. Benjamin Sherensky's home, which was also his place of business, was located just to the west of Regent's Park. His was one of the newer residential areas, which were expanding the boundaries of London so rapidly that maps were often out-of-date before they could be printed. It was, Niels thought, a pleasant neighborhood of colonnaded row houses, graceful despite a certain hasty sameness in their design.

The Russian was not a man to stand on ceremony. He opened the door himself in response to Niels's knock and beamed when he saw his friend.

"Come in, come in! I had little hope you would call so quickly, but your instincts have not faltered."

Speaking rapidly and leading the way into the house, Sherensky smoothed the napkin tucked under his chin. "I am having borscht. Come and eat with me."

The two men were soon ensconced in a pleasant, sun-filled room at the front of the house. A smiling maid brought another bowl of the glistening beet soup, so deeply red it was almost purple. Niels accepted a dollop of sour cream that set off both the color and flavor, as well as a scattering of chopped chives.

For several minutes, the men ate in silence. Niels put his spoon down first and did not restrain a sigh of genuine pleasure. "Been a long time since I've had borscht that good."

Sherensky grinned. He was a big man, fleshy without being fat, with dark hair and smooth plump cheeks. A careless observer would presume he was soft and might act on that misassumption. Depending on Sherensky's mood, it could be the fellow's last mistake.

"Considering that you never had borscht before you met me, maybe you aren't the best judge. But you're right all the same. My cook's all the way from Petersburg. Costs me the earth, and worth every penny."

Niels curled a hand around the glass of tea set before him, determined it was only scalding, and took a sip. "How long has it been? Two years . . . three?"

"Three," Sherensky said emphatically. "I saw you last in Washington. You bought that four-

116

teenth-century Venetian sword."

"An excellent piece."

"It is that. They knew steel, the Venetians." The Russian looked up from his borscht and grinned. "But I have something better this time. Much better."

Niels did his best not to look overly interested and suspected he failed. Sherensky pushed back from the table and rose.

"I thought of you the moment I saw it. Well, that's not strictly true. The moment I saw it, I thought *finally*. I'd been on the track of it, following rumors for months. But right after that, you were in my mind."

"Very good of you, I'm sure," Niels said dryly.

"No, I mean it. You will never forgive yourself if you let this go by. But come, see for yourself."

He led the way back to the ground floor where the high windows were covered with ornate metal grilles sufficient to discourage the most ambitious thief. Light filtering through the windows revealed a staggering array of weapons displayed on the walls, hanging from the rafters, laid out on long wooden tables or, for the smaller among them, set in glass-fronted cabinets. A fair-sized army could have equipped itself in what Sherensky was pleased to call his "little shop." An opposing army could have done the same equally well and the two could then have battled it out in Regent's

Park. The whimsical notion amused Niels. He was smiling when Sherensky moved aside suddenly and he saw . . . *it*.

A sword — of rare size and oddly compelling beauty. The blade itself was at least five feet long and the hilt added another foot. Only the most powerful of warriors could have wielded it. A design etched into the blade was in remarkably good condition for all its obvious antiquity. The hilt was oddly carved in a way he could not recognize. "How old — ?"

"Nine hundred years, roughly. That is my best estimate based on the circumstances in which it was found."

Ignoring his mounting excitement, Niels asked, "Which were?"

"It was found in Norway, south of Oslo, at a place that used to be called Sciringesheal."

Niels frowned. "I've heard of that."

"Really? The name hasn't been used in centuries, but never mind. There were other artifacts, including, if you can believe it, a book, sufficient to date it to the late eighth or early ninth century. The state of preservation is remarkable, but there is no doubt that it is old."

"Was it in a grave?"

Sherensky shrugged. "If it was, there was no body. Perhaps the warrior whose sword this was, went directly to Valhalla."

"Perhaps." He answered absently, trying to remember where he had heard the ancient name. His father? No, his father's mother, who

118

had died when he was very small. But before she did, she told the most remarkable stories that she claimed had been handed down generation after generation in the family. Looking back on those stories years later, he had assumed they were mere myth. But now, hearing a name directly from them, he had to wonder.

"What else do you know of the sword?" he asked.

"It belonged to a mighty warrior, a man called — oddly enough — the Wolf."

Niels laughed. "You really will say anything for a sale, won't you, Benjamin?"

The Russian put a hand over his heart in a gesture of sincerity. "I swear on the heads of my children, this is what I was told. His name lives still. He is said to have stolen a woman of rare beauty from England and made her his wife."

"How is it that no Viking ever stole a woman plain enough to crack a mirror?"

"They did, but they threw those back."

Niels laughed again, but inwardly he was mulling over the odd coincidence. His grandmother had spoken of a hero called the Wolf, long before her own grandson acquired the same name.

To the best of his knowledge, Sherensky had no children. Even so . . . "I may be interested in the sword," he allowed.

The Russian didn't try to hide his glee. "You and I both know you're not about to let this go to another collector. That is why, my friend, I sent word to you alone —"

He broke off as the same smiling maid stuck her head in the door. "Gentleman to see you, sir."

"What sort of gentleman, my dear?"

"The handsome kind, sir. *Very* handsome."

"Ivana has her own notion of what matters," Sherensky said with a grin. "Show him in."

A moment later, Andreas stepped into the room. He looked from one to the other and nodded cordially. "Gentlemen. Mister Wolfson, I thought I might find you here."

"Did you, Your Highness?" And why was that, Niels wondered? Was it possible the Akorans were curious enough about him to have him under surveillance?

"Rumor has it that Benjamin has returned from the Northlands with a rare prize. Mindful that you are a preeminent collector, I thought you might already have wind of it."

"Indeed, he does, Your Highness," Sherensky replied. For once, the wily Russian looked caught off guard. "But I had no notion that anyone else did."

Niels's fleeting thought that Sherensky had informed both of them in hope of igniting a bidding war, faded. The admission of ignorance had come too grudgingly to be false.

"Sailors have a habit of talking," Andreas said lightly. "And we are in the habit of listening. The fact is, I thought the sword would interest my uncle."

"The Earl of Hawkforte?" Sherensky asked. At Andreas's nod, the Russian said, "I understand the manor at Hawkforte houses a remarkable collection of weapons. Indeed, it has long been my ambition to see what is there. But all the arms have been in the Hawkforte family for generations, have they not? Nothing new was acquired from elsewhere."

"That is true," Andreas said, "except in the case of something that has gone outside the family and is brought back."

"This weapon is from the Northlands," Niels reminded him. He felt suddenly protective of the sword, as though he was somehow personally responsible for it. That was absurd, yet he could not shake the sensation.

"The sister of the first Earl of Hawkforte wed a Viking lord, a man called Wolf. If this is indeed his sword, it belongs — at least through marriage — to Hawkforte."

"A point I had not considered," Sherensky conceded with the sudden thoughtfulness of a man seeing both challenge and opportunity.

"We are speaking of events nine hundred years ago," Niels countered. "While it is true they are remembered within my own family —" He was stretching just a little, but thanks to his grandmother, not entirely.

"Are they?" Andreas looked surprised. "I thought few Americans knew much, if anything, about their forebearers."

121

"Why would you think that, Your Highness?" Niels inquired with mildness he did not feel. "We may rarely have been lucky enough to be able to keep written records, but we aren't without voices that can speak of the past."

"Of course." Rather to Niels's surprise, the Akoran prince took the correction with good grace. "I did not mean to imply that your claim was less than that of Hawkforte. In fact, if you believe you have a family link to the sword, Uncle Royce would likely want you to have it."

Sherensky stepped adroitly into the silence that followed this declaration. "Does that mean, Mister Wolfson, that I may look forward to an offer?"

"I will consider it." He would have the sword, but just then he was more interested in the prince. Andreas lacked the arrogance of European nobles he had encountered in the fulfillment of his professional duties. The Akoran seemed an intelligent, straightforward man.

Which meant he would be all the more formidable an enemy.

"Are you engaged for the rest of the day?" Andreas asked when they had taken their leave of Sherensky.

"I should pay my respects at the embassy, but it can wait."

"Good, perhaps you would like to join us. We are going out to Boswick for a picnic. We'll likely stay the night and return to London tomorrow."

Pleased though he was by this further evidence that the Akorans were accepting him into their circle, Niels did not reply directly. Instead, he said, "Princess Amelia's father, Prince Alexandros, is also the Marquess of Boswick, is he not?"

Andreas nodded. "That honor and others came to him through his English father."

"Then the ties between Akora and Britain go back several generations?"

"Technically, they go back much further. A distant relation of the present Earl of Hawkforte came to Akora in 1100 A.D."

"I was unaware of that," Niels said. And he was, despite having learned everything he could about the connections between the royal family of Akora and the powerful lords of Hawkforte.

"Is there any reason why you should have been?"

A collector of weapons pursuing his expensive hobby. Formerly an aide to a now-retired president. A man with no other reason to be in England, save personal amusement.

Certainly, a man with no particular interest in anything to do with the Akorans.

With an easy smile, he said, "One hears all sorts of things about Akora. It's impossible not to."

"That is true," Andreas allowed. He paused briefly, looking at Niels, who returned his gaze steadily. Slowly, the prince, too, smiled. "Coming with us?"

"I'd be delighted."

And so to Boswick. The elegant manor dated from the reign of George I and had, until recently, been a day's journey outside London. The new coaching roads made it reachable in mere hours.

"The wonder of the modern world," Amelia said shortly after the party departed down the long drive and through the high, wrought-iron gates. She rode a large gelding, almost as big as Brutus, and handled him with the same practiced ease she had shown at Smithfield. Her habit was emerald, replacing the crimson she had worn then. Vibrant colors suited her. Riding beside her, Niels thought she looked exactly what she was — a princess who also happened to be a damnably, if somewhat unconventionally, attractive woman.

He would do well to stop thinking about that.

"Do you have roads like this in Akora?" They were riding side by side, with the rest of the party bound for Boswick spread out in front and behind them. Rather to his surprise, everyone was on horseback, the Princesses Joanna and Kassandra included. Servants, he had been told, had left earlier in the day by carriage. He appeared to be the only guest, unless others were planning to join them at Boswick.

"We have roads," Amelia replied, "but they

are not macadamized like these. The road beds are dug deep, often eight to ten feet, filled with gravel, and finished with paving stones."

"They sound like the old Roman roads."

"I believe we took note of the Roman method and adapted it. All the same, travel in Akora is mainly by sea."

He knew that, had studied such maps as were available, including the most recent that revealed what the Akorans had kept concealed for so long. What had been thought to be a single island was, in fact, two large islands separated by an inland sea — the result of a catastrophic volcanic eruption thousands of years before. Amid the natural harbors that inland sea might well offer, the British were believed to seek a naval base.

"Do you sail?" Amelia asked.

"On occasion." He loved the sea, having discovered the Atlantic with astounded joy on his first trip out of Kentucky. It had been, in some strange way, a kind of homecoming.

"Do I detect an effort at modesty, Mister Wolfson?"

"I can handle a boat well enough," he allowed. "What about you?" He had seen how well she rode. Given her heritage, she was likely as adept with sail and rudder.

"I make an excellent passenger."

He laughed. "Now who's being modest?"

"No, I mean it. My mother, who is a marvelous sailor, has tried to teach me. Loving mother that she is, she pretends not to be frustrated with the results."

"You are close to your parents."

"I cannot imagine being otherwise."

"You are fortunate. Nothing is more important than family."

"Tell me about yours. Are your parents alive?"

"My father died when I was young. My mother remains in Kentucky, which she will not leave for all the world. Fortunately, she accepts that my brother and I are determined she will be comfortable."

"You have a brother? What is his name?"

Niels grinned. "I should explain that my father named the firstborn son. My mother claimed the right to name the second."

"Reasonably enough. Your father chose Niels for you and your mother chose . . ."

"She had — still does have — a great fondness for the tales of King Arthur."

"Arthur, then?"

"I'm afraid not. Her favor fell on Lancelot."

"Oh —"

"At a loss for something courteous to say, Princess?"

Amelia did not deny it. "I merely wonder what it is like to be a boy in Kentucky, or anywhere for that matter, named Lancelot."

"He did not answer to it for very long and will not now. While we were still very small, neighbors duped him Shadow because he was inclined to follow me about. He's been called that ever since, although he is as independent a man as I have yet to know."

"Was he in Washington with you?"

"On occasion. He . . . comes and goes."

"An adventurer?"

"You could say that."

Her horse shied a little just then, bringing her closer to him. He caught a hint of her perfume as she looked at him. "Like yourself?"

"I'm the staidest of fellows."

She laughed, a rich, completely genuine sound mercifully unlike the titters of simpering misses on either side of the Atlantic.

"I think not, Mister Wolfson. But I also think you are a man not given to revealing very much about yourself."

Score one for the princess, who could not have been more right about that. A bit of misdirection seemed called for.

"What makes you think there is anything of interest to reveal?"

Her gaze turned shrewd. "A man who has gone from the frontier of Kentucky to the council chambers of Washington can hardly claim to be without interest."

"Even to a princess?" He had not meant to say that. She . . . unsettled him. That was all there was to it. She was an appealing woman. Under other circumstances, he would have —

No, he would not have sought any sort of personal relationship with her. She was a woman for marriage and children. He had done very well avoiding that sort.

Which made it all the stranger why he couldn't seem to stop looking at her.

# Chapter Eight

"Please don't think I don't know what you are doing," Amelia said.

Her mother, seated beside her aunt in the drawing room at Boswick, smiled guilelessly. "I have no idea what you mean."

"You believe Mister Wolfson may be a suitor."

"What an idea," Joanna said. "Well, if you think of him in that light, dear —"

"I do not, you do. That is why you invited him here."

Her mother set down her teacup and folded her hands in her lap, a gesture Amelia had long since realized meant Joanna was measuring out her words with particular care.

"Isn't it enough that we have every reason to be grateful to Mister Wolfson *and* that he appears to be an interesting man and that he doesn't seem to know very many people in London, therefore would welcome the opportunity to widen his acquaintance? Isn't that sufficient reason for inviting him?"

"Yes, but that isn't why you did it."

Kassandra smothered a laugh and sent a meaningful look in the direction of the sister-in-law who was also her cherished friend. "She has you, Joanna."

"My own daughter. Oh, well . . . Look, dearest, where is the harm? If you truly do not care for him, we won't invite him again. But you seemed . . . that is, it appeared to me as though you rather enjoyed his company."

"I do," Amelia admitted frankly. "But I have no reason to believe that Mister Wolfson returns my interest." That was not entirely true. There were times when he looked at her in such a way that she was quite at a loss to breathe, much less think. But she was fearful of making too much of such moments, even in her own imagination.

Kassandra held out a hand to her niece, drawing her down beside her on the settee. Her dark eyes, eyes that at one time had seen the future, gleamed with tender amusement. "If you will pardon my saying so, Melly, you have a great deal of experience in discouraging men who tend to fawn or, worse yet, slobber over you and no experience whatsoever dealing with the other sort."

"What sort would that be?" Amelia asked, very low. She was torn between annoyance at her mother's and aunt's interference and desperate need for their wisdom.

"Mister Wolfson," her mother said slowly, "Mister Niels Wolfson . . . the Wolf . . . is an impressive man."

"So you have observed. Believe it or not, Mother, I, too, have taken note of that."

Undeterred, Joanna continued. "He is a man

130

in the way of your father and uncles, your brothers and cousins, in the way to which you have been accustomed all your life but have not been able to find outside your family."

"There are men on Akora who are strong, caring, protective, intelligent, who possess the qualities of the men of my family."

Kassandra nodded. "That is true. And we had hoped you might find yourself drawn to one of them. But that has not happened. I think you know why."

She did know, though she had never acknowledged it before. Were she to fall in love with and wed a man of Akora, her life would be on Akora. Her dreams of seeing much more of the world than she had already done, her unexplained yearning for another place she could not name, would all have to be forgotten.

Since coming to womanhood, she had held herself apart from the men of Akora. But among the men of England, she had found no one who drew her.

Until the night and the rain, and the dark of the road.

"You understand," she said quietly, "it is very likely nothing will come of your efforts."

Her mother and aunt exchanged a look Amelia could not decipher. They went on to speak of other things. Soon enough, it was time to dress for dinner.

For perhaps the dozenth time, Niels reminded himself that he soon might be at war with these charming people. In defense of his country, he could be called upon to kill one or more of the men. Or one of them might kill him.

He *knew* this, understood it to the marrow of his bones. Yet seated around the candlelit table, enjoying the excellent food and wine, but most particularly enjoying the company, the very notion of war with the Akorans was bizarre.

Could Andreas, a man who just then was winding up a genuinely funny story of which he himself was the butt, have actually plotted to blow up an American ship, slaughtering fifty-nine men in the process?

Could Prince Alexandros, who so evidently loved his wife and children that his hard face softened every time he looked at them, have conspired in such a plot?

And what of the Earl of Hawkforte and his countess, who were also present? What role, if any, could either of them have played in such an atrocity?

If there had been a time when Niels possessed the innocent naïveté of youth, he could no longer remember it. A degree of cynicism was his common starting point in any dealings with others. And yet, no amount of caution, doubt, or even outright suspicion could make him see the Akorans as the villains he understood they might very well be.

And then there was Amelia.

Candlelight gleamed off her bare shoulders. She wore a lacey sort of gown in pale ivory, showing more of a Spanish influence than the usual French. Her bosom was . . . emphasized. Well, no, not really. To be fair, it was just that she had lovely breasts and they likely would look exactly that were she to don sackcloth.

She laughed just then and a ripple of pleasure moved through him. Niels caught himself, took a breath, and did his damnedest to think of something, anything else.

War, chaos, havoc, death, destruction.

Amelia . . .

This was absurd. He had known any number of lovely women. None had ever affected him in such a manner. Was it that this one happened to be a princess?

He tried the thought and rejected it almost at once. He didn't care who she was, but he must care, or at any rate not forget. She was Akoran. He had to remember that, had to drum it into his mind until the pulse of desire building within him could be well and truly dampened.

"So I picked myself up," Andreas was saying, "dusted myself off, and did my best to apologize to the lady."

The company laughed and laughed harder still when he added, "Of course, I had trouble sitting down for the next week, but I made sure no one noticed."

"We noticed!" Luc exclaimed as Marc grinned. "Damn if we didn't."

"And kept quiet about it?" Andreas rejoined. "I think not. I would never have heard the end of it from the two of you."

The younger men tried denying that but gave up quickly enough. Joanna took the opportunity of a pause in the conversation to glance at her husband. "Darling, this has been wonderful, but it's been a rather long day."

Alex nodded and rose at once. He did not look fatigued, at least not to Niels, but then neither did the Princess Joanna.

"I'm rather tired myself," the Earl of Hawkforte said. He, too, stood and held out a hand to his lovely wife. "Shall we, my dear?"

Kassandra rose, smiled, and placed her hand in her husband's.

Very shortly, both couples departed amid cheerful goodnights and hopes that the "young people" would be able to amuse themselves.

Niels found himself staring at Amelia, who caught his gaze, dropped hers, and promptly raised it again. He was distantly aware of the others watching them, of Andreas, in particular, looking amused but vigilant. Subtlety and discretion were called for here. How unfortunate that he could not seem to muster either.

Whether from the cheerful obliviousness of youth or a more mature desire to ease them all out of an awkward moment, Luc asked, "Any chance you play billiards?"

"I've given it a try from time to time."

"Excellent!" Without further ado, Luc

pushed away from the table. Marc and Andreas did the same.

Niels also stood, but looked to Amelia. "If you have no objection —"

She appeared surprised by the very notion. "Of course not." Rising, she joined the others. "I'd love a game."

He could learn from this. Life offered many lessons in many different forms and he'd generally had the good sense to benefit from them. This was just one more example of that.

Sooner or later, a man's assumptions would always trip him up. That was the lesson here, albeit one he really had thought he'd learned long ago. Not so, apparently.

Amelia bent a little more, stretched out her slender arms a little farther, adjusted her hips beneath the ivory lace gown just so, and deftly tapped the cue ball. It bounced off the northwest corner of the table, struck the one remaining ball, ricocheted it across the smooth felt, and dropped the ball neatly into one of the six pockets placed at intervals around the table.

"Nicely done," Niels murmured.

She straightened, tossed her hair back over her shoulders and grinned. "Admit it, you're surprised."

"Not at all. I've known quite a few women who played billiards." Never mind that they were all ladies of decidedly easy virtue. "It's become the fashion."

"I warrant they didn't play as well," Andreas said as he set up the balls again. There were two, three including the cue ball, making for fast games with points scored for pocketing the balls or striking both at the same time. In the two hours or so that they had been playing, Niels had won a half-dozen times, as had Andreas. Luc and Marc each had three victories. All the rest, the considerable rest, were Amelia's.

"Perhaps not," Niels acknowledged, but absently. He was preoccupied with looking at Amelia. She was flushed and happy, twirling chalk onto the tip of her cue.

Her gaze met his long enough for him to become aware, however belatedly, of the silence that had descended around the room. In that silence, he saw the wash of color that came and went across her delicate skin, leaving her unnaturally pale. Abruptly, she put her cue down. "You must excuse me, gentlemen. I'm more fatigued than I realized."

Both her brothers frowned, but it was Andreas who asked, "Is everything all right, Melly?"

"Fine. It's just been a long day."

With a quick smile for them all and a last lingering glance in Niels's direction, the Princess of Akora departed.

Outside the game room, Amelia leaned against the wall, closed her eyes, and took a

136

deep breath. Her heart was beating far too quickly and if she didn't know better, she would have sworn that she felt light-headed.

She could not bear it. She had risked humiliating herself before members of her own family rather than reveal the impact a mere glance from Niels Wolfson had on her.

It was, of course, absurd. She was a perfectly sensible young woman. As attractive as the American might be — and there really was no arguing about that! — she was quite incapable of behaving like an addled schoolgirl.

Or so she most fervently wished to believe.

She had no hope of sleep in her present state and the solitude of her own room did not beckon. Instead, she went on through the high-domed entry hall, the ceiling festooned with gamboling cherubs, down a broad corridor and out the back of the house to the terrace overlooking the formal gardens. Leaning against the stone balustrade, she breathed deeply and sought the moon.

It had risen just above the tops of the trees, gilding their leaves and branches with silver. A soft breeze carried the scents of newly mown grass. Nearby, a fountain splashed. The fountain was a marvel of engineering, its broad marble base concealing a complex of water wheels that were turned by the falling water, which was raised in turn by the wheels back up the central tower to fall again, perpetuating the process.

As a child, Amelia remembered being endlessly fascinated by the fountain. She loved to sit on the edge of it, dangling her feet in the cool water and imagining the endless turning of the wheels hidden below. Once, by special request, she had been allowed to go with her father and the skilled craftsman who maintained the fountain into the chamber hidden in the earth, to see the mechanism for herself.

It fascinated her still, as did all things mechanical. She supposed that had to do with the mechanical boy her Uncle Royce had gifted her with on her birth and who — she always thought of him as who rather than what — had shared her nursery. He was still now, his gears and pulleys activated only a few times a year to keep him in good condition as he awaited a new generation to amaze and delight.

Beyond the fountain, in the fringe of trees, she heard the rustle of deer. She watched, scarcely breathing, as a small family emerged onto the lawn. A doe, her yearling daughter, and two fawns, astoundingly agile on spindle legs, their haunches covered with piebald spots. They moved out across the clearing, so bright in the moonlight that the shadows of trees stretched across it.

The deer gleamed white in the spectral light. Boswick was renowned for its albino deer. Had her father permitted it, visitors would have come from far and wide to see them. But Alex protected them as he protected so much else.

Amelia was well accustomed to protective men. Indeed, in her most truthful moments, she could admit that she took very much for granted such men and all they stalwartly provided.

What would Niels Wolfson protect? His country, that she did not doubt. The mother and brother of whom he spoke so lovingly. There was a startling softening about his eyes when he mentioned them.

What else? A wife? He had none. Children? He did not strike her as a careless man.

She thought of him far too much. Her mother and aunt . . . their plottings . . . she had meant it when she said it would all come to nothing. Yet her heart tugged in a different direction.

Foolishness. She should go to bed and she would, in just a moment. When she was done watching the deer.

"Are they white?"

She turned with an almost overwhelming sense of relief. He had come. As she had not dared to hope, yet had counted on all the same. How contradictory he made her feel. And contradiction heaped upon itself, how certain.

Moonlight heightened the hard lines of his face, emphasized the broad sweep of his shoulders and chest. He moved silently, a hunter.

"They are," she said and took pride in the steadiness of her voice. "Boswick is famous for them."

"I have only seen one albino deer before, and that was in Kentucky."

She was vaguely disappointed that the deer were not entirely new to him. She was so accustomed to people exclaiming over them.

"There were few left," she said, "until my father came. He paid the people hereabouts not to hunt them."

"I thought such hunting was forbidden."

"It has been for centuries, but it happens all the same, especially when there is a market for white deer hides. At any rate, the hunting stopped. He also realized that so much of the home forest had been cut down that they had little shelter. Their white skins make them more vulnerable to the sun, you see. Father planted many more trees, which have now grown. The herd has increased right along with them."

"They are beautiful," Niels said, but he was looking at her.

She was not beautiful. Not in the way of her Aunt Kassandra or her mother, although both laughed at the notion. What was beauty? A certain precise symmetry of feature, a difference of fractions of inches? What did it matter?

"Amelia —"

"Niels —" She smiled. "They call you the Wolf."

"That doesn't concern you?" He asked as though it should.

She shrugged. His eyes followed the movement of her shoulders. He seemed entranced by them.

"I assume you earned the name in some honorable way."

A swift look of pain crossed his features. "That depends on your definition of honor."

"I know precisely what honor is. It is not in the least questionable."

"There are those who would disagree, but never mind. Jackson gave me the name about the time he became president. It is not something I ever wanted."

The deer were nibbling grass, aware of the humans but unafraid. "Why did he call you that?"

He hesitated. "It is not something I speak of often."

She waited, willing him to take the leap, and had to control a smile of exaltation when he did.

"When he was running for president the first time, there were men who convinced themselves that a man of the people, as Jackson was, would be a great danger to the country. What they meant was that he would be a great danger to their ability to exploit the country to their own advantage, as they were accustomed to doing. Understanding that he had a good chance of winning, they conspired to kill him."

She had never heard a breath of this, but she was unsurprised all the same. Akora, generally so peaceful, was not entirely immune to the treachery and violence of ambitious men. Even so, she had to wonder how all this had touched Niels. "What did you do?"

"I killed them instead."

So simply said, yet she did not mistake what the words meant. "Yours is a nation of law, is it not?"

He nodded curtly. "There was no way to bring these men to justice. They were too powerful and they would not stop, not even when they realized that their intent was known. Arresting the men they hired did no good; they simply hired more. Worse yet, they were willing to kill anyone and everyone who got in their way."

"So you took the law into your own hands?"

He watched her carefully as she spoke, his gaze wolf-keen. She showed none of the avid excitement he had seen in women who had only heard rumors of what he had done, not the stark truth as he had revealed to her alone. Nor did she display any hint of the revulsion he had also encountered. Instead, she accepted the reality of his actions matter-of-factly. He added that to his admittedly small but growing store of knowledge about the Akorans.

Niels exhaled deeply, letting the words go. "I became judge, jury, and executioner."

"And you hated every moment of it?"

"No, not every moment. Every time I killed one of them, I felt . . . a certain satisfaction. There would be one less to threaten what was good and right."

"That being Jackson?"

"No, he is only a man, flawed like all the rest of us. What is good and right is the nation itself, and the notion behind it that all men are fundamentally equal. That no one, regardless of what wealth he may have or power he can buy, can undo that."

He glanced at the deer again, then looked at her. "I wonder if you can possibly understand?"

"I am a princess," she said, walking toward him across the stone terrace, diminishing the distance between them. "My uncle is the Vanax — you would say the King — of Akora. My father is his closest advisor. My mother is the daughter of the most ancient house in England, that which is called the Shield of the Throne but is really the Shield of England itself."

Closer still. She could see the sudden pulse of a muscle in his jaw, sensed the will he exerted to control himself. The thought of that supremely masculine will excited her. Did he but know it, she was born and bred to be the equal of such a man.

"On Akora, I live in a palace high on a hill."

"I know this —"

"No," she said and laid the palm of her hand flat against his chest, just there where she could feel the strong, steady beat of his heart. "Mister Niels Wolfson, you do not know what you think you know."

"We are as far apart as earth and moon. That I know."

"Do you think so? There is a pool on Akora where it is said the lover of the Moon drowned when he peered too closely at the Earth."

"A pretty story."

Strong, steady, but a flicker faster.

"Romantic. Do you believe in romance?"

He shook his head. "Not especially."

"What is this, then?"

His hard mouth lifted. She saw the amusement in his eyes and behind it, the fire.

"Passion," he said and reached for her.

# Chapter Nine

His kiss was very far from the tentative touch of a man uncertain of how a woman will receive him. He gave no quarter and offered none. His mouth took hers insistently, parting her lips, filling her with the thrust of his tongue. He tasted deliciously tempting, a heady enticement to her senses.

After the first stunned moment when she realized that the defenses proven so effective against other men had crumbled without murmur before the Wolf, Amelia simply yielded herself. She wanted everything he was, everything he made her feel. No, more than wanted, she yearned for it with a hunger she had barely acknowledged.

Time slowed, the world faded. There was only, as he had said, passion, and behind it, dare she hope, the stirrings of something more.

She could love Niels Wolfson. She could accept him into her heart and into her body without regret.

Instincts, honed in the sensual atmosphere of Akora, stirred. She moved against him, her hands running up his powerful arms before linking behind the thick column of his neck. Her mouth softened even further, accepting, coaxing.

This was insanity. He was a man of honor and strength lost in the heady kiss of a young woman who by all rights he should regard as untouchable. She was a virgin, wasn't she? Perhaps not at twenty-five, despite her unmarried status. Who knew with these Akorans? There were rumors that they were masters of the art of love. Mistresses of it, as well, or so it seemed.

He had to put an end to this and, to his credit, he did try. But scarcely had he managed to withdraw his mouth from hers, than his lips found their way down her throat to her exquisitely rounded shoulders. They were soft, as a woman's should be, but also shapely, well-defined, hinting that she lived a rigorous life. No reclining on silken pillows for this princess, he thought in the corner of his mind still capable of conscious thought.

Against his chest, the fullness of her breasts beckoned. He only just resisted the urge to cup them, finally drawing away with a sensation very akin to pain.

"Princess . . ."

"Amelia," she said on a thread of breath. He took some faint satisfaction from that, even as he struggled to breathe in turn.

He was rock hard, consumed by desire, requiring every ounce of his formidable self-control to avoid reaching for her again. All that was needed now was a glance out a window by her father or uncle or cousin or either brother, and the war he still hoped could be avoided would

146

come crashing down on them all for a ludicrously unanticipated reason.

His country could be dragged into war because he — a man trusted by two presidents and innumerable others in the highest positions of authority — seduced the beloved daughter of a royal house.

Or was seduced by her.

Strictly speaking, he wasn't quite sure which was more likely.

"Princess," he repeated firmly. "I apologize —"

"Whatever for?"

"The impropriety of my actions," he informed her resolutely. Better that than yield to the urge to laugh in response to the merriment he saw in her moonlit eyes. Passionate and good-humored. And that body and mouth, the undeniable pleasure he derived from the mere sound of her voice, the sense of almost boyish happiness with which she filled him.

The terrible problem she presented.

He took another step back, driven by a sense of self-preservation that was finally, however belatedly, making itself felt.

"This is not a good idea."

She smoothed her skirt and looked up at him chidingly. "You know, Mister Wolfson, if I were the ill-informed sort of young woman one commonly finds in England — poorly educated about certain matters — I might be wounded by your words. Heavens, I might even feel rejected."

"But you don't."

The smile she gave him was entirely feminine and wise beyond her years. "Happily, I had the benefit of a very good education."

And with that, the Princess of Akora offered her hand. "There is something I would like to show you."

Turn aside, make his goodnights, go back to the house. The sensible course was laid out right in front of him. He had only to take the first step —

He walked with her, holding her hand carefully in his, all too aware of how soft her skin was against his own callused palm. They walked past the silver splash of the fountain and across the lawn, near enough that the deer looked up and watched the pair in passing but still did not flee. Farther on was a path, just wide enough for two to stroll side by side. It led, beneath the moon-dappled branches of yew and oak, away from the great house to the banks of a small lake. In the center of the lake was an island and on the island was a gazebo in the shape of an ancient Greek temple.

"It was my special place when I was a child," Amelia said. She stepped forward, tugging lightly at his hand.

They came closer and closer to the lake. At the very edge of the water, he stopped. "You are hardly dressed for swimming, nor am I."

"Watch," she said and stepped out into . . . no, onto the water. Laughing at his surprise,

Amelia drew him one step at a time across the lake toward the island. He realized quickly enough that there was a bridge of stepping stones almost but not quite hidden beneath the surface of the water. She knew her way precisely, scarcely had to glance over her shoulder as she went backward holding his hand and his gaze, laughing in the moonlight.

"I had not thought you so cautious," she said at length when they reached the island.

"Neither had I," he admitted. Did she but know it, the Wolf was said to be a man who acted with such ruthless speed that an enemy would be dead before he knew himself endangered. That was, in its own way, merciful.

The temple gleamed white beneath the moon. He had come out of the world into some place entirely different. Yet the world remained, just beyond the borders of enchantment.

"You, on the other hand," he observed, "are very trusting."

"I am, in the right circumstances." She turned around, looking out over the lake. Her skirt swayed around her, drawing his eyes to the curve of her hips.

She turned again, saw the direction of his gaze and laughed. But her eyes, he observed in the moonlight, were entirely serious.

"Mister Wolfson . . . Niels . . . may I call you that?"

He was on fire for her, his blood hot and throbbing. A wry grin shaped his mouth.

"Under the circumstances, you might as well . . . Amelia."

She looked pleased by that. "On Akora, we almost never use titles. As often as I am in England, the emphasis on them is jarring."

"But Akora has a king and you are of the royal family."

"Not exactly. My uncle is the chosen ruler of Akora. His title, 'Vanax,' actually means 'chosen.' As for my family, it would probably be more accurate to say that we are servants."

He could not conceal his surprise. "You do not mean that."

"I do. We serve the country, the people, our heritage. Much has been entrusted to us and we endeavor to prove worthy of it."

How far would they go in that service, he wondered. To the gray, oil-slicked waters of Baltimore, to red, roiling fire and the screaming of doomed men?

"What is it?" she asked, seeing his face.

"Nothing." Aware that he had come perilously close to revealing too much, he moved swiftly to distract her. "Nothing at all," he said and drew the Princess of Akora — Amelia — back into his arms.

Old folks in the Kentucky hills spoke of moon madness. They said it made people do strange things. Just then, Niels was ready to swear they were right.

He could not let her go. He knew he should

150

. . . hell, he knew he had to, but knowing didn't get the job done. She felt so damn good, soft yet strong in her own way, leaning into his hands just like she wanted to be there more than anyplace else. Everything about her pleased him — the sound of her voice, the way she smelled, how she smiled when she was really happy.

What in God's name was wrong with him? He'd never been ruled by lust in his life and he didn't see why he should be now. Except maybe it wasn't just lust. Maybe his heart was involved as well.

Oh, no, definitely not! He was not a man for claptrap sentiment. Men and women each had something the other wanted. They struck bargains of all sorts to get it. Custom might dress that up in fancy trimmings, but he preferred unvarnished truth any day.

He wanted to lay his princess down, lift her skirts, and drive himself into her until they were both mindless with pleasure.

Now *that* was truth.

But he was a man, not a rutting boar. However hard she made him, however hot his blood, honor was there just waiting to be tripped over.

She moved against him as she had on the other side of the shore, in a world that grew more remote and meaningless with each passing moment. He sucked in his breath even as his arms tightened around her.

She couldn't possibly be a virgin. Virgins

were timid things likely to cry and carry on, making a man feel like a crawling snake just for doing what came naturally, or so he had heard. He had avoided such creatures all his life and had no mind to change now.

On the other hand, if she wasn't . . . He'd heard of islands in the South Pacific where it was said the women made love as easily and cheerfully as they did everything else. Perhaps it was the same on Akora. He had some trouble believing that, given that the Akoran men he'd encountered so far seemed very protective — not to mention possessive — of their women. But who was he to say what their customs might be?

Besides, she was a princess. Maybe the rules were different for them.

He sure as hell hoped so.

Of course, that didn't solve the problem of her family possibly being implicated in the murders of fifty-nine American seamen. If that were found to be true, it was certain to lead to war between their countries.

If it came to war, they would be on opposite sides. His loyalty to his nation was absolute and he did not imagine for a moment that hers could be anything less.

They might never have any but this stolen moment out of time. And if that was what lay in store for them —

"Amelia . . ." He set her back just a little, stared into her eyes, saw the passion in them, and felt his body tighten even further. "You know where this is going?"

She made a soft sound and laid her head on his chest. "I certainly hope so."

That pretty much did it for him. Niels took a deep breath, seeking control. A man had his pride. However desperately he hungered for her — and he couldn't remember ever feeling such need before — he was damn well going to make sure she had no cause for complaint.

She had led him to this place, but he led now. He was the man, after all, and buried deep within him was the need to conquer. Sweet conquest, sweet and hot, conquest of bodies clinging together, of clothes falling away, of moonlight bathing all.

She helped him, undoing the laces and ties his suddenly clumsy fingers couldn't manage, laughing over the boots and shoes in a way that made him shiver with delight. Such a woman. When had he met the like? Bold beneath the moon, on the hidden island, her hands on him and her mouth meeting his. He was dizzy with longing, weak with it, and yet stronger than he had ever been in his life.

Her breasts were exquisite, full and tantalizing, her nipples hard and dark against his callused palms. He had a sudden, riveting image of her suckling a child and tried to push it to the back of his mind, but could not. He was caught, knowing yet unknowing, in the fierce tidal pull of forces far beyond his own desire. Out there, beyond the world, immense power surged, in his body, yet far greater than it.

On the cusp of that power, driven by it, he thrust into her, past the barrier he had not thought to find, trying desperately to hold back, but drawn on by her own power, until he came at last to the place where somehow he was always meant to be.

"Amelia!"

His life flowed into her even as her back bowed, her nails digging into him as her eyes opened wide, reflecting the ancient moon.

It was done. There was no going back from it. The step she had taken was irrevocable and in that knowledge was a strange comfort.

Niels lay against her, for the moment — the precious, lovely moment — spent. This man of indomitable strength and will lay helpless in her arms.

She held him, feeling the beat of his heart and the heat of his skin against her own, his head heavy against her breasts, his legs twined with hers.

And she smiled despite the shock she felt at her own actions. Another being — surely not herself — seemed to have taken control of her. A woman of passion and desire, determined not to be denied. Nor had she been.

Her reward was pleasure — so great it still reverberated within her — and pain, more than she had expected, but insignificant against all else.

Was that not life itself, all in a moment there beneath the moon?

She was tired, suddenly, so much so that she doubted she could stay awake, yet she fought sleep all the same. Time was fleeting, the world too near. She had trespassed, they both had, in the shadow of the little temple. She would have to be careful, worst of all, of those she loved, who would not understand what she had done.

What they had done.

They would blame him, Niels — the Wolf. He raised his head just then and gazed at her. His eyes glittered with the hard sheen of steel. She was braced, already suspecting what he would say when the words came.

"This was a mistake."

That hurt, but it did not undo her.

"No," she said, still holding him, "it was not. I wanted you."

"Wanted?" Disapproval hardened his gaze. She plunged past it.

"Who knows what the future holds? Sometimes there is only the moment."

"Impulse." He spoke the word like a man who knew and infinitely distrusted the pitfalls of acting without thought.

"Fate," she countered. "Do you believe in that?"

He rose above her, holding himself on his braced arms, the muscles gleaming. Already, she missed his heat. "I don't."

"Why not?" The question was sincere. She was heiress to thousands of years of a people living what they believed was their destined course. To exist without such purpose, loose in the universe, was beyond her comprehension.

He struggled, seeking an answer, and finally said, "A man's fate is his own to make."

She smiled, fighting the urge to try to draw him back to her. "Of course it is, but the wise man knows where the current takes him and finds in its direction his own."

He turned his gaze from her toward the night. "Is that Akoran philosophy?"

"Knowledge," she said, and slipped from beneath him. The wind was rising and the night was growing chill. She reached for her clothes.

"You were a virgin."

He stood, luminous in the moon, still gloriously naked, gazing at her.

She shrugged, drawing her eyes from him with difficulty. "The choice was mine."

"It should also have been mine." He grappled with the thought that a woman could make such a decision for herself. "Why me?"

She rose before him, barely concealed by lace and darkness, her hair in disarray around her shoulders, her mouth full and soft. "Seeking a compliment, Mister Wolfson?"

"Niels," he said with bite. "It's an explanation I'd like, *Princess*. What you've just done — what we've done — may be acceptable by

156

Akoran standards but it sure as hell isn't acceptable by mine."

"I'm sorry to hear that." More than sorry. Pain was growing within her. Not regret, not precisely, for there was a sense of rightness to what she had done that she could neither fully understand nor deny. All the same, the intimacy they had shared too fleetingly was fast fading. She felt suddenly more alone than she had ever been in her life. Like a swimmer who had struck out into a tantalizing sea, only to be swept against rocky shores.

Niels reached for his trousers. "I have far too little control where you are concerned," he said.

She could have made some sophisticated remark about his control not seeming lacking to her, but she could not muster the energy for it. The full enormity of what she had done was sinking into her. She felt drained of strength, anxious only for solitude in which to hide the tumult of her emotions.

And yet, despite everything, or perhaps because of it, she could still smile. He sounded so purely and completely male — puzzled, vaguely irritated, somewhat uncertain, even vulnerable, though he would be loath to admit it. All because of a woman. Because of her.

"Before we go back," he said as he pulled on his shirt, "enlighten me, Princess. What is likely to be the reaction of your family — particularly of your father, brothers, and cousin, none of

157

whom strikes me as reluctant to pick up a sword — if they discover what happened here?"

She brushed grass from her skirt, gaining a moment. "There is no reason for them to know."

"That isn't an answer. Are such matters really considered so differently on Akora?"

"Yes —" That was true, so far as it went. Akora differed greatly from the England she knew, and yet there were aspects of human nature that did not seem to vary much at all. "And no." She met his gaze, resisted the instinct to soothe his stirring anger. "Their first impulse would be to kill you."

He did not even flinch, so far as she could see. But he did shake his head, as though at his own folly. "That, at least, I understand."

"You may, I do not. At any rate, you need not concern yourself. They will *not* know."

She moved away from him, anxious suddenly to be gone. In her haste, she stumbled. Niels's hand shot out, catching her before she could fall.

"Amelia —"

"Enough! You regret this. All right, I should not have lured you."

"Lured me? What are you talking about? I could have walked away at any time."

She turned, then, finding herself in his arms, which he truly had not meant to have around her. "Why didn't you?" she demanded, her eyes alight.

Why hadn't he? Why had he done what he knew was, by any measure of honor or simple sense, truly wrong?

Because she filled him with hunger beyond any he had ever known? Because he knew somehow that he would find with her pleasure beyond imagining?

Weak and poor excuses. Years — years! — of self-control, of discipline and determination, of ironclad principles and beliefs he had never thought could waver. Burned out in an instant. In her arms.

"Did you merely need a woman?" she asked, and her lip curled with her scorn. "Had it been too long between bedmates for you?"

"No! Don't think of yourself that way."

"Why not? Because you forbid it? Fie on you, I shall think as I will. You owe me nothing. Nothing! I chose you, I did as I wished, and I do not regret it. Be assured, Mister Niels Wolfson, you will be a pleasant memory."

His hand tightened on her, drawing her nearer still. "Oh, no, Princess. I am very far from being a memory of any sort. Feel this?" He closed the small remaining distance between them, holding her hard against him. "I am as real as you are ever likely to encounter, and what lies between us is very far from done."

"I say when it is done, not you."

"You think so? I don't."

They stood beneath the moon, glaring at

each other until he let her go. Very clearly and deliberately, releasing his fingers one by one, leaving no doubt that had he chosen — and when he did — he could hold her to him effortlessly.

She went across the bridge of stones, leaving him to follow.

Niels opted to swim across to the mainland. He found, in the cool night water, some small degree of ease for the burning heat of his body.

Body, not heart. He insisted that he had no heart, it having been frozen out of him in the icy winter when he pursued the men who would kill an ideal. Hunting and executing them one by one, as he himself grew rawer and wilder with each death. Until he emerged at last from that brutal time to discover that he had become the Wolf.

He strode, dripping from the lake, and stood beneath the moon, bathed in silver light, until he was sure the great house of Boswick slumbered. Only then did he enter its walls to seek his own uneasy rest.

# Chapter Ten

Shadow was waiting for Niels in the stable behind the rented London house. He was currying his horse with the smooth, rhythmic motion of a man who has done the same task so many times it no longer requires thought. Diablo stood still beneath his hands, but whinnied softly when Brutus entered. The stallions were brothers, rarely separated from birth and so inclined to tolerate one another. The human brothers were the same — usually.

"How was Boswick?" Shadow asked without interrupting his task.

Uncinching his saddle, Niels replied, "Well enough."

It was quiet in the stalls, but beyond he could hear the twilight city he had just ridden through after parting from the Akorans near their own residence. Amelia had not looked at him. Fine, so be it. He did not pretend to understand her, not for a moment, any more than he understood what had happened between them. He knew only that nothing — not the woman, not desire, not any other emotion he cared to name — would divert him from his mission.

He would do well to remember who and what he was — an American, Kentucky born, son of the wild hills, and beyond them of hard memories. It was a heritage he would never betray.

"What happened?" Shadow asked, glancing at his brother.

"Nothing." Niels hoisted the saddle onto its stand and drew off the blanket that was dark with the horse's sweat. Brutus shook himself and butted his head lightly against his master.

Moments passed with safe and ordinary chores — water poured into the trough, the feedbag filled, hooves checked.

Shadow set the brush aside and gave his attention to his brother. "No sign of the Angel?"

"I was the only guest."

"Waste of time, then."

"I suppose —" Never mind that it had changed his life, or at least his perception of it.

His brother shot him a hard glance. "You don't look yourself."

Just what he needed, Shadow getting sensitive. "And who else would I be?"

"Hell if I know. What's eatin' at you?"

"I went, he wasn't there, I'm back. There's nothing else to say."

"All right . . . You aren't ailin', are you?"

"For God's sake!"

"You had that ague a year ago."

"I had a fever for a couple of days. It was nothing. You're the one who damn near got killed."

"I know that," Shadow said quietly. "I also

know we've always looked out for each other. I know you better than any man on earth and I'm dead sure something's wrong." His eyes darkened. "It's not the woman, is it?"

Niels's fist tightened, his knuckles gleaming white. He was being a fool, but he couldn't seem to do a damn thing about it. "She has a name."

"Oh, damn, I knew it!"

"All I said was she's got a name. You could use it."

"Atreides, that's her name. It's Akoran, in case you've forgotten."

"Sweet heaven, I wish I could." So fervent were his words, that Shadow was struck silent.

When Shadow spoke again, his voice was low and tinged with regret. "I'm sorry for you. I wish things were different."

"It doesn't matter."

"Aye, it does. You care for her."

"It doesn't matter if I do or not. Nothing's changed."

Nothing, and everything. He didn't bother trying to go to bed that night. Instead he sat up, watching the glowing embers of the fire and trying to decide what could be salvaged from the hell of a mess in which he found himself.

He was at Benjamin Sherensky's house early enough to surprise the maid, Ivana, who opened the door to him. She took his measure quickly and stepped out of his way. "Mister

Wolfson, isn't it? Come in, then. I'll tell Mister S. you're here."

Praise be to sensible household staff who didn't stand on ceremony. "Thank you," he said and followed her direction to the parlor.

Sherensky joined him a few minutes later. He was still tucking his shirt into his trousers. "Is something wrong, my friend?"

A pretty day when a man's mere presence prompted concern for his well-being.

"Nothing a cup of your good coffee won't repair."

Ivana must have anticipated his wish, for she appeared again just then, bearing a tray. When she had accepted their thanks and bustled out, Benjamin said, "I have the greatest regard for the British, but their obsession with tea baffles me. They don't even serve it in a proper glass, as they should."

"A failing, to be sure. About that sword —"

They haggled, but only briefly. Both men knew Niels would have it. He paid a fair price and took due note, as he had before, that Sherensky did not press for more. The Russian was a man for the long term rather than the quick kill.

Business attended to and the coffee refreshed, Sherensky said, "Do you plan to be in England long?"

"That depends." Small talk had only held scant charm for the Wolf. He preferred to get right to it. "I wonder if I might impose on you for a favor?"

"Of course."

"This particular favor involves your silence not merely for a few days or weeks, but forever." Best to be very clear about that.

Sherensky's dark eyes widened slightly but, otherwise, the son of the steppes took the warning in stride. "Would this have to do with what really brought you to England?"

"What really brought me? Am I not a gentleman of leisure, lately retired from the service of my government and free to pursue my little hobby?"

The Russian laughed. "If you say so, my friend, although those who know you undoubtedly have difficulty seeing you that way. What is it you wish me to do?"

Niels hesitated but only for a moment. The die was already cast. "I'd like you to look at a drawing of a man and tell me if you recognize him."

"That sounds simple enough."

From beneath his jacket, Niels withdrew the sketch of the Angel. He laid it on the table near Sherensky. Shortly, the arms dealer said, "The nose is slightly wrong. Otherwise, this is Lord Simon Hawley."

Elation roared through Niels and with it heady relief so intense that for a moment he could not breathe. When he did, he said, "An Englishman? An English lord?" Not an

Akoran, praise be to God.

"Yes, yes, all of that. I believe his family's holdings are in East Anglia, although I doubt he spends much time there."

"What does he do? How does he occupy himself?" Already he was moving beyond his instinctive reaction, to cold, ruthless thought. The more he could discover of the man, the better to hunt him.

Sherensky shrugged. "I can tell you what he does not do. He is not one of those given to squandering his patrimony at the gambling tables. He is not a drunkard, and if he keeps a mistress, he does so discreetly. You could say he is well in step with these times, full as they are of reform. There are rumors that he has an interest in a political career. He has spoken to good effect in the Lords and been duly noticed."

"Does he show ambition regarding any particular ministry?"

"It is hard to say. He is a friend of Prince Andreas's, and some might think that indicates an interest in the Foreign Office, but it may simply be that the two young gentlemen enjoy each other's company —"

"Prince Andreas and Hawley are friends?" Relief, so briefly felt, ran hard aground on this bit of information and promptly shattered.

"So I understand. At least, they are seen together on occasion when the prince is in London." Sherensky frowned. "This concerns

166

you? But the prince has many friends. I would not presume that Hawley is any different from the great run of them. Indeed, it is possible that their acquaintance stems from Hawley's interest in the Princess Amelia."

"His *what?*" Despite his best efforts, Niels could not contain the raw disbelief and rage that roused in him. Even so, he managed some semblance of calm, lest he alarm the Russian.

"Rumor only," Sherensky said hastily. "Princess Amelia has had more suitors than anyone has bothered to count, but Hawley is shrewder than most. From what I hear, he hasn't actually offered for her, since the mere hint of an intent to do so has resulted in legions of young men being sent packing by the lady. No, he bides his time, remaining in the prince's circle and therefore in hers. Clever, no?"

"And why would Lord Simon Hawley think that the Princess Amelia would ever look favorably on him?" He tried to speak calmly but the best he could do was a snarl that came damn close to a teeth-baring growl.

The Russian shrugged his broad shoulders. "Most women marry eventually. Hawley may simply be planning to wear her down. He's around, her family is accustomed to him, he's titled, respectable. Marriages have happened for less reason than that."

Sherensky was fluent in English, but even so, he had not heard the expletive that broke from Niels. While it still scorched the air, the Russian whistled appreciatively. "I'll have to remember that one. There's no point in my asking why you're interested in Hawley, is there?"

Niels gathered up the drawing. "No."

Sherensky hesitated, but only briefly. Quietly, he said, "Be careful, my friend. I do not pretend to understand what is afoot here, but I doubt you would be involved were the stakes not very high. While I know nothing to Hawley's disrepute, his family has a long history of advancing through ruthlessness and treachery. If memory serves, they were ennobled by Henry the Eighth for their help in looting the churches and monasteries. Thus encouraged, they amassed a fortune by never allowing scruples to stand in their way."

"I appreciate the warning, but I am no stranger to Hawley and his kind."

"You will, all the same, take precautions?"

Niels assured him that he would. A short time later, sword in hand, he departed.

If he'd been in Kentucky, he would have found a tree — maybe a nice solid oak that had been around for a hundred or so years — and pounded on it until he felt better. In Washington, he'd have taken a boat out on the Potomac and rowed until exhaustion overtook rage. But he was in London — damnable London — and there wasn't a blessed thing he could do.

Except to go back to the house and face Shadow.

"Sherensky recognized him," he said without preamble. "His name's Simon Hawley. He's a British lord, but he knows the Akorans. Sherensky says he's a friend of Prince Andreas's and just possibly a would-be suitor of Amelia's."

"Damn," his brother said and put an arm around his shoulders. They stood for a moment in the silent communion of men whose love for each other is so absolute they wouldn't dream of mentioning it.

A little more calmly, Niels said, "I should have asked Sherensky right away. All this running around, trying to get close to them —" Too astoundingly close that for all that, even now, he couldn't manage to really regret it.

"Sherensky only got back to London a couple of days ago," his brother reminded him, "and besides, there was no guarantee he'd know. As for the rest, plenty of people might want to be taken for friends of the Akorans. There's no sayin' whether the Angel is or not."

Shadow, who had been so adamant about the Akorans' guilt, clearly was now trying to offer a ray of hope. Niels spared a moment to thank whatever fate had given him such a brother, before turning his mind to the task ahead.

"That's the first thing we have to determine, that and get a good grasp of Hawley's movements."

Shadow let his arm drop but didn't move away. "Where he lives, where he goes, he's probably in one or another of those clubs they've got here."

"Most likely. I especially want to know if there's anything he doesn't want known. Anywhere he goes where he doesn't want to be seen. Anyone he meets with."

"Besides the Akorans?"

"Besides them. I'll handle that end; you see to the rest."

"All right, but Niels, one thing: if he gets any sense that you're on to him —"

"He's a killer; I know that." He hefted the newly acquired sword, wondering suddenly about the man who had wielded it all those centuries ago. Somehow, it felt right in his hand. Quietly, he said, "Let's not forget, so am I."

"Don't compare yourself to him. Hawley's a murderer."

"There are some who would say I'm the same." It was the nightmare fear that gnawed at him amid memories of the men he had slain. He still dreamt of them sometimes, always the same dream. He was alone in a winter wood, the only sound that of his own breathing. Ahead of him was a clearing between trees, and there, a bloody circle marring new-fallen snow, spreading ever outward to engulf him.

"There are some who don't know their head from their ass."

Niels surprised himself; he laughed. Shadow always did have a knack for putting things in perspective.

"Where would a man go around here to get roses?"

"In April? You'll pay the earth."

"And they'll be worth every penny, especially if they help flush Hawley out."

"What exactly are you plannin' to do, brother?"

"Find out if Sherensky is right," Niels said, and went to ready himself for what had to come next.

"Roses," Amelia said. She stared at the flowers. In all fairness, they were lovely, with big blooms of a deep, velvety red and a heavenly scent. There were a great many of them in a crystal vase. There was also a card.

> *"That which we call a rose*
> *By any other name would smell as sweet."*
> *With thanks for a memorable evening.*
>                                    *Niels*

An oft-quoted line from Shakespeare's *Romeo and Juliet*, a thanks she would surely be asked to explain if her family learned of it, and his name scrawled in bold, black letters.

Her hand was shaking.

She tucked the card away swiftly beneath the lace ruche of her bodice and pretended to sniff the flowers. "They're lovely."

"Who are they from?"

Simon Hawley leaned against the mantel. He had arrived a short time before with apologies for his absence from the reception for Princess Victoria. He had ill-advisedly dined on French pork and was only now recovered. Amelia expressed sympathy even as she wished he was not there.

"Who did send them?" Andreas asked, when she did not reply.

Her cousin looked relaxed and in good humor, but he would expect an answer. The men of her family always did, in their well-intentioned protectiveness.

She folded her hands in her lap and bid herself to be calm. "They are from Mister Wolfson." Whose touch still lingered on her skin. From whom she had parted in defiant anger. And because of whom, though she was loath to remember it, she had wept in the cold, dark privacy of her bedroom when anger had burned away and left only hurt.

"Who is Mister Wolfson?" Hawley asked.

"Niels Wolfson, an American visiting London. He . . . was of assistance to me recently."

Hawley knew no more about her abduction than did anyone else outside the immediate circle of family and retainers. She intended to keep it that way.

"Was he?" the Englishman inquired. He

spoke mildly enough, but his gaze sharpened, in no way marring the perfection of his features that managed to be both masculine and beautiful at the same time. He had the sort of face that cropped up in paintings by the lesser Renaissance artists striving to depict an angelic ideal. As for his form, nothing was lacking there. Hawley was educated, pleasant, attentive to her without making a fool of himself, a friend of her cousin's, and seemingly acceptable to her family, for they did not hesitate to receive him.

Why, then, could she not return his interest?

Why was she drawn instead to a rough-hewn American who carried with him the sense of wild dangers and deeply rooted regrets?

Seeking distraction, she buried her nose in the roses, letting their perfume fill her. When she inhaled, she felt the crisp edge of the card against her breast.

A quote from *Romeo and Juliet*. Star-crossed lovers from warring families, doomed by circumstances beyond their control. Was there some significance to his choice of it, beyond the mere reference to roses?

She was assuring herself there could not be when a footman entered to announce that Mister Niels Wolfson had come to call.

"I don't believe you know Lord Simon Hawley," Andreas said as he did the introductions. Niels hesitated fractionally before accepting Simon's hand, or so it seemed to Amelia.

The men took each other's measure. Hawley's smile was a bit disparaging, she thought. Perhaps that was to be expected of a titled Englishman confronted by an American. The sting of old battles lost still lingered.

For his part, Niels was —

A sudden wave of cold moved through her. She blinked, looked again, and felt her stomach roil.

Behind the smile that did not touch his eyes, the Wolf was poised to kill.

In God's name, why?

Without hesitation, with no thought whatsoever for how they had parted, she stood and went to him. "Mister Wolfson, thank you for the lovely flowers."

For an instant she saw a bleak and terrible landscape in his eyes. The impression was gone so swiftly she wondered if she had truly seen it.

No matter, something was terribly wrong. Still keeping herself between him and Hawley, she gestured to the settee where she had been sitting. "Please join us."

He hesitated, clearly surprised by her welcome. Her fingers curled around his, a shocking breach of etiquette. She did not care. Hawley was watching them, as was Andreas. Let them both. Daring filled her, and with it, determination. She felt a sudden, unaccountable need to protect this man whom she might do better to think of as a danger to herself.

"What brings you to London, Mister

174

Wolfson?" Simon asked when Niels was seated beside Amelia. The Englishman remained standing. Looking at the pair, he frowned.

"I collect weapons," Niels said calmly, as though he was entirely at ease, when she knew him to be anything but. "This is a good place for that."

"Weapons?" Amusement flitted across Hawley's perfect features. "Don't you have enough of those in America? I thought there was scarcely a household that could not boast an arsenal."

"Probably not," Niels said agreeably. "We have learned the benefit of being ever vigilant."

"Did you get the sword?" Andreas interjected. He, too, was watching the two men, but for a moment, he directed his gaze to Amelia. Her cousin was also her dear friend. Scarcely a year apart in age, they knew each other so well they could often communicate with a glance.

Niels nodded. "I saw Sherensky this morning. Thank you for bowing out."

"Bowing out of what?" Hawley asked.

"Sherensky found a sword," Andreas said. "Apparently, it belonged to a great Viking lord, although the sword itself appears to be Moorish. Legend links it to our family, specifically to Hawkforte, but Mister Wolfson also has a family claim, so it seemed more proper that it go to him."

Before the explanation was finished, Simon's attention had clearly shifted, reminding Amelia that the Englishman had never shown any interest in the past. He was entirely, even ruthlessly, focused on the future.

"Do you plan to be in England very long, Mister Wolfson?"

"I hadn't," Niels said. He put his hand over Amelia's. "But it seems I will be extending my stay."

First the roses, now this? She ought to be delighted, yet she could muster only concern. Again, her gaze met that of her cousin.

"Simon," Andreas said promptly, "I've acquired a horse you must see."

"Another one?" Hawley looked less than intrigued.

But Andreas, bless him, was undaunted in his enthusiasm. He swept the Englishman before him, pausing only long enough to send a very direct look in Amelia's direction.

When the door had closed behind them, Niels rose. He walked a little way apart from Amelia and stood as though lost in thought until she said, "Would you care to tell me what is wrong?"

He should have realized that he'd have a damn hard time being near her. Playing the proper suitor when what he really wanted was to bury himself deep inside her called for acting skills he didn't have. Shadow, now, he was good at playing a role, could slip in and out of one with relish. Not so himself, who had only learned to tell a proper lie after he landed in Washington and found that that was one ability no man there could do without.

What had she asked? He ought to quit looking at her so intently and try paying attention to what she was saying instead.

"What was that?"

"I asked you what is wrong."

"There's nothing wrong."

Amelia sighed, a female sound redolent of patience. She rose and crossed the distance between them. Standing before him, close but not touching, she said, "Niels, I'm not very good at wiggling around things."

She'd wiggled some under him. Damn, he had to stop thinking of that!

"I'm more of a straightforward sort of person."

"That's fine, but what's it got to do with —"

"I know there's something wrong. Very badly wrong. I saw it when you came into the room."

He smiled at the recollection this prompted. "I used to have a great-aunt who thought she could tell what people were thinking," he said. "She'd be convinced they were filled with dread, when it wasn't anything a good belch couldn't fix."

His bluntness didn't faze her. She took it in stride. "This is different. There's something between you and Hawley."

How the hell could she know that? He'd let nothing slip, he was sure of it. Yet she seemed to see straight through him. That was damn disconcerting, to say the least.

"I only just met the man," he reminded her. "Besides, did it occur to you that maybe I'm a little anxious seeing you again? After all, we hardly parted on the best of terms after —"

"After you informed me our lovemaking was a mistake? How derelict of me. Without wishing to diminish the significance of what has passed between us, I would prefer that you not change the subject."

"Not change the subject —"

"Lord Simon Hawley."

"I hear he means to marry you."

Her brows rose. Winged, he thought they'd be called. "Is that what this is about . . . jealousy?" She looked amazed and very far from convinced.

"Now why would that surprise you? Haven't you ever seen two stallions go at it? Or a pair of rams? A couple of bulls — now there's a real set-to. Or how about some of those peacocks they've got in the parks around here? Ever watch them fight over one of those drab little hens? That's actually a pretty funny sight."

"Niels —"

"That's just how men are, Princess. It shouldn't come as a surprise to you."

"You want to kill Hawley. To do that for jealousy, you would have to be insane, which you are not."

"I want —" To start over, preferably with

some understanding of how the hell she was doing this and what he could do to protect himself from it.

"I'm sorry," she said, and just then she looked as though she meant it. "I don't mean to intrude. It just happens."

"What happens?"

His bold and passionate princess blushed. Maybe he'd better sit down again.

He led her over to the settee, sat beside her, and when he saw how she pressed her lips together, took both her hands in his. "Nice and slow, Princess. Just tell me what's on your mind."

"What's on yours?"

"You first."

"No, I mean what's on my mind is what is on yours, except not exactly. It's more a case of the quality of your spirit." As though to reassure him, she added, "I can't actually hear your thoughts or anything like that."

"You can't? Oh, well, then there's no problem, is there? Amelia, what the hell are you talking about?"

"It's a bit complicated." She tried to withdraw her hands but he wouldn't let her. She looked anxious and unhappy. Later on, she could be as independent as she liked, but just then he was going to hold on to her.

She took a deep breath, stopped trying to pull away from him, and said, "It's my family."

"Where are they, by the way?" He had

enough survival instinct left to want to be sure he knew where her father was, in particular. Alex Darcourt, Prince of Akora, didn't strike him as the understanding sort of parent who wouldn't mind that his daughter had gotten herself ravished practically under his own roof. He probably knew all sorts of inventive ways to kill a man, too.

"My parents are at the palace. The king has taken a turn for the worse. Luc and Marc are off seeing what mayhem they can get into. Andreas is here, as you know."

"That's fine, then." Andreas might seek to carve him into little bits if he got wind of what had happened, but at least it would be a fair fight. "Now what about your family?"

"It's our heritage, you see. In some generations, women are born with unusual gifts or abilities. In my case, I'm often able to understand what is in a person's heart. I don't really know how to explain it, but I simply *know*. I have since I was a tiny child."

"You're a good judge of people?"

"No, it's far more than that. It doesn't work with everyone. Some people are more closed off to me — Lord Hawley, for example. But not you, and not most others."

"Be hard to know what's in Hawley's heart since he doesn't have one." He hadn't meant to say that. It came out as he was grappling with what she'd told him. What had she said, exactly? What was it she thought she could tell him about herself?

"What makes you think that of Hawley?"

"Nothing, it's not important. It's good to be sensitive to other people."

She leaned back a little, the better to give him the full benefit of a chiding look. "Niels, how many *sensitive* people do you think would know that you want to kill Hawley?"

"I don't —"

"You do, and I want to know why."

"You're imagining it." He'd learned to lie; he could convince her. And besides, it wouldn't be good for her to know. Why he wanted to kill Hawley had to do with why he'd kidnapped her and just maybe why his country would go to war against hers. Definitely not anything he wanted to discuss.

"You're lying. I'm sorry to be so blunt, but that's the fact of it."

He was in trouble. Hell, he could practically feel the quicksand sucking him down. He'd never been in quicksand, but he'd heard about it, and for some reason it had stuck in his mind as something he definitely didn't ever want to experience personally. But there it was all the same.

For starters, he kept looking at her mouth. She had a beautiful mouth, full and soft, and it was all too easy to remember how it felt. Then there was her neck. It was long and slender. He seemed to remember kissing it a lot. And her shoulders. He'd liked her shoulders right from the start.

Then there was . . .

No, he wasn't going to think about that. He'd keep his mind on business instead.

The business of deceiving her.

"Now, Princess, why would I lie to you?"

"Oh, for heaven's sake!"

She was on her feet. How had she gotten there? He certainly hadn't let go of her, but there she was all the same, glaring at him.

He stood because a man didn't want to get caught sitting down under the circumstances. "Calm down, now. There's nothing to get upset about."

"Don't tell me that. Hawley is dangerous. If you try to kill him, he will hurt you."

The very notion made him snort derisively. "He can damn well try."

"I knew it! You do want to kill him."

"Give me strength! Please, Lord, just this once, hear me."

She softened a little and touched his hand. "Is it so very hard to tell me the truth?"

On the contrary, the problem was how very tempting it was to share his concerns with her. Amelia possessed courage aplenty, for all that he had ample reason to believe she wasn't overly burdened by caution.

"I don't like Hawley," he admitted, for that was truth enough.

"I have no intention of marrying him."

A straightforward sort of woman indeed. "Does he know that?"

"He has no reason not to know it. I have never given him the slightest encouragement."

Whereas she had lain with him in unfettered passion and joy. "Well . . . that's good."

"But you still want to kill him."

"Amelia, give this up."

He was convinced she was about to do exactly the opposite when he moved to stop her. Truth be told, he had other motives. High on the list was satisfying the raging hunger that had built in him with every passing moment in her presence. His mouth on hers, his arms holding her, the feel of her strong, supple body molding to his banished every other consideration.

Sunrise, sunset, a man just couldn't ask for a whole lot more.

She resisted very briefly before her passion met his own. He deepened the kiss, savoring her. She was warm, willing, unfettered by lies or pretense. A woman for the long haul.

Time ceased to matter; the world was of no consequence. There was only what they were able to find together. They were lost, enraptured in each other, forgetful of all else, when, through the red haze of passion, Niels heard —

"Sounds like a fine idea to me, Bolkum." Andreas spoke in the hallway just beyond the drawing room, mere yards away. "Let me know if I can help."

Then the door opened.

# Chapter Eleven

"Do you intend to speak with my uncle, sir?" Andreas stood just inside the door, his normally pleasant expression replaced by a hard frown and his voice dripping ice.

Amelia felt a sudden jolt of fear. She had known and loved her cousin all her life, but she had never seen him like this. He looked older somehow, somber and extremely determined.

Nervously, she stepped away from Niels, gathered herself together as best she could and attempted a reassuring smile. It did not work, in large part because Niels chose that moment to say:

"Under the circumstances, that would be a good idea."

"What?" She'd heard him wrong, she must have. "Niels, what are you — ?"

Andreas nodded but did not relax. "It appears King William really is dying. Prince Alexandros is likely to be very occupied the next few days."

"At the first possible opportunity, then," Niels said.

"Good . . . very good. In fact —"

"It is not good," Amelia interrupted. "It is most especially not good that the two of you are having this discussion when Niels and *I* have not had *this* discussion."

Her dear cousin looked at her with what gave every appearance of being genuine puzzlement. "What do the two of you need to discuss?"

"What do we need — ? Everything? *Something?*"

The Prince of Akora turned to Niels, who stood observing the unfolding scene with a slow, wry smile. "Do you need to discuss any of that, Mister Wolfson?"

"Seems like closing the barn door after the horse."

"My thoughts exactly. At the first opportunity, then. Good enough. Allow me to show you out."

"Andreas, you can't be serious!" Amelia exclaimed.

"Actually, Melly, I don't believe I've ever been more so. Furthermore, I'm sure Mister Wolfson understands perfectly."

She turned to the gray-eyed man who continued to regard her quietly. He looked entirely calm and at ease, utterly unlike her own self, who could scarcely breathe for the sudden pounding of her heart. "Do you understand, Mister Wolfson?"

He shrugged as though it was all very matter-of-fact. But there was a note of gentleness in his voice when he said, "It's right that I speak with your father."

Shocked by the speed of events and by his apparent seriousness, she took her courage in both hands, dug her nails into it and said, "Do you intend to offer for me?"

His smile deepened. It was a devastating smile, intimate and male, completely unfair. "From what I've heard, you don't take to that very well."

Though he tried to maintain his stern demeanor, Andreas grinned. "It is true that more than a few suitors have been disappointed."

"I daresay at least some of them were also relieved," Amelia muttered.

Both men looked at her but it was Niels who spoke. "Why would you say that?"

"Because . . ." She didn't have to answer him. She could turn the question away. It was too stark, too personal — especially in front of Andreas who, damn him, seemed to have no sense of time or place.

"Because I intimidate most men."

She hadn't said that! Please heaven, she hadn't blurted out the sad conclusion she had come to after so many years.

"Is that a fact?" Niels looked directly at her. He didn't appear shocked or surprised, and he very definitely did not look intimidated. In fact, unless she was dreadfully mistaken, he looked rather pleased.

"Hell, Princess, you just haven't been meeting the right sort."

And with that, he was gone, ushered out by her dear cousin, to whom she was going to have to find something most horribly dreadful to do.

★ ★ ★

Out on the street, breathing in what passed for air in London, Niels considered what had just happened. He could hardly have denied willingness to speak to Prince Alexandros. That would have brought the Akorans down on his head just when he needed to concentrate on Hawley. Moreover, he'd made a deliberate decision to use the Englishman's own intentions toward Amelia, coupled with Hawley's undoubted contempt for a commoner rival, to draw him out and trap him.

Even so, he'd be lying to claim it was purely devotion to his mission that had prompted him to say what he had. In the midst of kissing Amelia, he'd managed an actual thought. Amazing! If Hawley was *not* working for the Akorans, then he, Niels, would be free, once his duty to his country was done, to pursue his own desires. There was nothing he had ever desired in his life more than Amelia: the proud, passionate woman who had given herself to him with generosity and joy beyond any he had ever known.

Which left him where? On the brink of admitting to yearnings he had repressed for so long they seemed no longer to exist? They were stirring now with a vengeance, just when he needed to keep his mind most clear. The Akorans might still be guilty, there might yet be a war. But if they were blameless, if Hawley had acted alone —

If . . . Precious, fragile *if.* More than a mountain, the distance from the Earth to the Moon. What was that story she'd started to tell him, something about some fellow drowning? He'd have to see if he could avoid doing that.

A certain lightness infused his step as he made his way to his own residence. It faded when he found Shadow waiting for him. His brother appeared tired but pleased. "Hawley looked more than a little annoyed when he left the Akorans," Shadow said, reporting on the results of the surveillance the brothers had agreed to maintain on the Britisher.

"As well he might." Niels plunked himself down in one of the comfortable leather chairs that had played a part in his decision to rent the London house. A man's home, however temporary, ought to have decent chairs. "Where did he go?"

"His club. He was there for several hours, most of it spent with a pair of gentlemen, both English, titled, and associated until a year ago with the Foreign Office."

"What happened last year?"

"They got kicked out, although it was done very genteelly. Got to watch these British; they're masters at slippin' the knife in. At any rate, it seems the Prime Minister didn't care for some of their tactics."

"How did you come by this?"

"Servants tattle; amazin' what those people know. Hawley, whose family seems to be known for its ruthless ambition, is associatin' openly with men Melbourne banished from the government. Moreover, he's doin' this on the eve — or close to it — of the king's death and the ascent to the throne of an untried young woman likely to rely on Melbourne for her every thought. Now why do you suppose he'd do that?"

"Because he thinks he's going to win."

"Seems like. Question is, win what?"

"What's he likely to want?"

Niels thought for a moment. "If Sherensky is right, he wants what his family has always been after — wealth and power. They don't seem ever to have gotten enough of either."

"And maybe the fair princess in the bargain?"

The stem of the brandy snifter Niels held didn't snap, but it came very close. "He will never have Amelia."

Shadow raised his hands, palms out in a placating gesture. "It was just a notion. At any rate, we've still got to figure out who Hawley's workin' with. I'm sorry, Niels, but right now the Akorans still look like the best bet."

"No, they don't."

"You don't want to think so."

"It's true, I don't, but follow this: if Hawley did blow up the *Defiant* for the Akorans, they might reward him in some way, but they'd never let him get near Amelia. I've seen how close they are as a family and how much they love her. A man they knew to be a mass murderer would be the last man they'd consider as a suitor for her."

Which raised the uncomfortable thought at the back of his mind that they might not approve of him all that much, either. But he wasn't Hawley — he wasn't. All the men he'd hunted had amply deserved to die, not only for the crime of plotting Jackson's death, but for habitually mowing down anyone unfortunate enough to get in their way. He'd killed the murderers — for all that they usually worked through proxies — of innocent men, women, and children, not just of seamen whose only offense was to serve their country.

Shadow went over to the desk, pulled out the folder holding the drawing of Simon Hawley, and flipped it open. "If he isn't workin' for the Akorans, who is he workin' for?"

"I don't know," Niels admitted, "but I've got a suspicion. The likeliest outcome of the attack on the *Defiant* was — maybe still is — war between the United States and Akora, right?"

"That's what I've been tellin' you ever since it happened."

"Then tell me this: Who benefits from such a war?"

"We do, if we are to win, which we will."

"That's a big assumption. The Akorans are a warrior culture. They have several thousand years' experience protecting their country. They're also renowned sailors. Fighting on

190

their home territory and at sea, they'll be a formidable force."

"You can't seriously think we'll be beaten?"

"I think it's a possibility we had better keep in mind, or for sure we will lose. But let's say we win, what does that get us? Akorans love their country and their ruler. You know what 'Vanax' means? 'Chosen.' Not only that, but members of the royal family consider themselves servants of their people and I think they really mean it. We're not talking about some tyrant whose people would love to see the end of him. We'd need an army-and-a-half to have even a chance of holding Akora — and God help the men we send. They wouldn't be able to shut an eye, draw a breath, or relax for a moment."

"So we don't want to hold Akora, just hurt them for hurtin' us and maybe get a naval base out of it in the bargain. We could protect that well enough."

"Maybe, but there are a hell of a lot better places for us to put a naval base. We've staked out the Western Hemisphere for ourselves and we've let the world know it. So what do we want a naval base on Akora for? In the end, it wouldn't be worth the very high cost of getting it."

"Maybe not," Shadow acknowledged.

"Now suppose the Akorans win. What do they gain? They've proved to the world yet again how tough they are, but the world already knows that."

"They set us back some?"

"True, but how does that benefit them? We're not rivals or competitors in any way with the Akorans."

Shadow fell silent, looking again at the drawing of Simon Hawley. After a moment, he shrugged. "All right, you tell me; who benefits?"

"Who actually wants — and can use — a naval base on Akora?"

"Great Britain. They want an empire, always have. We stopped them in America, so they've got to look elsewhere."

"Right enough. Who can claim a special relationship with Akora by virtue of the marriages between the Akoran royal family and the house of Hawkforte?"

"Great Britain."

"If Akora were really up against it — say, in a war against one tough son-of-a-bitch country that was threatening to beat it — who would it likely turn to for help?"

"Great Britain." Shadow took a deep breath, let it out slowly. "Hell."

"Exactly. If Great Britain helped Akora win a war against us, and given that they already have a special relationship, they could bring a lot of pressure to allow a British naval base on Akora in recognition of their help."

"The Akorans would have to really think they were goin' to lose."

"A man who could blow up the *Defiant* could

harm Akoran interests as well."

"Hawley provokes a war, makes sure it goes badly for Akora, then Britain comes in and saves the day."

"And Hawley positions himself to get the credit. Whatever the Prime Minister might think of the man or his tactics, he'd have to reward him. Not only that, what you saw today may indicate that Hawley has allies ready to move into positions of power right along with him. If they're ambitious enough, they could undermine Melbourne's government and possibly even replace him."

"Hawley as Prime Minister of England?" Shadow winced at the mere thought.

"Stranger things have happened. Besides, I'm not saying any of this will actually work. All that matters is if Hawley *thinks* it will."

"If that's the case, you've just thrown a problem in his path."

Niels nodded. "Akora and the United States are supposed to be enemies, not lovers."

"What do you think he'll do?"

"Something foolish, I hope. In fact, I'm counting on it."

Shadow stood and reached for his jacket. "Seems like I'd better get back on post. Hawley moves, we want to know it."

"Be careful," Niels said as his brother went out the door.

He had a lot to think about — Amelia, Hawley, Amelia, the Akorans, Amelia. His instincts told him things were coming to a head, fast. He needed to be ready, but first he had to work out a few things in his own mind.

That being the case, he headed for where he'd always done his best thinking. He was just leaning back in the tub, stretched out to his full length after a good scrub, enjoying the steaming water, when there was a knock on the bathroom door.

"Sir?" the housekeeper called. "Sir? Sorry to disturb you, but there's a lady here."

A lady? How many people did he know who could match that description?

It couldn't be.

It was, as he discovered when he came into the parlor, his dark hair still damp and his shirt just barely tucked into his pants.

Amelia stood by the high windows, looking out on the garden. She was wearing a pretty suit in a shade of hazel that reminded him of her eyes, feminine without being gaudy, with a wide skirt and a jacket nipped in at her narrow waist. He'd never really noticed what women wore except when they wore nothing at all. With Amelia, he seemed to notice everything.

The nervousness behind her smile, for instance. Looking at him, she said, "The funny thing is that the expression 'to take the bull by the horns' isn't an Akoran saying."

"Should it be?" he asked. He had no trouble following her train of thought.

"Well, yes, we do that, after all. I mean, really

do it, take the bull by the horns. It's a sort of ritual and dance combined. And then also, some of us tend to be a bit headstrong, I suppose you might say."

"Headstrong?" He came closer. She was a little flushed. Good. He'd hate to think she was calmer about all this than he could be. "Is that how your family thinks of you?" he asked. "Or are they too busy tearing their hair out to care what word they use?"

"I just thought we needed to talk."

He cast a glance in the direction of the brandy decanter, but decided against it. He needed all his wits about him when he was with her. "All right, for starters we can talk about how you got here. I thought your father put more guards in place."

"Not to keep me in." The very notion seemed to appall her.

"So you just left and came here? Princess, you need a keeper."

"Do I?" Too late he saw her eyes flash, and braced himself. "Is that what you intend to tell my father? Is it your plan to volunteer for the position?"

"Sweetheart, I learned a long time ago not to volunteer for anything. Besides, you're just trying to change the subject. How did you get here?"

"In a carriage." At his doubting look, she said, "I am not such a fool as to walk unescorted through the streets of London."

Niels glanced toward the parlor door, wondering how sturdy it was. "So Andreas knows you're here?" If he didn't, and he found out, he undoubtedly would come to get her. He was likely to be in a dangerous mood when he arrived.

"No, and there is no reason why he should. Andreas is coping with a report from my cousin, Gavin, which arrived by ship from Akora this afternoon."

"Another cousin?" Just how many did she have — along with brothers, uncles, and who-knew-how-many guards, all no doubt sworn to defend her honor? Whatever qualms he had about the purity of his conscience did not extend to his courage. He knew he was the furthest thing from a coward. Even so, the thought of all those Atreides males descending on him was enough to instill a certain note of caution.

"Gavin is the eldest son of my Aunt Kassandra and my Uncle Royce. He is heir to the earldom of Hawkforte, but lately he's been spending most of his time on Akora."

"Writing reports?"

"I don't know what he's been doing. Mother and father are still with the king, so we are perfectly free to talk. I really must know what you intend —"

"Take a breath, Princess. Somebody must know you're here."

She hesitated a moment, then said, "Bolkum and Mulridge know, but they will say nothing."

196

"And why will they do that?"

"Because they are Bolkum and Mulridge. They've been with my mother's family . . . well, forever, and they seem to understand everything."

"Bolkum's that fellow who looks like a troll?"

"That's unkind. He has the sweetest nature imaginable."

"I didn't mean any insult. I'm sure as fellows like that go, he's better than most." He followed his own advice and took a breath. Damn, she looked good, but she had no business being there, and the sooner he got her home, the better.

"Did that carriage wait?"

"So you can send me on my way?"

"Fine, then, I'll saddle Brutus."

"Oh, that's a grand idea! Traipsing through London snuggled up in your lap. And just what do you think my family will make of that?"

He grinned despite himself. His mind was going the wrong way; he knew that. Hell, he knew it wasn't his *mind* doing it. But there it was all the same. "I think I'd better hope there's no Akoran recipe like the one I came across down in Mexico."

Her mouth twitched. "Which recipe was that?"

"Let's just say it involved certain parts I'll bet the ex-bull really would have liked to keep."

A little laugh escaped her, almost like a hiccup. She put a finger to her lips and looked at him. "Let me think . . . No, I don't re-member anything like that. We do have a very nice fish stew. It's called *marinos,* and you could say it's the national dish."

"Fish stew, huh? That sounds all right. I have to admit though, I prefer a good steak."

As though on cue, her stomach rumbled. She started, and her flush deepened.

"When did you eat last?" Niels asked.

"I haven't had much appetite since coming back from Boswick."

His senses were on alert, pleasurably attuned to her. "Oh, yeah? Why's that?"

"Are you mocking me?"

"A little, Princess. It's called teasing."

She relaxed, not much, but he counted it a gain even so. "I have brothers, cousins, all much in love with teasing."

"It's a way we have of righting the balance."

"I don't understand."

He was walking toward her, closing the distance between them, his fingers catching hers. "Yes, you do. If ever there was a woman used to having the upper hand, it's you."

"I have no notion of what you mean." She sounded piqued, but she wasn't pulling away from him, not the least little bit. Which was good, because he had no intention of letting her go. Not now.

Not ever?

"Teasing is a way of righting the balance, of making a man feel a little less like he's walking off into thin air every time he looks at a woman who stirs him."

"As I stir you?"

"You know damn well you do. Amelia, what happened between us —"

Her fingers brushed his lips. "Hush, Niels, no more talk of mistakes, please."

"I wasn't going to say that. What happened was the best thing I've ever known. You make me feel reborn."

She stared at him, her eyes suddenly luminous as she blinked away tears. "That is the loveliest thing anyone has ever said to me."

"You're probably used to hearing all sorts of nice things."

"Not like that." She was warm against him, soft and yielding. It would be so easy . . .

He stepped back, just a little, still holding on to her. "You said you're hungry."

Again she laughed, but this time she didn't try to hold it back. "Your housekeeper made it clear when I knocked that she was about to leave for the day. Do you propose that we fend for ourselves?"

"I'll have you know I can find my way around a kitchen. Well, the truth is, I'm better around a campfire, but I can manage."

She was taking off her little hat, setting it aside along with her gloves. And she was undoing the buttons of her jacket. "So can I, Niels Wolfson. I promise, we shall not starve."

★ ★ ★

He fried steaks found in the meat larder, kept cool with blocks of ice cut on the river in the winter and stored in layers of straw. The iron stove still held the heat of the day's fire, but Niels dismissed it in favor of the kitchen hearth and the embers glowing there.

"It's not all that hard to use a stove like this," Amelia said, eyeing it. They had acquired such a stove for the London house and she had seen it operated. If pressed, she thought she could manage it. But it was nothing like the large stone ovens she knew well on Akora.

"Too fussy," Niels said to her relief. "Can you manage those mushrooms?"

She could, coating them with oil she found in the pantry and placing them around the edges of the fire, turning them carefully so they would roast without burning. The housekeeper had left potatoes already cooked, still in their skins and protected by a moist cloth, probably meant as a side dish for breakfast the next day. Amelia made short work of the peels, sliced the potatoes, and set them in a skillet beside the steaks Niels was flipping over. He passed her a small wooden box with salt. She sprinkled a little on the potatoes and smiled. "A feast."

Outside, there was a sudden gust of wind and a smattering of rain. In the glow of the fire, he looked at her. "Will they miss you?"

"Mother and father will be at the palace until it is over, however long that might be. Andreas has too much sense to come near me just now. Besides, he's occupied with that report."

The steaks were done. He rose and held out a hand to her.

They carried the food back to the parlor and set it on a table in front of the fire. Niels went to find wine. When he returned, Amelia had lit candles and drawn the heavy velvet curtains over the windows.

When the wine had been poured, gleaming ruby dark in the crystal goblets, she took a bite of the steak and savored it. "You are an excellent cook."

"Thank you. You surprised me. I didn't think princesses did anything so ordinary as cooking."

"You concluded this based on your extensive experience with my kind?"

He accepted that it was her turn to tease and nodded. "Let's just say that I've met more than a few women in Washington, in New York, and in other places who thought they were princesses, or at least that they should be treated as such."

"Set up on a pedestal?"

"Something like that."

"We have many pedestals in the palace at Ilius. That's the royal city on Akora. When I was a child, I loved to climb them because they were more difficult than trees or walls. However, once I got to the top, the challenge was gone, and I was more than content to jump back down."

"Climbing the pedestal was better than being up on it?"

"Exactly, as I suspect the men drawn to such women know. The attraction is in the challenge, but once conquered . . ." She shrugged delicately and gave him a look he needed only a moment or two to interpret.

While he was doing that, he let out a satisfied sigh. He was feeling amazingly relaxed with this woman who could fire his passions with a mere look. "We don't have pedestals in Kentucky," Niels said. "And if we did, they'd only be good for knocking over." He moved a little closer to her. She was a contradictory thing, his princess, filled with courage but liable to trip over her uncertainty.

"Besides," he said, "last time I checked, you didn't strike me as 'conquered.' "

"Didn't I?"

He was smiling and couldn't help it. So much seriousness afoot, life and death really, and here he was, grinning like an idiot because she made him feel so good.

"Seems like I was the one lying there trying to remember how to breathe and then tripping over my own tongue." He was referring to his unfortunate comment about their lovemaking having been a mistake.

She was gracious enough to pretend it didn't matter. That was the mark of a good woman. Rip your hide off just once and then let the offense go. The world needed more women like that, but he only needed one.

"We ought to be getting you home," he said, because he really thought he should. Say it, that is. Actually doing it was another matter. But he had some control of himself, at least, and he knew what was right . . . or at least prudent.

"We ought to do that," she agreed, but she didn't look inclined to move. Her eyes met his. "Eventually."

Prudence was highly overrated. Now that he thought about it, he couldn't recall it ever doing him any good.

Care, now that was a different matter. He was more than willing to show her every care. What he really wanted, what drove him to take the wineglass gently from her hand and draw her into his arms, was the sudden, irresistible need to bind this woman to him in every way he could manage.

Before morning came. Before the world intruded.

Before she came to her senses.

"Last chance," he said softly against her hair. "I actually do have a carriage." The one he'd kidnapped her in. "It won't take more than a few minutes to get it rigged."

"Just try," she warned and raised her mouth to his.

The finely woven linen of his shirt was cool and smooth against her skin. She felt the brush of her hair, loosed and tumbling down her bare back. Her clothes were gone, fallen away beneath his hands. But he remained dressed, having gently but firmly denied her efforts to change that.

She stood now before him, naked but for the silken garters that held up her stockings and the rosy blush that suffused her skin. The firelight gleamed, and outside the rain continued to fall, but she was scarcely aware of either. This man — his scent, his touch, his power — engulfed her.

He did not lay her down, but leaned her instead against the table where they had dined. Smiling, he stepped back a little, surveying her.

"You look like a goddess."

His hand drifted between her legs, separating her thighs a little more, stroking the soft tangle of curls, damp with desire. "Aphrodite," he murmured, "rising from the waves." He touched his fingers to his lips first, then to hers. "You taste of the sea."

Again, she reached out to him. Again, he stopped her. "Soon," he said and stroked her, watching her response, quickening his touch as she stiffened helplessly, her head falling back as a soft, keening moan broke from her.

Pleasure still resonated within her when he lifted her, straddled her legs around his hips, and reached down to free himself. With a quick, driving thrust, he buried himself within her. She gasped, clinging to his broad shoulders as he drove into her again and again. Pleasure surged through her so powerfully that she was left shaking, her whole body quivering, held upright only by his strength.

Held, and controlled, for he was far from done, as she realized to her astonishment when he turned her, bent her over the table, and entered her very slowly, tantalizing her even as pleasure began, incredibly, to mount again before she could gain any respite.

*"Niels . . . I can't bear anymore!"*

"You can, you will." Amusement laced his words, but beneath them was the iron control of a man who would not be denied. Deep and hard inside her, he moved with tantalizing slowness, drawing out her pleasure until it became unbearable. Even so, her body lingered, caught by his will, until, finally, release came so intensely that she felt swallowed by swirling darkness.

When next she knew, she was lying on the rug in front of the fire. Niels lay beside her on his side, lightly stroking her hair. The man was an artist, a devil, a genius of the sensual. He was also naked, as she discovered when she moved against him. Flame gilded his magnificent body, reminding her of statues she had seen deep beneath the palace of Akora. But in place of cold stone was warm, living strength, irresistible to her. The languor so lately come upon her, which made even the lifting of her eyelids seem an effort, vanished as though it had never been. Hot, urgent desire flared again within her. He moved over her as she lay, heart pounding, looking up into his beautiful face, for he *was* beautiful in the way of wild places and windswept plains. She tried to catch him to her but he clasped her hands in one of his, drawing her arms over her head. "Not yet," he said, his breath hot against her skin as his tongue stroked her nipples, incredibly hardening them even further. She was teetering on the keen edge of pain, almost but not quite tipping over, her will, so strong, dissolving. Vaguely, she knew she was surrendering to him in some way she had not done before, letting him in not just to her body but to her heart and soul. The knowledge filled her with joy far beyond that of even the most intense carnal pleasure. Hot tears slipped down her cheeks as she reached out, taking him into her, taking the essence of his life, taking all he so generously gave, and in the same moment, giving of herself without restraint.

Some time passed — she had no idea how much — when she woke suddenly with a sense of exaltation. Sitting up, Amelia saw that the fire had burned down and that Niels was asleep. He lay on his stomach beside her, one powerfully muscled arm flung over her waist. She spent an enjoyable few minutes admiring him before the cooling air caused her to stir. Slipping carefully from beneath him, she stood and stretched with sensual pleasure. Every inch of her body felt vastly content. Every concern, every tribulation, every annoyance of life, large and small, was banished. She felt nothing less than wondrous.

And chilly. Shivering, she made quick work of feeding the fire, then donned her chemise because, after all, she was not used to wandering about naked. There was an afghan folded on the settee near the fire. She spread it over Niels carefully and was just a little disappointed when he did not wake.

The man deserved his rest, heaven knew. She, too, needed to sleep but could not manage it. Arms wrapped around herself, a seemingly perpetual smile on her lips, she wandered around the room.

The house was rented and the contents with it. Even so, she looked for some clue to the man who had come to occupy her every thought. She ignored the bookshelves, but the books on a table near the settee she picked up and studied. There were military treatises and works of history, all well-thumbed. There was brandy on the sideboard and something else that she sniffed, only to draw back abruptly. Rawer than brandy, yet not displeasing. Perhaps this was the Kentucky bourbon of which she had read.

The desk drew her attention next. She would never dream of intruding into his privacy, but there happened to be a folder thrown open on the leather surface. She glanced at the papers thus revealed and was idly surprised to see the drawing of a man.

Instinct, born in battle, woke Niels. He rose from the well of sleep reluctantly, but cheered when he saw Amelia standing nearby. She'd put her chemise on, but he could remedy that quickly enough. He was getting to his feet, the afghan sliding to the floor, when she lifted her head. The light in her eyes and the grim set of her mouth made him suddenly, keenly alert.

He stood, heedless of his nudity, and would have gone to her, but the look she leveled at him stopped him cold.

"Why," Amelia, Princess of Akora, demanded, "do you possess a drawing of Simon Hawley?"

# Chapter Twelve

There had been times in Niels's life when he had stood on the edge of a precipice, metaphorical or otherwise, and known that what he did in the next few seconds or minutes could determine all that came afterward.

There was the fog-strewn morning in the hills of Kentucky when he fell down an abandoned mine shaft, unused for centuries, and had the presence of mind in the final moments before he vanished into the earth to cry out for Shadow with all his might. That had saved him — along with a heaping of luck that let him land in one piece — and set them both on the road they had followed ever since.

There was the night not too long after that when he was fifteen, scarcely a man, and about to die. Then, a sure aim with a knife had saved him.

A winterscape in upstate New York near the palatial land holdings of the heir to Dutch poltroons, when the whistle of a bullet cut through the air just as he moved his head out of striking range.

A night in Washington and a conversation with the man about to be president, that had brought him here to the firelit room and the woman he wanted nothing more than to take in his arms and hold forever.

He could lie. He wasn't anywhere near as good at it as was Shadow, but he could manage in a pinch. He could tell her . . . what?

It didn't matter. There was knowledge in her eyes and the stirring of terrible pain.

"Amelia, listen to me."

He went to her, garbed in firelight, and took hold of her when she tried to evade him. Though she folded her arms, pushing away, and kept her face averted, he went on without pause.

"Simon Hawley is the man who blew up the *Defiant*."

Shock and curiosity overcame resistance. She remained stiff in his arms, but she did look at him. "You said the *Defiant* was an accident."

"That was the official finding, given to conceal what really happened."

"A lie —"

"A necessary one while we searched for the truth of what happened. Dying men described the man they saw setting the bomb. We had nothing but the sketch — no name, no notion of an identity."

"But you know now?"

"I know it's Hawley. I've known for a couple of days."

"It's inconceivable. Why would he do such a thing?"

He tightened his arms around her and spared just a moment to wish the words he was about to utter forever, unsaid.

"The *Defiant* was bound for Akora."

"Akora is closed to *xenos* . . . strangers."

"Jackson wanted it reconnoitered. He . . . we thought the British might be building a base there, and if they were, we wanted to know it."

She leaned all the way back in his arms, staring at him. "The *Defiant* was being sent to *spy* on Akora?"

Reluctantly, he nodded. "You know we've had a lot of trouble with the British . . . two wars, more than a few skirmishes. It's true that things have been better between us lately, but Jackson thought it was still in our best interest to know what the British intended. Plus, the truth is, his temper was piqued by Akora's refusal to open diplomatic relations with us."

"There is no British base on Akora. No permission for such a thing has ever been given."

"So far as you know."

"I would know! This is insane, spying on us when all we are interested in is maintaining our own sovereignty and way of life." She twisted hard in his arms. When he still refused to let her go, Amelia, his princess, stomped down hard enough on his foot to send pain shooting through him. "I will do worse," she promised.

"Sweetheart, there's no reason —"

"Let me go!" She raised her knee and very deliberately brought it into contact with the same portion of anatomy the hapless bull had wanted to keep.

Niels dropped his arms. He wasn't afraid — precisely — and he remained confident that he could have stopped her. He just didn't see any sense in riling the woman further when it was clear she was plenty riled already.

"You didn't know who Hawley was," she said as she began speedily to don her clothes. "Yet you came to London all the same? Why?" In the midst of fastening her skirt, she stopped and stared at him. "Because of Andreas? He was there when the *Defiant* was destroyed." Abruptly, all the color fled from her face. "My God, you think Andreas —"

"I did think," he corrected quickly. "At least, I entertained the possibility. An Akoran prince, present when everything happened . . . you've got to admit, it made sense to suspect him."

She was breathing hard, still staring at him, horror growing in her eyes. "You killed the men who wanted to kill Jackson. You hunted them —"

"I came to find the truth, that's all!"

"How can I believe you? You have killed before; you can again. I swear to you, I will never let you harm my family! No matter what my feelings for you, I will never —"

"You have feelings for me?" The notion was absurdly pleasing under the circumstances. "I mean, besides hurt and anger?"

"Do I have — ?" She looked toward the rug in front of the fire where they had so lately lain.

"What passes for your brain? A poor and curdled thing?"

"Now, sweetheart, a man just likes to know, that's all. Especially under the circumstances, I think it's a good thing for us to — you know — talk about things the way you wanted to."

He thought that sounded rather good and was pleased with himself for thinking of it, but mainly he was just walking toward her, slow and easy, the way he'd come up on a wild horse he didn't want to spook.

She looked at him warily and he thought she was about to refuse, but suddenly her face crumbled. "Oh, Niels, this is so *awful.*"

He could stand up to a lot of things — hunger, cold, exhaustion, the nearness of death. But the tears of this proud, strong woman went right through him.

"Sweetheart, don't," he murmured, taking her into his arms. "It will be all right, you'll see. We'll work this out."

He prayed he was right, but whether he was or not, he was bound and determined to console her.

Trouble was, she wouldn't let him, at least not entirely. Looking up at him, she said, "I am not a fool, Niels Wolfson, and I have little taste for fooling myself. You did not come into my life by accident."

He had dreaded this and had hoped she wouldn't make the leap she just had. But there was no help for it now except to manage as best he could.

"You are a good man; I know that beyond any doubt. But part of that goodness is your unshakable service to your country. You have killed in that service. I have to wonder if you would also . . ." Her voice broke and she looked away. ". . . love in its service, or at least pretend to."

He was dumbstruck. What exactly was Amelia suggesting? "You think I . . . we . . . what happened between us was some kind of strategy?"

"It's an unpleasant thought," she acknowledged.

"Oh, good. I'd hate to think you were chipper about thinking I was a —" A what? A contemptible, crawling worm of a man who would use a woman in such a way? But she didn't think that. She'd said just the opposite.

"— a whore?" He only just managed to get the words out. Stunning though the notion was, it did fit with what she seemed to be saying. Besides, he had to figure that was better than a worm. He'd known whores who were fine people. Of course, they'd been women. Could a man be a whore? He'd heard of strange things in his time, and why the hell was he thinking of all this right now?

"I didn't make love to you because of the mission I'm on. I did it despite that. The fact is, I just don't have a lot of control around you."

His body was cheerfully making this evident right then. With a mutter of disgust directed entirely at himself, he let go of her, seized his trousers, and pulled them on. He got as far as buttoning them when he noticed she was smiling.

That was better than crying. Still, he was having a hard time keeping up with her see-sawing mood. She seemed to feel the same, for just then she said, "I'm sorry to be this way. I'm normally very levelheaded."

"This is a tricky situation. It's enough to turn anyone's heels up."

"You're very understanding."

"Not usually, but you seem to bring it out in me. Look, Amelia, what we need to do now is get you home."

She shifted a little on her feet, exactly as though she was digging her heels in. "So that you can do what? Go after Hawley?"

"That's the only way to end this. But I'm not looking to kill him, not if I don't have to. There's a ship in port, an American ship. It'll take him back to stand trial."

"Won't the British government have something to say about you making off with one of their lords?"

"The truth is, Melbourne and the rest will be glad to have Hawley off their hands. He's trouble for everyone."

"And the suspicions about Akora? Will all that just go away?"

"President Van Buren has enough to deal with. The last thing he wants is a war. The fact that Hawley is British instead of Akoran will be a godsend."

"Hawley won't go quietly. He's a dangerous man."

"I know that, Princess." Niels reached for his shirt. "That's why my brother's watching him."

But, in fact, Shadow was not, as Niels discovered when he headed out to the stable to saddle up Brutus. His brother was lying in a bloody heap on the garden path.

Amelia ran from the house, her skirt bunched in her hands and her heart beating frantically. Rain pelted her, but she was unaware of it. All she saw was the dark shape of Niels, kneeling on the path. All she heard was his cry of anguish.

She skittered to a stop beside him and stared down in horror. He held a man of whom she could see very little, but the stench of blood was unmistakable.

"Who? . . ." she gasped as she flung herself onto the ground next to Niels.

"Shadow. My brother . . . Goddamn it, I knew . . . shouldn't have let him —"

"Where is the wound?" She searched frantically with probing hands, desperate to find it. Her seeking fingers encountered the hilt of a knife.

*"Eleos."* Even as she summoned mercy, she knew nothing would save this man except swift

and certain action. Obeying instincts she had scarcely known she possessed, she thrust the bunched fabric of her skirt up against the wound, hoping thereby to stem the flow of blood, at least enough to gain them a little time.

"We must get him inside and summon a healer."

"I'm not setting some butcher doctor on him! I'll tend to him myself before I'll let that happen."

They could argue about it later. Niels carried his brother into the house as Amelia followed along, awkwardly to be sure, but managing to keep firm pressure on the wound. Once inside, Niels went directly to the kitchen. He laid Shadow on the wood plank table near the fire, as Amelia quickly stripped off her skirt. In her chemise and blouse, she looked around frantically for a lamp. Once she lit it, the full extent of the injury could be seen. The knife was buried just below and to the left of the heart. A few more inches and —

Niels seized his brother by the shoulders. "Damn it, Shadow, don't you die on me!"

Amelia laid her head against the injured man's chest. "His heart beats regularly, but it is weak. The knife missed his lung."

Niels stared at her. "How do you tell that?"

"I can hear it. We must stop the bleeding and try to prevent him from going any deeper into shock."

"You know all that?"

"I know what anyone knows. Any Akoran," she amended.

"I've heard that about Akorans. You know ways to heal that we don't."

"We've tried to share what we know. The problem is, no one wants to listen to us."

"But you can help him?"

"A proper healer can help him. I am not that. I just know what everyone is taught." She looked down at the man, seeing him more clearly now. He was a year or so younger than Niels, light-haired and extremely pale as his life's blood drained away.

"Word must be sent to Andreas. There is always a healer at the London residence. Andreas will bring her."

"A woman?"

"Many of our healers are women. Does that make a difference to you?"

"Hell, no. I don't care who saves him, just as long as someone does." Abruptly, Niels bent his head. "I sent him out, agreed he should watch Hawley while I —"

"Dallied here with me?" His anguish and his remorse came as a wave breaking over her, almost breaking her in the process.

"Regret will not help your brother," the Princess of Akora said. "If the knife shifts, it will pierce his lung. We must remove it, but to do so is dangerous. It may be all that is preventing him from bleeding to death."

"The healer —"

"We can wait for her, but every moment is precious. I think it is better done now, but in all truth, I could be wrong."

"He's still bleeding."

They looked down together, watching the darkness spread across Amelia's skirt.

"Bring more light," she said and closed her eyes for a moment, fighting for strength.

"I have no gift for this, but I have learned."

Amelia's hands, long and slender, moved in the light as she recalled the teachings of her Aunt Brianna. *You must spread yourself, the essence of what you are. Let yourself grow thin, even transparent, so that you can truly feel without barriers.* Wife of the ruling Vanax, an orphan come shipwrecked to Akora, Brianna was the adopted niece of a brilliant healer.

It had seemed impossible, though she had tried. But now it must not be. Now she must do it somehow, she must find the path to heal the man who, moment by moment, slipped further from them.

"We need more cloths," she said. There was so much to do that she hardly knew how to explain it all. "Hot water, very clean cloths, thread of some sort — very strong thread — needles, more light, and we must raise his feet with pillows, books — anything — but his feet must be higher than his head."

"Can you manage here while I — ?"

"Yes," she said, because she could say

nothing less. Not while the man she — loved? — oh, admit it! Loved. Not while the man she loved was in the throes of such torment.

"Go," Amelia said and turned all her attention to Shadow, aptly named, slipping too quickly from her.

Niels was back at once with all she had asked for except the hot water. That would come soon, for he had fed the fire in the hearth and hung a kettle above it. Not content with that, he tackled the iron stove.

The lamps, lit all around her, made the air hot. Amelia wiped an arm across her forehead and watched the slow but steady seep of blood from the wound. The nearness of death was a rank and terrible presence. Nausea filled her, but she beat it back as she leaned closer. A little of the blade protruded above the wound. That was good; it had not sunk as deeply as it might have. Perhaps Shadow had fought off his assailant. Certainly, he had the strength and sense to make his way back to the house before losing consciousness. Now if only she could remove the knife without prompting more bleeding —

Her hand shook. That would not do. She took a breath, willing herself to stillness. "Is the water hot?" Her voice sounded unnaturally high and thin.

"It is." He was very close, near her right shoulder. She took comfort from that, steeling herself. "Put the thread in the water and the needles in the flame."

She thought he might object at what could seem like a waste of precious time, but instead he said, "I have heard of this."

"Who from?"

"My grandmother. She also heated a knife or anything she was going to use to cut a wound. Some people mocked her for it."

"She was a healer?"

"No, not really, just a woman who could do what needed to be done. She carried a lot of lore around in her head."

"A wise woman. Would that I were the same."

"You seem to be doing all right."

His comfort, given as it was from the depths of his own despair, glowed within her. She steadied herself, waiting through the long moments until she judged that the thread and needles had been heated enough. Finally, there was no longer any reason to wait.

"It must be now," she said quietly.

Niels nodded. He took up a position opposite her. "What can I do?"

"Hold him still and be ready when I remove the knife. If blood spurts —" She did not finish what she had been about to say. The look on Niels's face made it clear he understood. If that were to happen, his brother would be beyond hope.

She wished most fervently that she had listened more carefully to her Aunt Brianna, to

Brianna's Aunt Elena who was a renowned healer, to her own mother, to everyone and anyone who knew the smallest bit about healing. All that time out riding, exploring, reading, thinking, dreaming . . .

Please God, let her hand stay steady.

She gripped the hilt and pulled.

# Chapter Thirteen

The bleeding had stopped. Scarcely able to believe it, Amelia bent a little closer. The cloth she had most recently pressed to the wound was stained red, but far less so than those that had preceded it. Relief filled her, but only briefly. Far too much remained to be done.

As Niels held a lamp high to cast a circle of light, she worked slowly, methodically stitching the wound. The work was painstaking and difficult. She had to pause twice when she felt her senses swimming dangerously out of focus. But finally, miraculously, she was done.

Shadow breathed shallowly but regularly. His color remained poor but his skin was a little less cold than it had been when they first brought him into the house. Her shoulders slumped with relief. She swayed against the table and might have fallen if Niels hadn't been there to catch her. Lowering her into a chair, he said, "Don't move. I'll be back as soon as I have him settled."

Amelia nodded and leaned her head back. Her eyes were closed when she heard Niels leave the kitchen, carrying his brother. The battle with death had left her dazed. Exhaustion hovered at the edges of her consciousness, but she did not succumb to it. Later there would be time to rest, but right now, much more remained to be done. She had to send for a proper healer, convince Niels to accept help from the Akorans in capturing Hawley, hope Andreas would understand why she had gone to the man who had yet to speak with her father. So much, yet she was eager to get started. She was on her feet when Niels returned.

"How is he?" she asked.

"Better than he would have been if you hadn't been here." He came across the room and took hold of her shoulders, drawing her to him. For just a moment, she thought she felt him tremble. His voice was low and husky. "Damn, Amelia, what would I have done without you? I've tended wounds, but none that serious. Like as not, he would have died."

"Don't think of that," she said softly. "I am here and together we will work out what must be done. You said he was following Hawley?"

Niels nodded. "He was, or at least that was his intent."

"London is dangerous at night. We should not overlook the possibility that he might have been attacked by a robber or even more than one."

"There's a chance of that," Niels acknowledged, although he sounded skeptical. "But Shadow handles himself better than most men. The only way I can figure anyone could get a knife into him is if he was lured into a situation where he couldn't protect himself. Ordinary robbers wouldn't be capable of that."

As he spoke, he released her and turned to the table. In his absence, the wick of the lamp had burned lower. He raised it slightly, increasing the light, and reached out for the knife still lying where Amelia had put it after pulling it out of Shadow's body. Niels's hand was almost on it when he stopped suddenly.

"What's this?"

She peered around him at the blade she had scarcely noticed while all her attention was focused on the wound it had caused.

"These carvings here on the hilt," he said. "I've seen them somewhere."

As well he had, for the same proud bull's horns were emblazoned on the banner that hung above the entrance to Amelia's own home. The royal symbol of Akora was engraved on the hilt of the knife that had almost taken Shadow's life. It could not be — yet even as her mind cried out in denial, she felt the sinking weight of truth and understood its implications.

"Niels, it doesn't mean —"

"An Akoran knife," he interrupted. Slowly, he lifted the weapon, turning it over in his hand so that the light gleamed on the steel still stained with Shadow's blood. His eyes were hard as he looked from it to her. "My brother may yet die because of a wound inflicted by an Akoran knife. The innocent Akorans who couldn't possibly have anything to do with what happened to the *Defiant*."

"We did not have anything to do with it," she insisted. Looking at the knife, she added, "There has to be an explanation for this."

His gaze hardened, growing shuttered. She could feel him withdrawing from her and reached out a hand in entreaty. "Niels, listen to me, Shadow was following Hawley. There's no reason to believe he could have encountered any Akoran, much less fought with one."

"Unless that's who Hawley was with," Niels said, although he did not move away from her touch. "He's no stranger to you people."

"He also is no friend. He is merely an acquaintance. We have many acquaintances, in England and elsewhere. We make certain to know men who aspire to power so that if they ever attain it, they will not come as a surprise to us."

"Well and good, but it doesn't change anything. This is an Akoran knife."

Deliberately, he removed her hand from his arm. "I appreciate what you've done for Shadow, but it's best for you to leave now."

Her throat tightened. This couldn't be happening. Niels's suspicions about her family, so lately put to rest, were returning with a vengeance. It was the wedge that would tear them apart if she let it. Desperately, she said, "He isn't out of danger. You still need help."

"We'll manage. Go home, Amelia."

"Niels, please —"

"Go home!" When still she did not move, he said, "For God's sake, how clear must I make it to you? If an Akoran wielded this knife, how am I or anyone else supposed to believe that Akora was not responsible for the *Defiant*? And if that is so, it will be your country against mine to the bitter and bloody end." He yanked a cape off a nearby peg and threw it around her. For a wrenching moment she was reminded of how he had wrapped her in his cloak on the rain-swept road.

His hand closed hard and unrelenting on her arm, drawing her to the garden door neither of them had thought to close. Beyond it she saw only darkness. His words were a lash. "I will do what I have to, Amelia, and you will hate me for it. Now go out to the stable, saddle Brutus, and get the hell away from here. Away from *me*."

She went, but only because he shoved her out the door and slammed it hard behind her. Pelted by rain, Amelia stood in numb disbelief through the space of several heartbeats. Niels a danger to her? A danger to her country? She had known of the possibility, but so confident was she of her family's innocence and his own honorable nature that she had not allowed any such concern to deter her for a moment. Now it loomed before her, a harsh and unrelenting reality.

Revulsion gripped her. She would not be afraid. She would not! All her life she had been told: Know your fears, they can be valuable, but never, ever yield to them. Courage first and always.

But courage seemed far beyond her capability just then. Half-blinded by tears, she found the startled horse in his stall and led him out. Once astride him, she spared a last anguished glance in the direction of the house before urging Brutus to a gallop.

She entered her home through a back door after turning the stallion over to a stable hand. Head high, enveloped in the cape, she sped past the guards who were far too well disciplined to react to her sudden and decidedly unorthodox appearance. A quick inquiry informed her that Andreas was still in the study. Good. Dealing with him just then was utterly beyond her.

However, she had no choice but to deal with Mulridge. The black-garbed woman was in the hall directly outside Amelia's rooms, looking for all the world as though she was waiting for her.

"Is that blood I smell?" Mulridge asked, the nostrils of her beaked nose flaring.

"Probably. I need a bath, very hot and with an absolute minimum of conversation." Hearing herself, Amelia blushed. It was not like her to sound so high-and-mighty. More gently, she said, "I'm sorry, it's just that it's been a difficult evening." To grossly understate the case.

"Stormy, too much energy in the air. The water's heated, I've checked."

Amelia did not ask how Mulridge had anticipated her wish, much less her arrival. The ageless retainer often seemed a step or two ahead
of the rest of them. In her rooms, she went
straight to the large closet, shut the door behind her, and stripped to her skin. Wrapped in
a thin silk robe, she emerged into the bathing
chamber. Mulridge had set the taps to fill the
large, shell-shaped tub that dominated the
room. Steam rose past the marble walls to the
ceiling, which was painted to resemble the sky
above the royal city of Ilius at the summer
equinox. A sudden, fierce longing for home
gripped her. She shoved it aside, something to
think of later.

"When did you eat last?" Mulridge asked.

The mere thought of the meal she had shared
with Niels and its aftermath made her stomach
roil. "I'm not hungry."

"Cook made that rice pudding you like."

Amelia looked up, meeting the eyes of the
wise woman who had been there all her life.
"With dried cherries and raisins?"

"The very one."

"I could eat that."

Mulridge gave a satisfied nod and went to get
the pudding. When the door had closed behind
her, Amelia dropped her robe and sank into the
blissfully hot water. It came not courtesy of the
thermal streams that heated water in Akora,
but thanks to a gas-fired furnace in the base-

229

ment of the house, a recent and deeply appreciated innovation.

The heat loosened muscles in her shoulders and back that were painfully knotted. She leaned forward, resting her head against her updrawn knees. Never in her life had she felt so afraid or so lost. Of course, she'd had scant opportunity to feel either. Her life to this point had been singularly unchallenging. Loved, protected, privileged, she had tried her best to be a good person, but she had never really been tested. Until now.

Tears trickled down her cheeks. She brushed them aside but they kept coming. Alone in the tub, her sobs muted by the rushing water, Amelia wept. For herself, though that shamed her; for the men of the *Defiant*, where all this had begun; for Shadow, who hovered so near to death; and ultimately for Niels, in whom she feared regrets were mounting. When she was done, she lay back in the tub, wearied by the deluge of emotion. She was at real risk of drifting off to sleep when Mulridge knocked.

"Come out of there before you pass for a prune."

Amelia emerged into her bedroom, wrapped once more in the silk robe, to find the lamps lit and a cheerful fire holding the rainy spring night at bay. Mulridge disappeared into the closet, returning with Amelia's discarded clothes.

"Any point asking why you came home

without a skirt?" She lifted the cape and sniffed it. "Wearing a man's cape. He likes good tobacco, by the way." She tossed the bundle onto the floor. "Is it his blood?"

Amelia sat down at the table in front of the fire. She dug a spoon into the pudding. "His brother's."

"Then why are you here?"

Mulridge never had been one for beating around the bush and neither was Amelia. "Niels told me to go home."

"When did you start doing what you're told?"

Amelia swallowed the sweet, soothing confection and took another spoonful. "I wasn't that bad a child, was I?"

"Not at all. I personally can't abide the sort who look like butter wouldn't melt in their mouths. They're always the ones bound for trouble and blaming others for it. But never mind. Do you want to talk about what happened?"

"Not especially. It's completely miserable and I'm all at sea over it."

Mulridge looked relieved. She'd never been one for a lot of talking. Indeed, she had a habit of referring to talkative people as "damn starlings."

"Good thing the king's dying," she said.

Amelia didn't have to ask her meaning. She knew perfectly well that the king's distress was the source of her own freedom to go and come without explanation. So long as Andreas remained preoccupied, she could continue to do so. She only hoped whatever was in that report from Gavin was both intricate and urgent.

She scraped the last of the pudding onto her spoon and swallowed it. Whether thanks to the bath, the fire, the food, or a good cry, she felt better. Not immensely, but enough to consider what had to be done. Her thoughts now possessed a clarity they had been sadly lacking. Shove her out into the night, would he? He'd just see about that.

When it came right down to it, the decision about what to do was remarkably easy, perhaps because she truly could envision only one choice.

"I'll need some supplies," she said.

Mulridge nodded. "I'll see to it."

The black-garbed woman was turning away when Amelia caught her hand. "Thank you."

A thin hand touched her hair lightly. "I've faith in you, little chick."

"Please, God, it's not misplaced."

"It's not," Mulridge said simply, and went to gather what was needed. In her absence, Amelia dressed. She chose a plain but sturdy skirt and jacket in a green-and-gold plaid that she was more likely to wear at Hawkforte while clambering over the ancient walls or exploring the nearby caves with her cousins. The clothes were comfortable and she associated them with happy memories, a comfort in itself. Her hair was still damp from the bath. She brushed it out, twined it in a single braid and left it hanging down her back. Because she did not know how long she would be gone, she tucked a nightgown, extra undergarments, and a few toiletries into a black valise.

Just before she went from the room, she noticed the roses Niels had sent. One of the maids must have brought them up. She hesitated a moment before snapping off a blossom and tucking it beneath her jacket.

Mulridge was waiting for her downstairs with the supplies. Amelia took a quick look through them and was satisfied. She didn't ask how they were acquired without the notice of the healer in whose quarters they were generally kept. Mulridge had a talent for coming and going without being seen.

"Andreas will finish whatever has him so engrossed and emerge eventually. He'll wonder why I am not here."

"What do you want me to tell him?"

Amelia hesitated. She was an intrinsically honest person. But these were desperate circumstances and they seemed to call for desperate measures.

"A lie. I can't see any alternative. If you would rather not be a party to it, I'll write a note for him."

Mulridge smiled faintly. "You're a good girl. My conscience is my own affair. Tell me you're going to Boswick."

"What?"

"Just tell me that."

"I'm going to Boswick."

"Then that's what I'll tell Prince Andreas you told me. But you must promise me you'll be careful. First sign of trouble, you be fleet on the wing."

Amelia put the supplies into the valise. "I have nothing to fear from Niels."

"I don't think you do, either, or I wouldn't let you be going like this." Without warning, Mulridge threw out her arms and hugged her fiercely. Just as quickly, she let her go. "Be off, then, before I change my mind."

Amelia went. Brutus seemed a little surprised to be roused from the strange stall so quickly after being put in it, but he was, for all his size and power, a remarkably patient horse. Or perhaps he merely sensed they were going home. Certainly his trot quickened as they turned the corner near Niels's house.

Having left there only a few hours before, in the most unpromising circumstances and not at all certain she would be allowed back in, Amelia hesitated. She took Brutus to the stable around the back and saw him settled while she wrestled with her nervousness.

"No more disturbances tonight, boy," she said as she untacked him and made sure he had fresh water.

He nickered in response and butted her side gently. At least the horse approved of her. Satchel in hand, she turned up the garden path toward the house. The air smelled blessedly of damp grass and nothing else. The rain had stopped. It would be morning soon. Already she heard a few birds stirring beneath the eaves.

The door through which she had so lately been thrust, was in front of her. A last, treacherous urge to retreat, swept over Amelia.

She raised her hand and knocked.

Niels lifted his head slowly. He was sitting beside the bed where Shadow lay, having kept vigil over his brother ever since Amelia's departure. Shadow was restless. Twice he had called out in apparent agitation, but his words, if they were that, were impossible to discern. At least his skin remained cool and he did not appear to be in pain. That would come later. In anticipation of it, Niels had brought up a bottle of bourbon. He distrusted laudanum, even if any were available, and there was nothing else.

Staring at his brother, lying pale and for the moment unmoving on the bed, he felt swept by a wave of disbelief. How had it come to this? How had his brother come so close to losing his life while he, Niels, dallied with Amelia? Assuming, of course, that dalliance was the correct word for the most intensely sensual experience of his life. Never mind he had failed in his duty to protect Shadow, a duty Shadow himself mocked, but which Niels, as the older brother, felt keenly. Better to be dead himself than to see Shadow in such extremes.

The strength and certainty that had maintained him in so many dangerous circumstances were gone. He felt hollow inside, the mere husk of a man waiting to be blown apart by the first decent wind that came along. Worse yet, he couldn't muster the energy to object.

But he could, and he damn well would, do his duty.

He was straightening the covers over Shadow when he heard the sound again. What was that? A branch banging against an outer wall? It must be, for surely no one would be about at such an hour.

Oddly, it sounded like someone knocking.

He straightened further, his senses suddenly alert, and listened. For a moment, there was nothing more. Until softly, almost plaintively, he heard:

"Niels . . . Niels, let me in. I've brought supplies to help Shadow. You have to let me in . . . for his sake."

He was dreaming. Having done everything possible to earn Amelia's hatred and scorn, he could not possibly be hearing her outside his door, asking to be let back in.

"Niels!"

More like demanding, actually.

He went down the stairs very quickly and yanked the door open so hard that she was caught by surprise. Fist raised, she swayed toward him.

He stepped back, resisting the instinct to catch her in favor of the far greater wisdom of not touching her. She caught herself, lowered her hand, straightened her skirt, and would have entered if he hadn't blocked her way.

"What in hell are you doing here?" he demanded.

For just a moment, her lower lip trembled. It damn near undid him. Another second and he would have been in real danger of crumbling. Fortunately, she recovered herself and gave him a good strong glare.

"Didn't you hear me? I've brought supplies for Shadow."

"Shadow's fine."

"Really? And just how did this apparent miracle occur? Was there a visitation of some sort, the fluttering of wings, any hint of an angelic chorus?"

"Don't be sacrilegious."

"Don't you. We both know he isn't fine. Now stand aside."

His manner softened treacherously. She looked so damn good standing there, the wind blowing stray wisps of her hair around her face and her color high. That she was there at all was the miracle and that, he was sure, was no sacrilege.

"I sent you away for a good reason, Amelia."

"Oh, yes, an excellent reason. You think my country and yours are enemies, we're going to war, and you and I are bound to hate each other. Well, let me tell you something, Niels Wolfson, that's all nonsense. What's more, your brother is going to recover, wake up, and tell you so. When he does, I want to be here to see it happen. I'll treasure every moment."

"Have you ever once in your whole life thought you might be wrong?"

"Actually, I am frequently wrong, but not about this. I am not wrong about my family, my country, or you. Now let me in!"

There were tears in her eyes. They belied her stalwart determination even as they tore at him. When had he ever received such unalloyed trust except from Shadow, who did, undeniably, need her help?

He stepped aside but did not shut the door. "Where's Brutus?"

"In his stall, untacked, brushed down, and probably asleep by this time."

"Did I see you ride out of here on him astride and without a saddle?"

"What if I did?"

"It was a damn foolish thing to do."

"Not on a horse that well schooled. Why were you looking, anyway?"

"A man has to look at something."

He could practically feel her taking his measure. Whatever she thought she saw must have satisfied her, because abruptly she smiled.

"So he does. Where's Shadow?"

"Leave what you've brought. I thank you for it. Now go home."

"I wouldn't dream of it. As I said, I want to be here when you find out how wrong you are. The stairs are through there?" She gestured toward the hall and quickly moved past him.

"How did I ever doubt that you're a princess?"

"I really have no idea. It does seem as though it would be glaringly obvious." She was across the kitchen, then through the door to the hall and out of sight. He was left feeling vaguely stunned and treacherously happy. And strangely enough, he thought he smelled roses.

"How has he been?" Amelia asked as she set the valise down in the bedroom and looked at the man lying motionless in the bed.

"A little agitated but otherwise all right."

"Any sign of fever?"

"Not so far."

"You know it is likely to come unless we can prevent infection. I brought ingredients to make a poultice. Is there water here?"

He pointed toward the ewer on the dresser. "It's cold by now. Do you want hot?"

"That would help." She was taking off her jacket. As she did, a crumbled rose fell onto the floor. He bent to retrieve it.

"What's this?"

She snatched it away, tucking it into a pocket of her skirt. "Nothing."

"One of the roses I sent you?" He could scarcely believe it — yet what other explanation could there be?

"The roses and the note — 'A rose by any other name.' What did that signify?"

"A line from *Romeo and Juliet*."

"I know that. Why choose it?"

"No particular reason, it just sprang to mind." Fruit of his hard-won education, first with borrowed books and stolen hours, then in more recent years with tutors. They might have thought themselves hired to assure he would be at no disadvantage in the world of the privileged and powerful, but they rapidly came to realize that their true purpose was to assuage his endless thirst for knowledge.

"Doomed lovers torn apart by the conflict between their clans," Amelia said. "Dying before they have scarcely had a chance to live. You were trying to warn me . . . or yourself."

"You're reading too much into it."

She shrugged, clearly unconvinced. "As you wish. The water?"

He went and managed not to vent his sheer male frustration on the pots, at least not too much. He banged them only a little, which was certainly preferable to slamming his fist through the nearest wall. When he returned, she was sitting beside the bed, her hand holding Shadow's.

"He is growing warmer."

Niels touched his brother's brow. His face hardened. "The fever has started."

"Then we must stop it," she said and opened the valise.

# Chapter Fourteen

Whatever it was that Amelia was crushing with that mortar and pestle, it stank. As discreetly as he could manage, Niels edged over toward the window and cracked it open. The fresh air helped a little, but not all that much.

"What is that?" Niels asked, trying to breathe through his mouth.

She turned her head aside, gasping a little. "The rotted rinds of a fruit that grows on Akora. Awful, isn't it?"

"Rotted? Shouldn't it be fresh?"

"Oh, no, they're useless until they rot."

"You're not putting that on Shadow."

"I most certainly am. It will prevent infection."

"It'll kill him."

"That's insulting, Niels."

"I'm sorry. I didn't mean you want to kill him. I just don't see how that can help him."

"As nearly as I understand, something grows on the rotted rinds that kills whatever causes infections. At least it does most times."

"My old gran swore by spiderwebs to stop bleeding."

"I've heard of that. There's also snake venom that will slow the heart during very delicate surgeries."

"Surgery? Butchery is more like it."

"Not on Akora. Here, hold this." She handed him the mortar with its noxious contents. He grimaced but held it for her.

With great care, she undid the bandage over Shadow's wound and looked at it critically. "It is as well we are doing this."

"You're sure there's nothing else?"

"Nothing as effective." Taking the mortar from him, she carefully spread the poultice around the edges of the sutured wound. Merely touching the stuff called for courage, in Niels's opinion. When she was finished, he set the remains outside on the windowsill. Dawn was breaking. The servants would be arriving soon.

"I'm going downstairs for a few minutes," he said. "Do you have everything you need?"

Amelia nodded. "For the moment, unless you want to make tea."

He should have thought of that. She'd had no more sleep than he had, yet she'd come out in the night, despite all he'd done to prevent her, to help his brother. When had anyone behaved so generously toward either of them? Their father was no more than a faint memory. Their mother — a good and strong woman — had yielded her sons to the harsh reality of life while yet they were little more than children. There hadn't been any choice, given their circumstances and their own natures. Since then, he and Shadow had been self-sufficient, making their own way, doing well for themselves and their country, but expecting nothing from the world that they didn't wrest for themselves.

And now? He knew without having to be told that Amelia was behaving toward them as she would toward members of her own family. She refused to let any obstacle, most particularly his own suspicions, stand in her way. The vast love he had sensed among the Akorans had been extended to himself, and from there, to Shadow. It was a startling and humbling realization. Worse yet, it was almost irresistibly seductive.

He made the tea, as well as coffee for himself. While he was about it, he set bread to brown in metal racks near the fire, found butter and jam, and located a tray. It was all very domestic, very pleasant. A secret dream. He almost laughed. What his enemies — and they were legion — would give to know that the Wolf fancied himself an ordinary man with a wife and children, caring for them in the simplest yet most important ways.

He had scarcely ever admitted the desire to himself, and when he had, it had seemed so unlikely as to be pointless to pursue. He was who he was — a hunter and killer, a man who got the hard things done.

All the same, he could make a decent pot of tea.

Setting everything on the tray, he returned upstairs. The smell had eased. He could breathe without regretting it. Amelia looked grateful, then surprised. "Toast, too, with jam?"

"It was close at hand. Besides, you need to eat."

"You'd get along with Mulridge. Her answer to anything is a full stomach."

He waited until she had eaten, then asked, "When can I expect Andreas to come after you?"

She dusted crumbs from her fingers and did not look at him. "He thinks I've gone to Boswick."

"Why would he think that?"

She did look at him then, and her gaze was steady. "Because I lied. What was it you said, a 'necessary' lie?"

This from a woman he was certain valued honor above all else. He should never have come into her life. The cost to her was far too high and likely to grow higher still.

"The servants will be here soon," he said because he had to think of something else. "I'm going to pay them for the week and send them off."

"It's probably just as well. The fewer who know about Shadow, the better."

"And about you."

"Yes, that as well, at least until this is over."

Whenever and however that would be. He made one last try. "It isn't too late for you to leave."

"Yes, it is," she said and slathered more jam on the toast.

By dawn, Amelia was asleep. She drifted off,

sitting beside Shadow, her hand still on his. Some little time passed before Niels realized she was no longer awake. When he did, he set aside his coffee mug and looked at her. Watching her unobserved was a luxury he had not hitherto experienced. Her lashes lay thickly against cheeks he thought too pale. The thick braid of her night-dark hair hung over her shoulder. He watched the slow rise and fall of her breathing. She had worn herself out — the indomitable spirit he had come to know so well was stilled briefly. A wise man would take advantage of that.

There was a little smear of jam on her chin. He wiped it away gently. She did not stir. Lifting her in his arms, he stood for a moment, letting himself simply feel — without doubt or concern, without duty or honor, with nothing more than simple, honest emotion.

Luxury heaped upon luxury.

Quickly, before he could think better of it, he carried her across the hall to his own room. There he laid her on the bed and removed her boots. Resisting the temptation to go further, he covered her and withdrew, closing the door softly behind him.

An hour or so later, Shadow stirred. He called out, but again the words were unintelligible. Niels moved quickly to soothe him.

"It's all right," he said, touching his brother's arm. "You made it back; you're safe." He had to repeat that several times before Shadow eventually calmed. He lapsed again into what Niels had to hope was a healing sleep.

At least the fever showed no sign of worsening. Niels was surprised by that. Perhaps there was something to Amelia's rotted rind after all. The Akorans were rumored to be great healers, just as they were said to be skilled in many other areas as well. War, for instance.

If it came to war . . .

His mind shied away. He was tired and there was no point dwelling on such things. Even so, the thought lingered, conjuring images he could have done without. The morning passed slowly. Twice he got up to check on Amelia. She was sleeping deeply, as she had been when he took her from the safety of the life that should have remained hers.

He'd had no right to do that. He thought he had, justifying it out of the greater right of his country, but he'd been wrong. What he had done had been wrong. Yet look where it had led.

She was there, close to his hand, despite everything.

God, how he wanted that to continue. How he wanted her to be with him each and every day.

What had she said? *You did not come into my life by accident.* How much did she truly know? She was intelligent, and she came from a long line of people extremely adept at judging their circumstances. Otherwise, how could they have survived?

Did she truly grasp the full extent of what he had done, yet did not rail at him for it?

An honest, straightforward woman who was also a puzzle. He saw himself suddenly, a child playing with a wooden maze. Made by his father? He did not know. In memory, he was trying to get a marble to roll along the correct path. It was difficult, frustrating . . . enthralling. By dint of perseverance and a certain delicacy of touch, he had succeeded more often than he'd failed.

He shut his eyes for a moment, opened them to notice a flash of color emerging in the morning light. There, on the floor, he found the rose. It must have fallen from Amelia's skirt, where she had thrust it. He picked it up and sniffed it. The petals were wilted, but the perfume remained strong and heady.

Romeo and Juliet. His stalwartly nonromantic soul cringed at the thought. Yet he had written that, plucked it from memory on impulse.

She was right; he had been trying to tell her — and himself — what lay ahead.

Death and the tomb.

He had seen *Romeo and Juliet* at the Bowery Theatre in New York three springs ago. Shadow had been in the city and wanted to go. They'd taken two "ladies," sisters who were thoroughly congenial. He remembered thinking

247

the play would be tedious. How wrong he had been. There were those who claimed *Hamlet* was Shakespeare's greatest play, but the prince of Denmark was a self-centered bore going on and on about what was really a very straight-forward matter. Kill the uncle, marry the girl, certainly don't let her wander off and drown. Romeo . . . now, he was all right; a good man with a sword and not afraid to love. Impulsive, though, and ill-fated. Fine enough on the stage, but not for real life.

Shadow loved both plays, cherished anything to do with the theatre. He'd have been an actor if his life had worked out differently. Just lately, before the *Defiant*, he'd talked about buying a share in a New York theatre or perhaps spon-soring a traveling company. Please God, let him live to do both.

Restless, he went over to the window. The rain was gone but clouds lingered. The air was damp and cool. Beyond the immediate grounds of the house, the life of the city went on. Lorries rolled past, carriages as well. If London ever slept, it was in the wee hours, and briefly.

The house itself was quiet. In the absence of servants, there was none of the usual bustle. He could hear the sounds of the city all the more acutely. Notice, too, the sudden flutter of movement in the trees just between the house and the street. Weary, he squeezed his eyes shut, opened them, saw nothing exceptional.

A phantasm of his tired brain. He had experienced the same before, when fatigue played tricks on even the most agile mind. He left Shadow long enough to make more coffee, drank it, and stayed awake. The day aged. Toward noon, Amelia awoke.

For a moment, she had no notion of where she was. The ceiling above her was a pale blue; the curtains were dark blue velvet. None of that was familiar. She lay, staring up at the ceiling, as her mind slowly cleared away the lingering wisps of dreams. When it did, she sat bolt upright.

*Shadow.*

Throwing back the covers, she jumped from the bed and was halfway across the room before she realized she was in her stocking feet. Grabbing her boots, she hurried out into the hall.

Silence hung heavy in the house, alongside dancing dust motes. Pausing to listen, she heard nothing save for the distant sounds of the city. Only the light streaming through the tall window at the far end of the hall confirmed that it was day.

Urgency seized her. Unsure of exactly where to go, she opened the nearest door and looked in. Niels sat beside the bed. His eyes were closed as though he slept, but the moment she opened the door, he was alert.

"What?"

She had the sudden sense of coiled strength

capable of exploding without warning. Quelling a tiny spurt of anxiety, she said, "It's just me." Aware suddenly that she was straight from bed, uncombed and unwashed, she made a stab at smoothing her hair, then realized she was still carrying her boots and set them down. "How is Shadow?"

"His fever hasn't worsened. That stuff you put on him must be working."

"Has he awakened?"

Niels shook his head. "He's called out a time or two but it doesn't amount to anything."

"You can't understand him?"

"Not a word." He got to his feet, running a hand through his thick black hair. "What time is it?"

"I don't know." She went over to the window and peered out. "Afternoon. I should not have slept so long."

"You needed it. I would have wakened you if Shadow worsened." As she watched, he stretched his long, hard body, then ran a hand over his jaw and grimaced. "I need a shave."

She thought he looked all-too temptingly male, but this wasn't the time to mention that.

"I'll stay with Shadow."

He nodded and went from the room, leaving her to the quiet of her own thoughts. Before they could intrude too much, she checked Shadow carefully and was satisfied that his condition had not worsened. That was saying a great deal. If they could stave off the twin enemies of fever and infection, the natural strength of his own body would have a chance to heal him. If . . .

The water in the pitcher near the bed was cold. She risked a few minutes to run down to the kitchen, poke up the fire, and set a pot to boil. Glancing through the kitchen window, she was surprised to see Niels in the garden.

"I thought you had gone to bed," she said when she opened the door.

He turned, frowning. "I needed some fresh air."

A pleasant breeze blew from the west, holding off the city stench. Yet he looked . . . braced. Yes, that was it, he looked like a man braced for trouble. Or perhaps he was merely tired and her imagination was running roughshod over her better sense.

"You should lie down," she said.

Slowly, Niels nodded, but even as he came toward the house, he glanced over his shoulder toward the line of trees that bordered the garden.

"Are you looking for something?" Amelia asked, standing aside for him.

"I thought I saw someone."

A ripple of concern moved through her. "Who?"

"No one." He shut the door, closing off her view of the road. "I'll heat more water."

"I've started a pot." She nodded toward the

hearth. "Would you mind bringing some up when it's ready?"

He assured her he would and she left him to it. Climbing the stairs, she paused and glanced down toward the kitchen. Niels was crouched beside the hearth, testing the water. Looking at him, her heart quickened. Did men know their own beauty? She doubted it. They thought beauty was the province of women, but they were wrong. She could close her eyes and retrace in memory the curve of his jaw, the planes of his chest, the powerful muscles of his thighs and buttocks. Feel the rough-smooth texture of his skin, hear the low, hard sounds he made when pleasure was upon him, even smell the musky scents of their bodies intermingling.

All right there on the steps from the kitchen while she was supposed to be tending a gravely injured man. Heat swept over her, partly desire, partly embarrassment for her own susceptibility.

She climbed the stairs and was sitting beside Shadow when Niels brought the water. When he was gone again, having promised to at least lie down, she washed her face and hands, then uncovered Shadow's wound. The edges were red and hot-looking, but that was to be expected. There was no sign that the infection was spreading. She replaced the bandage with a fresh one, then poured a little of the tea Niels had also brought, onto a spoon. Carefully, she put the spoon to Shadow's lips.

"Drink," she said softly and let a little of the liquid trickle into his mouth.

He did not swallow and she had to wipe the tea away. Still, she tried again, speaking to him softly, calling to him wherever his spirit dwelled now, drawing him back to the world.

"You must drink even if it is only a little. You will live, you will, and your body needs this. Drink, Shadow, for your brother. Niels is here, close by, worrying for you. Please, he needs for you to live. Don't leave him."

Nothing. He did not hear her or he could not respond. With no fever, he could live for a while without fluids, but eventually he must have them or he would die. If he did not revive enough to drink . . .

Pushing the thought aside, she soaked a cloth in cool water and gently bathed his face. He, too, needed a shave, but his beard was much lighter than his brother's. One fair, the other dark. Yet she suspected they were much alike, for all their outward differences.

With a sigh, she got up and walked a little way around the room. Her body was restless, her mind even more so. She straightened a carpet by the bed, set a picture to better rights and noticed that the door of the wardrobe hung open a little. When she tried to shut it, the bolt would not catch. Something blocked it from closing.

A boot. A very large black boot and its mate. Shadow was a big man, but the boot belonged to a giant. Or did it? The sole was un-usually thick. A man standing in it would be inches taller than his true height.

Tall enough to wear the oversized black coat that also hung in the closet?

And the black wig along with . . . yes, it was a beard. The sort an actor would wear.

She had known, or at least suspected. She just hadn't wanted to think about it very much.

*I am the man on the road in the dark and the rain.*

So Niels had said, and so he was, but not by chance. Every step had been carefully planned. He had insinuated himself into her family, made them grateful to him, the better to assess their guilt and do what he felt he must.

She was not a fool. She knew it was all dif-ferent now. Or at least it could be. Her gaze went to the man lying in the bed. When he woke, when he began to speak, what would he say?

She had to believe she knew. That confidence was her armor and her shield. Her family would never — never! — commit such an atrocity as had befallen the *Defiant*.

Her father, her uncle, her cousins, and brothers were all men of the most rigorous honor — Akoran men, warriors sworn to pro-tect Akora at all costs. But not by stealth and treachery. Not by murder.

Niels had believed that until he found the Akoran knife in his brother.

There had to be an explanation. Hawley had been in the London house many times. He must have found the knife there and stolen it. Shadow would confirm when he awoke that no Akorans were involved in the attack on him. Wouldn't he?

Her head hurt. She sat down again and tried to think what to do. The wound was stitched, infection held off, there was no sign of shock or other injuries. Moving the covers back a little, she bent her head and listened to Shadow's breathing. It seemed stronger than before and when she moved her head from one side of his chest to the other, the sound was the same. Thank God for that. If the knife had struck one of his lungs, his chances for recovery would be that much less.

She tried again to give him a little tea and again was unsuccessful. Refusing to be discouraged, she spoke to him softly, telling him who she was and why she was there.

"Your brother is a stubborn man. He sent me away, but I, too, am stubborn. I will not let you go. You are far too young to leave this world and certainly not courtesy of an Akoran knife. Where were you, Shadow? What happened to you?"

It seemed just then that he stirred a little, but the impression was fleeting and she could not be sure. After a moment, she went on, "You were following Hawley, weren't you? Trying to discover his plan? Was there a fight or were you tricked?"

Beneath her hand, the muscles of his arm seemed to tighten. She took a breath, willing patience. "How did you make it back here? What strength and courage did that take? Be strong now, Shadow. Come all the way back."

Nothing, no sign he heard her. Or . . . was there? Did she mistake wish for reality or was there truly a slight flicker of movement in his jaw? "Come back," she said again, entreating him, and was rewarded suddenly when his fingers closed around hers.

Startled, she drew back a little but did not break contact with him. Taking his hand in both of hers, she pressed hard. "All the way, Shadow. Don't stop now. Please hear me. We need for you to wake. Niels needs it. He must hear what you have to say. You must tell him —"

She broke off suddenly when Shadow jerked hard. For a horrible moment, she feared she had hurt him. That fear fled, to be replaced by one even greater, when he suddenly cried out.

"The Akorans! Niels, the Akorans! Be careful . . . don't let —" A spasm of coughing seized him. It passed quickly, but in the aftermath his voice was faint and weak. Still, she could make out the words clearly enough. They were the same.

*"The Akorans! Niels, the Akorans!"*

This could not be. It was impossible. Shadow could not be trying to warn his brother about her family. He could not mean that they were responsible for the attack on him.

Yet anyone else, hearing those words, most certainly would believe that was exactly what he meant.

Niels would believe it.

She could leave him in ignorance, say nothing, and pray that when Shadow spoke again, it would be with far greater lucidity. She could do that.

No, she could not.

Honor and love, both, demanded what she knew beyond any doubt was right.

A terrible coldness seemed to descend over her. She set Shadow's hand down gently and rose. Slowly, weighed by dread, she turned to leave the room and find Niels.

Only to discover that he was already there, standing by the door she had not heard open.

# Chapter Fifteen

"He is not conscious," Amelia said quickly, "not really. You cannot assume his meaning."

Niels did not move. He remained where he stood, leaning against the doorframe, his arms crossed over his broad chest. He had shaved, but he looked no more tame for it. Or any less dangerous.

"He could be trying to warn you that the Akorans are innocent," she said, "and you should be concentrating all your attention on Hawley."

"He didn't mention Hawley."

"He is unconscious! He doesn't know what he's saying. For God's sake, Niels, this is too important —"

He did move then, crossing the room in quick strides to stand before her. His eyes were bleak, his face hard. "I know damn well how important it is. Move aside."

She hesitated, but finally did as he said. There was no point provoking him any more than he already had been. He took her place beside Shadow and spoke gently.

"It's Niels; I'm here. Talk to me, Shadow. Tell me what I need to know."

His brother sighed deeply but did not respond. Niels tried again. "Speak to me. Who did this? Who is the enemy?"

Amelia held her breath, fearing what he would say, but Shadow remained silent. His head tossed a little from side to side, but he showed no awareness of anything going on around him.

"Did you drug him?" Niels demanded suddenly. He straightened and looked at her.

"No! Of course not. What are you talking about? I was about to get you." When he did not respond, she said, "Don't you doubt me, Niels Wolfson! I feared you'd jump to all the wrong conclusions about what your brother had said, but I meant for you to know all the same."

He shrugged as though it was of no importance. Damn man! "Perhaps you were. He spoke once; he will again. I'll be here when he does."

"Fine, just fine. You sit with him. You hear what he has to say. You jump to any conclusions you choose. I'm —"

"Going home?"

How could she when home would forever be where he was?

"No, I am *not* going home! I am going down to the kitchen where I will be making *soup*. Unless, of course, you think I'm likely to *drug* it!"

She was perilously close to losing control, but that didn't appear to trouble Niels. Indeed, her tirade seemed to provide a measure of relief. Or perhaps it was her intention to stay that did that.

"I'll risk it, Princess," he said softly and resumed his seat beside his brother.

Amelia went down to the kitchen. More correctly, she stomped down. She could not remember when she had ever been so angry . . . or so afraid. What had Shadow meant? He couldn't possibly have been trying to warn Niels about her family . . . could he?

No, he absolutely could not have been, and she was a fool to indulge such an absurd thought for even a moment.

But Niels thought so, or at least entertained the possibility. That, she could not deny. Nor could she truly blame him for it. First the *Defiant*, now this. He had every right to believe the worst. And he had no right. Why couldn't he believe in her as she did in him?

He did not have her gift. It had led her to see the quality of the man from the beginning and that, in turn, had led to actions she would never have taken under other circumstances. Well and good, but it solved nothing now. She was as blind as anyone now, struggling in the dark to cope with a situation that might soon spiral out of control.

What better time to make soup?

She tied an apron around her waist and got to it. A few firm blows with the cleaver separated the chicken she found in the larder. She put the pieces in a kettle along with water, salt, and pepper, then hung the kettle from a hook over the fire. While the chicken simmered, she peeled potatoes and carrots, and added them to the kettle. As all that cooked, she found apples, peeled them, mixed dough, and rolled it out. When the apples were cooked down with cinnamon and sugar, she assembled a credible pie.

"Don't give me any trouble," she muttered to the iron stove. Judging the fire in it to be about right, she slipped the pie in and hoped for the best.

At loose ends until the soup was further along, and not eager to return upstairs, she explored beyond the kitchen. Finding a butler's pantry, she located a surprisingly expansive collection of wine and selected a decent claret. Opening it, she poured an inch or so into a crystal wine goblet and drank it down — purely for tasting purposes, of course.

When she was eighteen, she'd gotten drunk.

Heavens, she hadn't thought of that in how long? Still, the memory must have lingered, because she'd never done the same again.

Honey wine, it had been; mead that legend had it was introduced to Akora by the Hawkforte ancestor who arrived there in 1100 A.D. It had given her the most horrible headache she had ever experienced.

She'd been with her cousin, Gavin, and her brothers, Lucius and Marcus, the lot of them eating and drinking around a roaring fire on a beach not far from the palace at Ilius. They'd had a grand time, until the following morning. It all seemed so long ago, in a much simpler and more innocent time.

She felt so much older. Childhood was behind her, but even youth itself seemed tenuous now. So much was at risk — life, death, honor, hope. She took a breath, drawing deep from the strength that, she reminded herself, was the true gift she had received.

When she returned to the kitchen, the soup was ready enough. She drew out the chicken on a slotted spoon, carefully skimmed away the fat, removed the skin, separated the meat into shreds and returned it to the kettle. It was good work that kept her hands busy and her mind mercifully stilled.

Her father had taught her to cook. Not that her mother wasn't able in the kitchen, but Joanna herself said that her husband was by far the better cook. He'd started with *marinos,* the dish so loved by Akorans, but little by little, Alex had revealed culinary mysteries of all sorts to his beloved daughter. It was understood between them that she would not prattle of this. He was a warrior and leader, second only to the Vanax. Yet there was no denying it, he had a deft hand with a sauce.

The soup needed none, but she decided it would benefit from dumplings. She mixed the batter and dropped spoonfuls of it into the simmering liquid. That done, she was left with nothing to do but go upstairs.

Perhaps she should reconsider the wine. A white might be better. No, she was merely delaying, and that was cowardice.

She loaded up a tray, balanced it carefully, and climbed the stairs. Niels was standing near the windows. He turned when she entered and came to her, taking the tray.

"You really did make soup." He looked surprised.

"Undrugged soup or would you like me to try it first?"

"I spoke out of turn."

It was more apology than she expected, and it went a long way toward mollifying her. In all fairness, the man had reason to be suspicious.

"I think we should try to get Shadow to eat some of this," she said.

"He hasn't taken any of the tea."

"He needs liquids." She set the tray on the table beside the bed, laid a napkin over Shadow's chest to protect him from the hot soup, and carefully filled a spoon. When it had cooled so that it no longer steamed, she set it to his lips.

Nothing.

Behind her, Niels asked, "How long . . . that is, how long can he live without liquid?"

"I don't know. It helps that he has no fever, but it would be better if he took some of this."

She tried again. Shadow's lips moved, but only slightly, and the soup trickled away.

"This isn't working."

"Be patient." She tried again, still without success. Was it cruel to persist and risk disturbing an ailing man? Or was it better to continue? She had only her instincts to guide her.

Once more, she filled the spoon with broth and held it to Shadow's mouth. Very softly, she said, "Please, just try."

Carefully, she slipped the liquid between his lips. For a moment, nothing happened. Then, quite unmistakably, she saw the muscles of his throat work.

"He swallowed!"

Niels looked at her with the eyes of a man who wants desperately to believe but cannot. "Are you sure?"

"I saw it. Look." She offered another spoonful with the same results.

"Is he conscious?"

Amelia shook her head. "No, not really, but he has some awareness, however slight. Swallowing is a reflex that is born in us. That much he has recovered."

"Can he speak?"

"If he can, he will, and please, God, it will be soon."

"Amen to that."

She fed a little more of the soup to Shadow. When he had taken all she thought he could manage, she turned her attention to Niels. "This soup is for you, too."

"I'm not hungry."

"You don't have to be hungry to eat soup. It will do you good."

"What about you?"

"I will if you will."

He sat as she handed him a bowl. This he ate while watching her do the same. "It's good soup," he said after a while.

"Thank you."

"How does a princess learn to cook?"

"I'm an *Akoran* princess. That's different from whatever you may think."

"Why is it different?"

"Because of who we are. Our history has made us different."

He filled both the wineglasses she had brought and handed one to her.

"Because you've been so isolated out there in the Atlantic?" he asked. "The Fortress Kingdom, alone and inviolate, beyond the Pillars of Hercules. Nothing seems to touch you. Until recently, no one even knew much of anything about you."

"But we have known the world," she countered. "We have always sent people out into it to learn whatever might be of use to us. And we have welcomed those who came shipwrecked to our shores, offered them new lives beyond any they could know elsewhere."

"Laudatory, I'm sure. It still doesn't explain why a princess can cook."

"Cooking is enjoyable and useful. Besides, people should know how to look after themselves."

"Princesses included?"

"Most definitely. I told you my family are servants of Akora."

He nodded. "You did say that."

"Did you believe me?"

He hedged, "I didn't *not* believe you. It just seems odd. I've spent enough time in Europe to understand why my ancestors left. Royalty, aristocracy, nobility, they're all just people whose forebearers were aggressive enough or lucky enough to get an edge over everyone else. Why is it different on Akora?"

She sipped a little of the wine and chose her words with care. "My family, the Atreides family, had its beginnings on Akora after the volcano exploded, ripping apart what had originally been one island."

"This was about three thousand years ago?"

She nodded. "We are called Atreides because that was the name of our . . . founding father, I suppose you could call him. He was the leader of a band of warriors from the Greece Homer wrote of, long before the Classical Greece with which people are more familiar. Like so many men then, they were also traders when they could be, as well as hunters and fishermen, well accustomed to doing whatever they had to do in order to survive. Atreides and his men were at sea when they were caught in a terrible storm. Usually storms in the Mediterranean blow from west to east, but this was a cyclonic storm, what you would call a hurricane. It hurtled them westward. By the time it was over, they were very far from any land they knew. But they were adventurers, and Atreides convinced them that instead of turning back, they should take advantage of the opportunity and keep going. Eventually, they found themselves near the Pillars of Hercules, what we call Gibraltar on the European side and Mount Hecho on the African side."

"Didn't men then believe that was the edge of the world?" Niels asked.

"Some did. We know there was argument about whether or not to go on, but Atreides prevailed. He had heard of a land beyond and to the north of the Pillars — we know it as the western shore of Europe — and he wanted to explore there. But shortly after Atreides and his men entered the Atlantic, they witnessed an immense explosion off toward the western horizon. A huge cloud of ash quickly overtook them, effectively blinding them. With fresh water almost gone and no way to take sightings from either the sun or the stars, Atreides did the only thing he could do. He headed toward the glow still visible to the west, praying that when he got there he would find both land and water."

"What did he find?"

"Hell. The volcano had torn the island in two, drowning the vast center of it. Everything else was covered with lava or on fire. The devastation was so complete that there was not a single tree left standing."

"What about survivors?"

"A handful had taken shelter in caves where there were springs of fresh water, but they faced a slow death. They had no food; all the crops had been destroyed. They couldn't fish, because all the boats were gone."

"They must have been glad to see Atreides and his men."

"Perhaps they were initially. But Atreides was a warrior from a violent culture. The original Akorans were a peaceful people. Their surviving leader was a young priestess named Lyra. A clash between her and Atreides was inevitable."

"Which she couldn't win."

"You're certain of that?"

Niels shrugged. "Atreides had the food, the only way of getting more food — his ship — and weapons. Moreover, he was a trained warrior. Obviously, he would win."

"If you know that your defeat is inevitable, should you just give up rather than fight for what you believe in?"

"No, of course not."

"Lyra believed that her people should not just accept conquest and enslavement as the price of survival. She thought the two different peoples could combine their strengths and work out a better way."

"She convinced Atreides of this?"

"Eventually she did. The two of them forged a personal relationship that helped them to overcome their differences, which made possible everything that followed."

Niels set down his glass and looked at her. "So, ultimately, this is a love story?"

Amelia nodded. "The first great love story of Akora, but only the first. Many others have followed."

Abruptly self-conscious, she looked in Shadow's direction. "I think he's resting more easily."

Niels did the same, then asked, "Was Lyra also your ancestor?"

"Yes, she was."

He reached out across the distance separating them and twined his fingers through hers. "I'd lay odds she'd be proud of you."

Her throat tightened. "That's very nice of you to say, Niels."

He didn't reply, but he did lift her hand and lightly kiss it.

When Amelia returned to the kitchen, still smiling softly, she smelled the apple pie. She had forgotten all about it and was surprised to find it merely done, not charred. Setting it on a rack to cool, she tidied the dishes, then decided to make coffee to go with the pie.

She was spooning coffee beans into the hand-cranked grinder when she heard a sound in the direction of the larder. Thinking that perhaps one of the servants had come in after all, she went to greet him or her.

But she never got there. Halfway to the larder, she was seized from behind. A cloth was pressed over her face. She smelled a cloyingly sweet scent and knew nothing more.

A few minutes later, Niels came downstairs. With his brother resting comfortably, he felt a need to find Amelia. Being near her, seeing her, hearing her voice had all become startlingly important to him. The man known as a lone wolf wanted the comfort of her presence.

But she was not in the kitchen or the nearby larder. Nor was she in the garden as he determined when he went to check. There was a damp dishcloth on the kitchen floor. He picked it up as he looked around the room. A pie was cooling on a rack. There were coffee beans in the grinder, but no ground coffee. The dishes were washed and dried, but not put away.

"Amelia?"

No answer. Only the faint rustle of the breeze in the trees beyond the house.

He moved quickly through the ground floor, looking in every room. Several more times, he called her name.

"Amelia!"

When there was no response, he went down the stairs into the basement. There was no conceivable reason why she would have gone there, but he had to look all the same.

He searched the upper floor of the house as thoroughly, thinking she might have returned

270

to sit beside Shadow or perhaps had fallen asleep.

But Amelia was not to be found.

Again he went outside and this time looked in the stables. Brutus was there, as was Shadow's mount, but the horses were alone.

In the garden once again, Niels stood unmoving for several moments as he struggled to come to terms with the only conclusion available to him: Amelia had left the house. She was gone.

He had urged her to go, demanded it, really. Instead, she had come back and insisted on helping. Even if she had changed her mind, she would not have left without a word to him.

And she wouldn't have left a dishcloth lying on the kitchen floor. His princess was much too tidy for that.

Amelia had not left under her own volition. Who had taken her, then? He had thought earlier in the day that he sensed someone moving around the periphery of the house, near the garden wall. A member of her family? But surely Andreas would simply have burst in and demanded some explanation for her presence, probably at the point of a sword.

Hawley? The thought chilled him. He had intended to make himself the bait, hence the delivery of the roses and his own appearance at a time when Shadow's surveillance suggested the Britisher might be calling on Amelia. It had seemed to work, but he hadn't counted on

Amelia coming to him, staying near him, per- haps inadvertently putting herself in Hawley's path.

His fist clenched. Hardly aware that he did so, he rammed his hand hard against the wall. It hurt, the pain serving to clear his mind. Dis- tracted by the crisis with Shadow, he had not considered that Hawley might strike so quickly, or so daringly.

But had he? Or had Amelia sensibly recon- sidered her involvement with a man who might be her family's enemy?

Should he accept that she was gone and focus his attention on bringing Hawley to jus- tice?

Or trust that she would not have left him willingly and put her safety above all else?

Duty or love?

In the end, the choice was easier to make than he would ever have believed possible.

# Chapter Sixteen

"Oh, sir!" the maid, Ivana, exclaimed when she opened the door in response to Niels banging against it with his foot.

Carrying Shadow, he stepped into the hall. "Is Benjamin here?"

"He is, sir. I'll go and fetch him." Before she did, she added, "There's a spare room up the stairs to the left. Perhaps you'd best put the gentleman in there."

Niels did as she suggested and had Shadow settled on the bed when Benjamin Sherensky appeared. The arms merchant was in shirt-sleeves, as usual. He looked concerned but calm.

"What's happened to Shadow?"

"He was stabbed. I need to leave him with someone I can trust."

Benjamin nodded brusquely. "I'm flattered. May I point out that the Akorans are the most renowned healers in the world? They are right here in London."

"He was stabbed with an Akoran knife."

Sherensky's eyebrows rose into the vicinity of his hairline.

"Amelia swears her family cannot possibly have had anything to do with it, but they aren't bound to be feeling very charitable toward me.

273

In any case, I thought it best to come here instead."

All this was said in a rush. There was so little time. He had to be gone, had to hope for the best, had to do what was so very difficult for him — trust anyone other than the very man he now had to leave.

Ivana appeared in the doorway, bearing a tray. She brushed past them, set the tray down, and put a hand on Shadow's forehead. "No fever, that's good. What happened to him?"

"He was stabbed," Benjamin said.

"The wound has been stitched," Niels told her, "and there's something on it to prevent infection."

The maid looked at him over her shoulder. "Is it working?"

"It seems to be, he also took a little soup. Look, I'm sorry, but I have to know if he can stay here and then I have to go."

"Of course he stays here," Benjamin said. "Do not insult me by suggesting otherwise. I will look after him as I would my own brother."

To the best of Niels's knowledge, Sherensky did not have a brother, but he was relieved all the same. "Thank you." He nodded to include Ivana, who had pulled up a chair and settled beside Shadow, clearly intending not to be moved.

Sherensky went with Niels to the front door. "When your brother wakes, what do I tell him?"

"That I have gone after Hawley."

"Lord Simon Hawley?"

Niels nodded. "Shadow will understand."

At the door, the men clasped hands. Sherensky said, "Be careful, my friend."

"I won't forget your help, Benjamin."

The Russian grinned. "Then I will dance at your wedding. Go."

Niels went. He unhitched Brutus from the carriage, left it and Shadow's mount in Sherensky's driveway, and rode hard for the Akoran residence. Far later than he would have liked, but far sooner than most any other man could have managed, he was admitted.

"What precisely are you telling me?" Andreas demanded. He stood by the desk in the library. The collar of his shirt was undone and he was without a jacket. He looked as though he had been up all night. There were a great many papers spread out over the desk. They appeared to be covered with diagrams, equations, and notes of an indiscernible nature.

All this Niels saw in swift assessment. He could not tarry longer to notice more. Nor could he avoid what had to be said. "Amelia did not go to Boswick. She came to me. She has been staying in my London house, helping to care for my brother, Shadow, who suffered a knife wound. Now she is missing, and I have come to find her."

He expected to have to repeat at least some

of what he had just said, on the assumption that Andreas had probably stopped listening about the time he heard that Amelia had gone to Niels instead of to Boswick. But the Akoran prince surprised him. His eyes flared but he said nothing before he stalked to the door, banged it open, and shouted something in what Niels took to be Akoran. Moments later, there were a great many people in the hall.

Very shortly after that, Andreas stalked back into the room. His hands hung at his sides, his fists clenched. "My cousin is not here."

The last faint hope Niels had kept alive, vanished. "There is a possibility that Simon Hawley has taken her."

"Hawley? Why?"

Briefly, Niels told him. As he did so, he laid the drawing of Hawley on the desk. Andreas picked it up, looked at it, and tossed it back down.

"I will say this once, I had nothing whatsoever to do with what happened to the *Defiant*. I would take your suspicion that I did as a mortal insult but for the fact that I realize you are *xenos*."

"I would take it as a mortal insult that my brother is lying wounded by an Akoran knife but for the fact that I realize the knife might have been stolen," Niels countered sharply. He was rewarded by Andreas's start of surprise.

"You have this knife?" the prince asked.

Niels withdrew it from a sheath at his belt

276

and laid it beside the drawing. Andreas took one quick glance and said, "It is my knife. I missed it several weeks ago."

"Hawley again . . . I think. If I'm wrong, if you people aren't what Amelia has sworn to me that you are —"

"I suggest we postpone any discussion involving my cousin, Mister Wolfson. I have sent word to my uncle, and our men are readying themselves. We will depart as soon as Prince Alexandros arrives."

"Fine. Hawley's no doubt got a place here in London, but I don't think he'd use it for this. There must be a country estate —"

"We are familiar with Simon Hawley's holdings, Mister Wolfson. Let me be clear: 'We' does not include you. *You* have already done quite enough."

"You can't expect me to sit on my hands while Amelia is in danger."

"Frankly, I don't give a damn what you do. We'll settle with you later." And on that cheerful note, the Prince of Akora departed.

So, too, did Niels. There wasn't much point in staying. Andreas didn't seem like the sort who would reconsider letting him go along, and there was at least an outside chance that Prince Alexandros would decide that the man who had compromised his daughter shouldn't be walking around free.

He would have preferred to work with the Akorans, but so be it. The Wolf was well accustomed to hunting alone.

Beyond the gates of the residence, Niels reined Brutus in and considered what to do next. The Akorans would quickly surround and search the locations associated with Hawley. They were highly trained, well-armed, and fiercely determined. No doubt they would get the job done. Where, then, should he turn his own attentions?

Where else might Hawley go?

Shadow had followed the man and had mentioned several places he frequented, but none of them was the sort where Amelia might be hidden. If Hawley had a bolthole, he hadn't resorted to it while Shadow was on his tail.

Which left what? London was a vast city, and beyond it stretched villages, manors, estates, shires, a seeming infinity of places offering anonymity for the commission of any crime.

Or did they?

He had discovered for himself, when searching for a place to conceal a purloined princess, that the countryside abounded with forthright people who took it for granted that they should know the particulars of anyone newly arrived in their particular part of the sceptred isle. They weren't nosy, precisely, but they nosed out information with a combination of straightforward questions and keen observation.

In point of fact, he'd had a difficult time finding a sufficiently secluded house and then had only stumbled on it by accident when he took a wrong turn down a road.

Hawley's family holdings were in East Anglia, too far from London to make taking Amelia there practical. Over a journey of that length, there would be too many opportunities for her to escape or at least summon help.

No, it had to be somewhere closer. Near the country estate he was likely to have within ready reach of London, as most wealthy and ambitious men seemed to do? But surely that would be too obvious?

What was Hawley's goal? If he really did have Amelia, why had he taken her?

For the same reason he had taken the knife — and used it. To spark war between Akora and America. That had to be what he ultimately wanted.

How would kidnapping her accomplish that?

If America — or an American — was blamed.

Brutus shied, unhappy at standing still too long. Niels looked around at the bustle of the city and realized the day was passing swiftly. It would be twilight soon. He was as impatient as the horse, but even as he set Brutus to a gentle trot, he forced himself to think. If he guessed wrong —

But he mustn't think of that. He must think instead of what Hawley wants. Put himself in the man's shoes, as it were, no matter how distasteful that was. Hawley might well intend for whatever happened to Amelia to be laid at

Niels's door. She had been taken from his London house to . . . where?

His country house? Was that possible? It was the only other place in England that could be associated with him, save for the nearby house he had rented surreptitiously. But his connection to that house was buried deeply under layers of false names intended to conceal it from vengeful Akorans. Hawley wouldn't know of it, but he could have learned of the other house, the one Niels had rented openly.

There was only a handful of property agents in London who dealt with the sort of house he engaged. The friendship of a powerful lord — and the right amount of coin — would appeal to any of them.

If he was wrong —

Then her family would find her. He had to believe that, or there would be no reason to draw his next breath. Damn, this love business turned him inside out!

He set his spurs to Brutus, who really needed no encouragement. Man and horse surged on as one.

Being kidnapped once was an experience. Twice was another matter altogether. Much as she would have liked to manage some amusing quip, if only for herself, Amelia had none. What she did have in more than ample quantity was fear. Stark, stomach-clawing, bone-chilling terror.

How strange. The first time, she had been far more angry than afraid. Even when she thought the "Irishman" had let her see him because she was going to be killed, she had still not felt more than a tiny fraction of the fear she felt now.

It was because of Hawley. The man she had never been able to know. He sat across from her in the carriage, perfectly garbed, not a golden hair out of place, observing her with a sardonic smile.

"Feeling better, Your Highness?"

"There is a stabbing pain in my head, and I have the disconcerting notion that I am about to vomit, but other than that, I am fine."

He made a small grimace of distaste and moved a little farther away from her. "I regret if I overdid the chloroform," he said with the air of a man who regrets nothing, "but you do understand, I had to be sure."

"Oh, I understand perfectly. You are a mass murderer who is trying to provoke war between my country and America. For this, you will die."

When he scowled, Lord Simon Hawley was not in the least handsome. A lesser woman might have reconsidered the wisdom of provoking him, especially shackled as she was at both the wrists and ankles, but Amelia did not quail. Let him know what it was to face a princess of Akora.

"To think there was a time I considered marrying you," he said.

"A foolish dream that never would have come true."

"A nightmare, more like it. You are a thoroughly unpleasant woman."

Amelia inclined her head. "Considering the source, that is a compliment. Niels will realize I am gone. He will alert my family."

"Ah, yes, your family. I wonder how charitably they are feeling toward the American at this moment. Will he be so crude as to tell them that he's had you? Oh, don't try to deny it. I saw for myself when you were so attentive to him in the drawing room."

"I wasn't about to deny it."

"Really? No sense of shame at all? I've heard you Akorans have no morals."

"You know nothing of us. If we are to have a debate about morals and who has them, I assure you, you are going to lose."

Hawley leaned back against the tufted leather seat, pressed the tips of his hands together and gifted her with a cold smile. "Perhaps it has escaped your notice, Princess. I am not the one shackled and bound. You are here for one reason and one reason only — as bait. Serve your purpose, cause no trouble, and you may yet survive."

Amelia ignored the small, treacherous leap of hope that followed his seeming assurances. She knew better than to believe anything said to her by an enemy. Instead, she focused on what really mattered.

Bait. He intended to use her to get to Niels. To lure Niels into a situation where he would not be thinking about his own safety because he would be concentrating on hers. She could not, of course, allow it to happen. But how to stop Hawley?

Leaping from the carriage had not worked well for her before, and was out of the question now. Though she did cast a glance in the direction of the door, she did not seriously consider it. Being shackled, she would have no chance to escape.

Which left . . . what? Even as her mind puzzled over the problem, her gaze shifted to the sheathed object on the seat beside Hawley.

"What is that?" she asked.

"Nothing, certainly not your affair."

"It looks like a sword." Indeed, it was the correct shape for one, although she could not really tell because of the black cloth that concealed it.

A sudden thought occurred to her. "It isn't Niels's sword, is it?" Not the one he had secured from Benjamin Sherensky.

Simon Hawley, with no evident regrets for having murdered fifty-nine men, flushed. "I happened to come across it while waiting for you to appear. It isn't the sort of sword that should be in the possession of such a man."

"It belonged to one of Niels's ancestors."

"That's nonsense. It obviously belonged to a great Viking lord."

"You stole an Akoran knife, the one you used to stab Shadow. Now you've stolen this sword. Is that something you go about doing, Lord Hawley? It's not enough to be a murderer, you must be a thief as well?"

She had gone too far and knew it the moment the words were said. But she could not regret them. Not even when Hawley reached across the small distance separating them and cuffed her so hard across the face that she was thrown into a corner of the carriage.

"Bitch," he said with chilling calm. Rubbing his knuckles, he settled back and remained silent through the rest of the journey.

So, too, did Amelia. Her face throbbed, but the pain helped her to focus. The windows of the carriage were covered, but there was enough of a gap for her to see that it was dark outside. She had no idea how long she had been unconscious, therefore no notion of how far they were from London. If only she could get some sense of where she was, she might be able to formulate a plan of escape.

In the back of her mind, she knew how very unlikely it was that she would be able to do any such thing, but she refused to surrender to what were, admittedly, grim odds. Instead, she continued staring through the tiny gap in the curtain, hoping against hope that she would see something, anything that might help her.

Despite her determination, she was unprepared when the carriage suddenly passed an inn — not just any inn, but one she happened to know. The Three Swans. The very inn Niels had taken her to after finding her on the road.

She had been held only a few miles away. In good order, they passed a house she believed she knew, although she had not seen it so clearly as to be sure. But if it was, where, then, could they be going? The answer flooded her mind.

Niels had been coming from his country house, the one he had rented after arriving in London, when he found her. She recognized at once why Hawley would be taking her there.

To implicate Niels in whatever was to happen to her, all assurances not to the contrary.

"Where are we going?"

Hawley roused himself unwillingly. He looked at her as though she was the greatest trouble on earth.

"To my country house."

"You live here?" The coincidence seemed impossible. Niels hadn't known Hawley's identity when he arrived in London and rented the house. When she played billiards, she did what any good player did, instinctively calculating the odds of making any shot. The odds of Niels and Hawley happening to have residences in the same neighborhood struck her as next to impossible.

Far more likely that Hawley was lying, to lull her into a false sense of hopefulness. He had no way of knowing what had transpired, or that

Amelia could recognize any aspect of her surroundings.

That much advantage she had. But how to make use of it?

"How will Niels know to seek me here?"

"I will send word to him. Now be quiet."

She had some time, then, at least until morning. If not for the shackles binding her —

"Lord Hawley?"

"I said to be quiet."

"I am most dreadfully uncomfortable."

"So you said. If you still feel inclined to vomit, kindly stick your head out the window. And please note," he said with a sneer, "that the carriage door is chained."

"As am I, and that is why I am feeling so uncomfortable. No doubt it is also to account for my unseemly behavior." She lowered her eyes, then raised them again to look at him with a small smile.

Where warriors rule and women serve.

Poor Lord Hawley. He had no notion at all of Akoran women. Her ancestress had risen from a destroyed land into the arms of a brutal conqueror, to tame man and future both. The same blood flowed in Amelia's veins. The same determination guided her.

"Do not think to gull me," Hawley warned.

"Of course not. But surely these chains aren't necessary. I can't escape."

"That would not prevent you from trying in order to protect Wolfson."

"Protect him? Why would I wish to do that?"

"You are in love with him."

"In love?" She laughed softly. "I thought you a man of sophistication." Heaven forgive her for what she must do. "Unlike Mister Wolfson, who was a . . . pleasant diversion."

"Are you trying to tell me that you don't have feelings for him?"

"Do you have reason to believe that I have feelings for any man? Surely you know how many suitors I have rejected."

"I'm not certain of the precise count."

"Truth be told, neither am I, but it is a significant number. I am a princess, Lord Hawley. It is only natural that I indulge myself."

His gaze remained skeptical, but she saw the beginnings of unwilling interest. A man so steeped in evil would be drawn to see it in others. "Then you have no objection to my doing away with Wolfson?"

"Mister Wolfson believes my family was involved in the attack on the *Defiant*. Not to put too fine a point on it, but he thinks you were our tool. There is every chance that he will go back to Washington, inform his president of this, and cause a war between Akora and America. Above all, I wish to prevent that."

"You went to his house and helped his brother."

"Of course I did. One keeps one's enemy close, the better to observe him."

"I do not believe this. You are a woman with

a woman's heart. You are not capable of such a stratagem."

"I do not doubt your knowledge of women, Lord Hawley." In fact, she thought he knew very little of her gender and appreciated even less. "However, I remind you that I am both Akoran and royal. How is it you imagine my family has held power through so many thousands of years? Do you think we breed weaklings?"

"Your family does have an impressive record." He spoke grudgingly.

"Impressive? We have accomplished what no other family in history has done. Not merely to hold power through the millennia, but to acquire wealth as well, vast wealth. With all respect, Lord Hawley, compared to us, your family crawled out of the cave a week ago. As for Mister Wolfson . . ." She shrugged lightly. "The less said, the better."

"You mean this? You were merely amusing yourself with him?"

"Why should that surprise you? Men have been doing that with women for eons."

"But women don't do it. At least, not young, unmarried women."

"Princesses do, Lord Hawley. An Akoran princess does." She lifted her arms, jangling her shackles. "These are ridiculous. *You* are in danger of being ridiculous. What is it you want? Besides the death of Mister Wolfson, of course."

"What I — ?"

"Please tell me you haven't done all this without a clearly formulated goal."

"No, of course I haven't. I want a British naval base on Akora."

"Why?"

"Why? It will be good for my country."

"You want to do *good* for your country?"

"What I meant was that the man who secures such a base can use it to climb to greater heights."

"Oh, well, then, I understand perfectly. You had me worried for a moment, Lord Hawley."

Deciding she had made a sufficient beginning, Amelia leaned back and closed her eyes. She could feel Hawley staring at her, but she gave no sign of it.

At length, the carriage turned into a drive and soon thereafter came to a halt. Hawley stepped out. She heard him have a word with the driver, then the door opened again and he reached for her.

# Chapter Seventeen

Niels had visited his rented country house no more than a handful of times, the lease existing only to provide an explanation for his presence when he appeared to "rescue" Amelia. Now he approached it cautiously. The night was cool for late spring, and cloudy. It occurred to him that in the time he had known Amelia, the moon had waxed to full and was now waning. Only a sliver cast its light through the clouds, providing ample shadows through which he moved.

He left Brutus tethered to the gate and walked on, quickly and with a keen sense of purpose. The house was removed from the road down a long allée framed by oaks. There were no servants in residence, but there were lights. Not many, only a few on the ground floor and farther back, above the stables, enough to give hope that his desperate gamble had been right. Either that or squatters had taken possession. Not impossible in an England where dire poverty lived cheek-by-jowl with almost incomprehensible wealth, but not overly likely either.

Only a lifetime of discipline enabled him to resist the urge to enter the house immediately. Instead, he moved slowly around it, concealed by the trees, taking the measure of what

Hawley might have in store for him.

He would not make the mistake of underestimating Hawley's cunning; the man had, after all, blown up the *Defiant* and escaped Baltimore without detection. But he did not believe that the Britisher was expecting him quite yet. He would have the advantage of surprise, for whatever that might be worth.

The overgrown garden in the back gave way to a slight incline that led to the rear kitchen door. The door had been left locked and remained so. Niels eased in the key, turned it carefully, and opened the door. The hinges creaked, but only faintly. Beyond, the kitchen lay in darkness, its old stone walls holding the chill of an unoccupied house in which the fires remain unlit.

He stepped in and shut the door behind him. Waiting while his eyes adjusted, he listened for any sound. He heard nothing but the rising wind whispering through the young leaves of the trees.

He left the kitchen and moved silently into the hallway beyond. A short flight of steps led up to the main floor of the house. The third step from the bottom creaked, as he discovered when he stepped on it. Instantly, Niels froze and listened again.

Far off toward the front of the house, a door opened.

"Is something wrong?" Amelia asked. She

managed to sound mildly concerned rather than hopeful.

Hawley did not answer at once. He stepped into the hall beyond the drawing room, stood for a moment, then returned and shut the door again. "Everything is fine."

Pointedly, she raised her hands, which were still chained. "Would that were so. These are most frightfully uncomfortable."

"That is regrettable."

"I don't blame you for not trusting me. Under the circumstances, I wouldn't, either. But surely you could at least undo the ones around my ankles, allow me to move around a bit more easily."

"The better to escape?"

Amelia laughed. "Escape to where, Lord Hawley? Out onto the road in the night, in the middle of nowhere? How precisely would I manage?"

"You seem quite resourceful."

"How kind, but the truth is that I am far too fond of my own well-being to place it at such foolish risk."

The man who had struck her so brutally in the carriage smiled faintly. "You know, I almost believe you."

"Well you should. I have been cosseted my entire life."

"I would say spoiled."

"As you will. Do you truly believe I would place myself at risk for Mister Niels Wolfson?"

"Cold-blooded *and* cold-hearted?"

"Traits I should think you would admire, Lord Hawley. Now, as to the matter of these chains —"

"When I put those on you while you were unconscious" — he paused long enough for that unsavory image to sink into her — "it occurred to me how very easy it would be to take someone weighted down in such a way and toss her into the nearest river."

"On Akora, there are divers who go down into the deep caverns of the Inland Sea, where the most succulent oysters and urchins are to be found. They wear weights around their waists to enable them to descend more quickly. I have dived with them."

"What extraordinary customs you have."

"Perhaps you will become better acquainted with our customs when there is a British naval base on Akora."

She had the satisfaction of seeing Simon Hawley jerk with surprise, but, to give the man credit, he recovered quickly. "Are you by any chance . . . attempting to negotiate with me?"

"Why should that startle you?"

"There is no point to it. You have no authority."

She smiled faintly. "Authority breeds responsibility. One is held accountable for one's actions. I have something far better — influence." Pointedly, she said, "We are a very close family. My father loves me, as does my uncle, the

Vanax. Love makes men malleable."

"You expect me to believe that you would use such influence on my behalf?"

"I would if our objectives happened to coincide. You want a naval base and — I imagine — even more importantly, you want the credit for it. I want —"

"What?"

"Independence. The freedom to make my own decisions and live my own life precisely as I choose. Forgive me for being crass, but that involves money."

"Your family is fabulously wealthy."

"But I am not. I require wealth of my own."

The advantage of dealing with a man of such venality was that he was prone to believe others were as low as he was.

"You do understand," he said, "I had no choice but to do as I have done. In the final analysis, you will be well shorn of Mister Wolfson. I rather think your family might ultimately be disposed to thank me."

As he voiced the delusions she had encouraged in him, he reached into the pocket of his waistcoat and withdrew a small key. Approaching her with a lingering degree of caution, he indicated that she should lift her legs. This she did, managing not to show her revulsion at his touch. When the chains were removed from around her ankles, Amelia smiled and held out her arms. "Is there any possibility you will also remove these?"

He straightened, returning the key to his pocket. Lamplight glinted off the brilliant gold of his hair. He looked more than ever like the conventional rendering of an angel, which she supposed only proved how misleading appearances could be. Indeed, in Hawley's case, they were a profound perversion of reality.

"None," he said. "I am prepared to make your situation moderately more comfortable, but that is all."

"What a shame." She rose, sighing, took a step toward him and stumbled.

He caught her, holding her at arm's length, and frowned.

"I'm most terribly sorry," Amelia said.

Without taking his eyes from her, Hawley patted the pocket of his waistcoat, confirming that the key was still there. "No harm done."

"Do you mind if I walk a little? My legs are a bit numb."

"All right, as long as you don't go near the windows."

She did not, staying instead so close to him that she brushed against him in passing.

"Do you know," she asked, "that every year at least a few *xenos* are shipwrecked on Akora?"

"Really?" Hawley spoke with an air of utter disinterest.

"We get all sorts — sailors, of course, but also bakers, tailors, candlestick makers, thieves — quite a variety."

"Do you never run out of things to say?"

"An ability to make conversation under stressful circumstances is one of the skills required of a princess."

"Even so, be quiet."

Amelia turned away so that he could not see her satisfaction. She might have told him of the old Akoran saying: if you wanted to meet someone, all you had to do was wait at the palace, because eventually everyone came there. Even the thieves did so — at least one in particular, who had turned his light-fingered skills into a new vocation as a magician, to the delight of the palace children, who begged and pestered until he showed them how certain things were done. Amelia had proven particularly adept, so much so that her mother had felt compelled to caution her never to put such skills to mischievous use.

There was nothing in the least mischievous about her purloining the key to her chains. She intended to put it to quite deadly purpose.

Flattened against the wall just beyond the drawing room, Niels listened to the murmur of conversation. The closed door was too thick for him to make out any words, but he recognized Amelia's voice. That alone was a great relief, though it also posed problems. If she was near Hawley when Niels attacked, she might be harmed.

He made an instant decision and slipped from the hall, leaving the house the way he had come in. Going carefully, he circled round the outside of the building until he came to one of the drawing room windows.

Hawley hadn't bothered to light a fire, or perhaps the man genuinely didn't know how to do such a plebeian task. But he had lit several lamps, and by their light, Niels could see the two people in the room clearly.

Amelia was standing near a table on which lay a long object wrapped in black. She had her back to the window, facing Hawley. That scion of aristocracy regarded her cautiously. They exchanged a few words before Amelia turned toward the window. Niels had only a moment to take in her appearance before fierce anger engulfed him.

She was hurt; he could see the bruise on one side of her face. And she was chained. That murdering piece of scum. Hawley couldn't die hard enough. Before tardy reason reasserted itself, Niels's hand had gone to the knife encased in a scabbard concealed beneath his shirt. He was ready to surge straight through the window, glass and all.

But he did not. Instead, he took a breath, eased his grip on the knife, and waited until the worst of the hot roar of rage subsided. Not until then did he trust himself to move.

And not through the window, but back into the house. He had hunted men in the countryside and in the city, across fields and through woods, down alleys and along boulevards, but never before had he hunted as he did now. Never with such cold and relentless intensity of purpose. He needed ground that favored him, cover, and a means of limiting his opponent's movements. The house offered that and more.

His goal, at least initially, was to draw Hawley away from Amelia. Thus he chose a point well removed from the drawing room, toward the back of the house in the direction of the kitchen. There, deep shadows plunged the hallway into almost total darkness. Niels lit a candle taken from the kitchen, grimaced at the stink of the match, and quickly surveyed the hall. The ceiling was far lower than in the formal rooms, being no more than eight feet above his head and crossed by exposed wooden beams. Clearly, no expense had been wasted on an area expected to be frequented only by servants.

To the rear of the hallway was an arch leading into an empty larder. Niels gauged the distance from there to the kitchen and in the opposite direction to the drawing room. What he calculated satisfied him.

Snuffing out the candle, he moved by memory and touch back toward the kitchen. Wrapping his jacket around his hand, he smashed it through the window near the door. The distinctive sound of breaking glass filled the room and echoed down the hall.

"What the hell — ?" Hawley yanked open the

door and stepped out into the hallway. At the same moment, Amelia reached for the key concealed in the pocket of her skirt. If she acted quickly, she might have a chance of undoing her chains. Before thought could become deed, Hawley turned back, crossed the width of the room and seized her arm. "You will come with me, madam."

He thrust a lamp into her hand and pushed her out into the hall ahead of him. Amelia protested — loudly enough to warn anyone who might be listening. "Whatever are you doing, Lord Hawley?"

Keeping a firm hold on her arm, he said, "Investigating the remote possibility that we have guests."

"I really don't see how that could be. No one could have the faintest idea that we are here." Except Niels, please God, and that seemed far too much to hope for.

"Even so, I find it best to be sure."

They reached the kitchen without encountering anyone and saw the broken glass littering the floor.

"Perhaps an animal tried to get in," Amelia suggested, quelling her own urge to believe otherwise.

"Perhaps —" Barely had Hawley spoken when he whirled around suddenly, still holding Amelia in front of him. She gasped as the firelight gleamed off the knife in his hand.

"What are you — ?"

"Do you think me a fool or does someone else? Which is it?"

Despite the fear that threatened to choke her, Amelia said, "I have no idea what you are talking about. And why ever do you need that knife? You are in danger of seeming like a child fearing the bogeyman."

"Be quiet! No one could have guessed that we are here, and yet —"

"What about the driver?"

"Who?"

How like Hawley to give no thought to those who served him. "The man who drove the carriage that brought us. Can you trust him?"

"He is a hired man. He knows nothing of what is happening here."

"Are you sure? Servants can be so treacherous." In fact, she thought nothing of the kind, but any sowing of doubt in Hawley's mind could only be beneficial.

"That is true," he allowed. "I was going to have him take a note to Wolfson in the morning, but I've said nothing to him of that. Even if he wanted to betray me, he had no opportunity."

Amelia shrugged. "He could have enlisted the help of a friend."

The lamp she held cast only a thin circle of light. Beyond it lay impenetrable shadows. But in them she thought she caught a faint glimpse of movement. The impression was fleeting and most probably the result of her own desperate yearning. Still, it strengthened her resolve.

"Unlikely —" But not, apparently, impossible. At least not in Hawley's mind.

"Besides," she said, pressing her advantage, "how did you happen to hire the man? He might have crossed your path deliberately."

For just a moment, she thought she had gone too far, but Hawley was heir to generations of a family that had gained wealth and power through the time-honored means of conspiracy and guile. Betrayal was as common to them as air.

"Where are we going?" she asked as he pushed her back down the hallway.

"Alas, I must leave you briefly, my dear," Hawley said. "But not before assuring you will be secure during my absence."

"Not those chains again."

"I'm afraid so."

They reached the drawing room. Hawley shoved her into a chair, picked up the discarded chains, and looped them through the links still securing her wrists. He glanced around for something sturdy to fasten her to. His gaze fell on the heavy mahogany desk. Satisfied, he wound the chains around one of the thick legs, fastened them, and stood back. "That should assure you are here when I return."

"Just see that you do," she instructed. "I have no wish to remain in so undignified a position any longer than I must."

Looking down at her, he essayed a faint smile. "Always the princess. Is it possible you are becoming more appealing to me?"

Sweet heaven, she hoped not! "I don't think so, Lord Hawley. Remember how much I irritate you."

"That is so, yet seeing you like this —"

Her skin crawled. She had never experienced such a sensation before, indeed, had thought the expression no more than a quaint saying. But in reality, it was all too accurate. Moreover, whether from the lingering effects of the chloroform or a mixture of sheer terror and disgust, she felt overwhelmingly nauseous. The effort to remain smiling in the face of such discomfort almost surpassed her training and discipline.

Almost, but mercifully, not quite.

Hawley brushed her bruised cheek with the back of his hand. "Chained . . . on your knees . . ."

Revulsion filled her. She looked away from him and forced herself to breathe slowly and deeply.

"Shy suddenly, Princess? How unlike you."

Keep silent, say nothing, give him no excuse to linger.

Hawley laughed softly. "Don't fret. I'll be back swiftly."

She swallowed against the bile in her throat, watched as he went from the drawing room, shutting the door behind him. Still she forced herself to wait, listening to the fading sound of his footsteps moving down the hall. If he changed his mind, came back —

When she had delayed as long as she dared, Amelia fumbled in the pocket of her skirt for the key she had taken from him. For a horrible moment, it eluded her and she feared it was gone. A sob of relief broke from her when her fingers closed on it. She gripped the key hard, desperate not to drop it, and turned it toward the lock holding the chains around her wrists. Carefully, painstakingly, she slid the key in and turned it.

The lock opened. Suppressing a cry of victory, she slipped the chains off and sprang away from the desk. She had to flee, get word to Niels, warn her family, all this she thought in the scant moment before the drawing room door slammed open.

# Chapter Eighteen

"Niels, thank God!"

He crossed the room with quick strides, glanced at the chains lying on the floor and said with some surprise, "You're free."

Overjoyed to see him, she could not restrain her pleasure, although the urgency of their circumstances had to take precedence. "Hawley is here."

"I know, I've seen him. He's gone to deal with the driver."

"Who is innocent —"

"And who has fled. I warned him off. Hawley will be back in minutes. We have to get you out of here."

His hands closed on her shoulders, compelling her to look at him, which she was doing in any case. He was so beautiful, this man, in the way of wild places. She wanted to lie in his arms, feel him deep within her, watch him as he slept.

She wanted to swell with a child they made together, hold that child in her arms, watch him or her grow in joy and love.

Something of her thoughts must have been evident to him, for his eyes were suddenly heavy-lidded and sensual. He took an unsteady breath and gathered himself. "Amelia, listen to me. There is a house about a half a mile from here. You must have passed it on the way. You'll be safe there."

"Oh, yes, a house —"

"It will look familiar to you. I should explain why."

"For heaven's sake, Niels, I know why."

"You know?" It wasn't often that she could surprise him. Despite all else, she relished it.

"We can discuss all that later. For now, know I do not want to leave you."

His hands hardened on her. "You must."

She saw it then in his eyes, the knowledge that he would kill Hawley. It was, she thought, an entirely sensible decision. But Niels shied from her seeing that part of him, the hunter who had stalked his country's enemies, delivering them into the hands of Almighty justice.

"Go," he said again, and pushed her toward the French doors.

He had opened one and she was outside, standing in the damp, night-swept garden when Hawley returned.

In a single movement, Niels slammed the door to the garden shut and turned to face Hawley. The Britisher had already drawn his knife. Niels remained unarmed, or so he appeared. He moved slowly but steadily toward the other man, his hands loose at his sides, showing no hint of either hesitation or fear.

"Bad move, coming here," Niels said, almost pleasantly. "Or did you really think it wouldn't occur to me where you'd gone?"

"I expected you to come." The Britisher glanced around the room while trying to appear not to do so. "Just not quite so soon. Where is the princess?"

"Gone. And by the way, that was another bad move. You should never have involved her, and you most especially shouldn't have hit her."

"Chivalrous, Mister Wolfson?" Hawley sneered. "I'm always entertained by the pretensions of Americans, but you, in particular, amuse me. I've made it my business to learn about you. A man of no family, no heritage, no stature, and yet inexplicably you have attained a position of influence. I can only conclude that Americans are content to be ruled by their own rabble."

"We're not content to be ruled at all, but I wouldn't expect you to understand that." Niels looked at the knife pointedly. "Are you planning to use that or do you just want to chat?"

Hawley's face darkened. He stepped closer to Niels. "You are far too troublesome to leave alive."

Horror filled Amelia. Although she could not hear clearly the words the men exchanged, she had no doubt at all about Hawley's intent. What she could not understand was Niels's behavior. She had seen men fight many, many times. Of course, that was on the training fields and in the occasional impromptu matches of which her brothers were so fond. But that couldn't be so very different from the real thing, could it?

Hawley lunged. Amelia choked back the cry she was wise enough not to utter.

Niels stepped smoothly to one side, bent slightly — and straightened with a blade in his hand. Where had it come from? But thank God he had it and —

Hawley recovered and came at him again, snarling. He might have done Niels the great good turn of running directly into the knife had he not seen it just in time.

"Not quite the fool, Wolfson?"

"Not entirely. Come on, then."

They circled, taking the measure of each other. Hawley moved closer, his fingers moving eagerly on the hilt of his knife. He lunged again, his blade scraping the air within inches of Wolfson's chest.

Amelia could bear it no longer. She eased the door open and stepped just into the room. Her need to be close to Niels in such terrible circumstances drove her, but she kept herself very still, determined not to distract him in any way.

"Where did you learn to fight, Wolfson?" Hawley demanded. "Bar brawls? I watched a self-styled Gypsy king gut an opponent, then hired him to teach me how to do the same."

Again he attacked, and again Niels just barely evaded him.

"You are outmatched, American, and you are going to die."

Niels did not reply. All his attention was focused not on Hawley's knife, as Amelia would have thought, but on the Britisher's . . . shoulders? How much experience had Niels really had in such combat? Was it possible he was more adept with a rifle or perhaps even a bow and arrow? Perhaps the knife was not his weapon . . . perhaps —

Hawley attacked again, and this time Niels went down. A silent scream tore through Amelia, but wait, he was on the ground, rolling, putting distance between himself and Hawley as the Britisher reacted too slowly to stop him. An instant later, Niels was on his feet. Hawley turned to face him across the width of the room. The Britisher frowned.

"Why draw this out, Wolfson? I'm the better man. My kind always will be."

"Your kind," Niels said quietly as he lifted his arm and took aim, "needs killing."

In the instant just before he released the knife to fly its true course, Amelia moved. She did not mean to, indeed hardly realized what she had done. But the motion, slight as it was, was enough to distract Niels minutely. The knife still struck Hawley, but only in the shoulder, not a killing blow.

The Britisher screamed in pain and shock. He slapped a hand to the bleeding wound and stared from it to Niels in disbelief. "Damn you! You filthy bastard!" Knife in hand, he lunged at the man who was now unarmed.

Amelia moved, or rather, she flew, for truly she did not feel the ground beneath her. In a single desperate leap, she reached the table, snatched the black cover off the sword and lifted its heavy blade in both hands. It was far too heavy for her to throw, but she could send it sliding across the floor straight to Niels, who grasped it smoothly, lifting it with ease. It settled into his hand as though made for no other.

Hawley drew up short, gaping at the sword that had appeared so suddenly in the grip of the man disinclined to die at his bidding. He gasped, turning, and his gaze fell on Amelia.

"You! You bitch! I should have killed you right off." He reached out, seized her, and held her as a living shield between him and Niels, who paled suddenly.

"Drop it!" Hawley screamed. He put the knife to Amelia's throat. "Drop it or watch her die!"

Fear closed over her, a true and terrible thing, for she could feel the pall of death edging close and closer still. But beside her terror rode another and far stronger emotion. She saw with a brilliant clarity the essential goodness of the man she loved, the future she longed for with all her being, but which seemed to be slipping moment by moment from her grasp.

"He will kill me anyway," she said, her voice calm and steady despite the sorrow overwhelming her, the courage of generations of women flowing through her, the rock on which her strength was built.

"Still trying to save him?" Hawley said. "You stupid fool! Don't you understand yet? Haven't you realized? I went to Baltimore at your family's bidding. I blew up the *Defiant* because your family paid me to! If he lives, if he goes back to America, there will be war between Akora and America. And just who, dear stupid Princess Amelia, do you think will be the first to die? Your father, your brothers, your uncles, and cousins, all those you love so well. They will die in front of American cannons, shot by American rifles, pierced by American swords. No doubt the bold Mister Wolfson, here, will account for a goodly number of them himself."

Hawley's arm tightened around her throat. She felt his hot breath close to her ear. Like the beguiling serpent, he hissed, "He has to die, Amelia, so that all those you love can live."

Niels's eyes were shuttered. With each word Hawley spoke, the man she loved was sealing himself off further and further from her. Wrenching despair filled her. There was so much she longed to say, to tell him . . . so much —

Through the tears that suddenly threatened to blind her, she cried out.

"Niels, kill him!"

Choice made, die cast for the man she loved and had to trust to find the truth even without her. There was a single cold and silent moment when all the world seemed to hang suspended, and then —

A whoosh of sound, strangely like the murmur of a deep and ancient voice. The touch of steel passing by her cheek almost like a caress.

The smell of iron engulfed her even as her back was suddenly hot and wet. She had a moment to realize it was Hawley's blood she smelled, before, with what most surely had to be his last strength, he slashed the knife across her throat.

He was in a nightmare and there was no way out. Hawley was dead, may he burn in hell. The ancient sword lay shattered into pieces, its tip protruding from his body.

Amelia was barely conscious. She lay on the floor, her eyes wide and staring, blood oozing from the cut in her throat.

"Don't move," he said as he knelt beside her. "Don't talk. Don't do anything. Oh, God, Amelia, I'm sorry!"

His hands were shaking. She covered them with her own and looked at him intently. He needed no special insight to guess what she would be telling him if she could. Hawley had implicated her family in an act of war committed against the United States. To protect them, she might well have acquiesced in Niels's own death.

But she had not. She had offered up her own

311

life to stop the man trying to provoke a war between her country and Niels's.

Her sacrifice humbled him even as it filled him with rage. He couldn't let her see that, had to conceal it while he got ahold of the situation, got her somewhere safe, where she could be cared for properly.

"I paid the driver," he said, "to take word to your family. They should know where you are by morning."

She began to nod but the effort must have pained her, for she winced.

"Don't," he said again, more urgently. Quickly, he stripped off his jacket, tossed it aside and yanked his shirt out of his waistband. With a quick rending, he tore a strip of linen from the shirt and used it to bind up the wound to her throat.

"Not exactly up to Akoran standards," he said, "but it will have to do for the moment." Lifting her, he carried Amelia quickly from the drawing room, away from Hawley's body, and through the wide entry hall.

"We can't stay here. The house hasn't been equipped. There's no food, no fuel, no way to take care of you. The other house is no better; Shadow cleaned it out. That leaves the inn." He stopped and looked down at her. "Can you make it there, do you think?"

She nodded, but her face was white and there were half-moons of darkness beneath her eyes.

"Hold on, then," he said grimly and carried

her down the long driveway to where he had left Brutus. That good horse picked up his head when he saw his master. He stood rock still as Niels lifted Amelia into the saddle and swung up behind her. The journey to the Three Swans Inn seemed interminable. Amelia soon appeared to be asleep, but Niels wasn't convinced. He suspected pain and shock were sapping what was left of her strength. Before they were halfway to the inn, moonlight revealed a thin line of blood soaking through the improvised bandage. He cursed under his breath and spurred Brutus on.

The redoubtable Mistress Porter did not take kindly to being awakened in the wee hours of the night. Most particularly, she did not care to have her rest broken by barking dogs, shouting stable boys, and the sight of her portly husband, stumbling out of bed in his nightshirt to bang the shutters open and demand to be told what in 'ell was 'appening.

They ran a proper inn, as she reminded him, and it didn't do to disturb the guests with such goings-on.

"It's that Mister Wolfson," Portius Porter informed her as he stumbled into his pants. Cheeks flushed with excitement, he added, "Looks like he's got a woman with him again."

"I won't have it! I don't care how much coin he has to spread about. We have to think of our reputation, we do!"

"You didn't give it all that much thought

when you was working the stews of Southwark, Thalia, dear. Best hurry. Looks as though there's something wrong."

"Now see here, sir," Mistress Porter began when she came face-to-face with Niels in the main room of the inn. "We can't be having this —"

"The lady is injured. I need clean warm water, soap, and bandages."

"Injured? Let me see — Oh, sweet Lord!"

Niels brushed past her and mounted the stairs. "Quickly, if you please, madam."

Quickly it was, and all in good order, wide-eyed maids bustling in with steaming water and fresh linen, while Mistress Porter herself presented what she described as "the leach's chest."

"There's fine medicines in here, sir," she assured him. "Acquired at no small expense. But truth be told, I can't say what to do for the lady." Staring at Amelia, who lay motionless on the bed, she said, "Is that her throat what's been cut, sir?"

"It seems so. Is there a doctor in the neighborhood?" Much as he loathed the bastards, he'd try anything to help Amelia.

"There was, sir," Mistress Porter replied. "But he was a bit too fond of the gin. Sir . . . we don't want any trouble with the law."

So focused was he on Amelia, that it took a moment for him to understand the woman's words. "There won't be any," he said finally. He would see to that. After he saw Amelia safely reunited with her family — please, God, let that be soon — he would go to the authorities, inform them of Hawley's death, and explain his part in it. Whatever repercussions there might be, did not interest him. Nothing did apart from the woman lying here so pale and helpless, so unlike her indomitable self. Brought to this by his own actions.

Guilt twisted in him. He said something, unaware of his own words, and ushered Mistress Porter from the room. When the door was closed, he gently undid the strip of linen from Amelia's throat, cleaned the wound, and carefully rebandaged it. That done, he lay down beside her, taking her gently into his arms. She stirred slightly, but he did not believe she was awake. It was just as well. There was nothing he could do for her now except watch and wait . . . And pray.

He'd never been much of one for praying. There just didn't seem any point. But he prayed then, without ceremony or form, simply opening his heart and mind.

His message was simple in its purity, stark in its desperation: Me, not her.

Take his life, not Amelia's. He had done what he had come to do. Hawley was dead, no longer a danger to anyone. His mission was fulfilled. He was ready and more to lay down the burdens he had carried for his country. Life was sweet, to be sure. Hell, it had never been sweeter. But that didn't matter. She had so much to live for, so much to give to the world and those lucky enough to be loved by her.

Me, not her.

He fell asleep thinking it, intending to stay awake but drifting off all the same, his arms close around her, his heart beating to the rhythm of hers.

And woke to the sting of a sword point against his throat.

"Get up," Andreas said. He spoke quietly, clearly mindful of the woman sleeping beside his quarry. His eyes were hard, his hand steady.

Glancing down at the blade that would, with the slightest effort, make real his plea to the Divinity, Niels said, "Amelia is hurt."

"Pray she recovers. If she does not, you die."

That seemed fair. Moving with utmost caution, Niels slid from beneath the sword point and stood. Careful to keep his hands in sight, he surveyed the man who had eluded the keen senses and survival instinct that had thwarted so many enemies over so many years.

"I must have been more tired than I realized."

"You've had an eventful few days, haven't you, Mister Wolfson?" Without the pretense of expecting a reply, Andreas continued, "We found Hawley. You killed him?"

Niels nodded. "He said he was working for you."

"He lied. Who wounded Amelia?"

"Hawley. He used her as a shield. When I went for him despite that, he slashed at her throat."

"You would have sacrificed my cousin's life."

He could have said that she had called on him to do just that and if he had not, in all likelihood she would have been killed by Hawley anyway. But he was a man long accustomed to shouldering responsibility. "I did my job."

Andreas gestured with the sword. "Move."

"I never wanted to harm Amelia."

Andreas looked at his cousin and most particularly at the makeshift bandage around her throat. "I can kill you where you stand, Mister Wolfson. No matter how good you are — and I've learned enough about you to acknowledge that you are very good, indeed — I'm still the one with the sword. Believe me, I know how to use it. Now go."

Amelia stirred fitfully beneath the covers Niels had drawn over her. She would wake in another moment or two, drawn by their voices.

And do what? See him in conflict with her cousin? Have to somehow muster the strength and courage to mediate — even to choose — between him and her own family?

He could not allow that. Not in the least, because he had no expectation whatsoever that she would choose him. The hunter and killer, the man in the dark and the rain.

And so he went, out of the room, away from her, into the bleak day.

He had fleeting impressions — of Mistress Porter standing shocked and silent as she was confronted by bare-chested Akoran warriors on horseback, Prince Alexandros among them, staring at Niels grimly as he was prodded from the inn; of a woman in a white tunic hurrying inside, a servant following after her with a chest; of Hawley's body slung over the back of a horse, shorn of ceremony or dignity; and of Brutus, stalwart Brutus, waiting for him.

He went under escort back to London, guarded by Akoran warriors who remained silent throughout the journey. He was taken, as he had expected, to the Akoran residence. And there he was deposited in a small room in the basement, secured behind a locked and barred door. The room boasted a bed and a commode, nothing else. Guards brought him water and food. After that, he was left alone. He had ample time and more to reflect on everything that had happened and everything he might have done differently. It was not a pleasant experience.

The better part of a very long day passed before the door opened again.

A woman stood on the other side of it. She was tall, thin, and garbed entirely in black. Her eyes were small, dark, and bright. She looked him up and down at her leisure.

"You are Mister Niels Wolfson."

"I am. You are?"

"Mulridge, sir."

"Amelia mentioned you. How is she?"

"All things considered, she is well. Come with me."

They climbed the basement stairs to the hall. Niels looked around cautiously. He would not have been surprised to find himself surrounded by guards, but there were none.

"It's very quiet," he said.

"The king is dead. Prince Alexandros and Prince Andreas have gone to the palace to pay their respects to the new young queen."

"And Amelia?"

Mulridge hesitated a moment. She folded her hands and looked at him down the long beak of her nose. "She has returned to Akora. She left on the morning tide, accompanied by her mother."

He was still absorbing this when she added, "Prince Andreas left something for you." She gestured to a box on a table near the door.

Niels walked toward it with proper caution. The box was of a polished wood he did not recognize. It opened readily to his touch.

Fragments of metal gleamed in the light streaming through the entry hall windows. The pieces of the Viking lord's sword. Killing Hawley, the ancient weapon had shattered. It would never be whole again, but it had fulfilled its purpose. Of this he was entirely sure.

What message did Andreas intend by leaving it for him? A gesture of respect from one warrior to another? Or a reminder — as though he needed any — of why Amelia was gone from him.

"Thank you," he said simply, and with it went from the house.

Ivana opened the door just as Niels raised his hand to knock on it. She took one look at what he realized belatedly must be his disheveled appearance and, good woman that she was, stood aside to admit him.

Without delay, she said, "Your brother is awake, sir. He has no fever and I'd say he's doing remarkably well."

"Thank you," Niels replied, and for just an instant, his vision blurred. He blinked it clear and followed the maid upstairs to the room where Shadow rested.

His brother was sitting up in bed, looking pale still, but far more himself than when Niels last saw him.

"Damn," Shadow said when he entered, "you look like hell."

"Me? I'm not the one who got a knife stuck in me."

Shadow shifted self-consciously. "Anybody can make a mistake."

"Hell, I'm not blaming you. How do you feel?"

"Fine. I feel fine."

"He needs a great deal more rest," Ivana said firmly.

Shadow bestowed upon her a smile that had melted feminine hearts from one side of the vast American continent right through to the other. "What I really need is more of your excellent beef barley soup."

"Oh, well, I suppose a bit more of that wouldn't do you any harm." Clearly pleased, the maid hurried off.

When she was gone, Niels sat down beside the bed and looked hard at his brother. "Who did this to you?"

"Hawley and those bastards I saw him with at his club. They were on to me and I didn't even know it." His expression left no doubt that being caught unaware hurt more than any actual wound.

"Let it go. We found an Akoran knife in you."

Shadow raised an eyebrow. "I didn't see any Akorans."

"I think Hawley stole it. He stole my sword."

"That sword you got from Benjamin? He stole it? My God, a man can't crawl much lower than that."

Niels agreed, but he shrugged all the same. "Doesn't matter. Hawley's dead."

"Your work?" When Niels nodded, his brother looked pleased. Even so, he said, "Are there likely to be repercussions?"

"I'd have thought so, but the last I saw of Hawley, what was left of him was slung over the backside of an Akoran horse."

"You'll have to explain to me how that happened. Where's your princess, by the way?"

"She's not my princess." Much as he longed for her to be.

"The hell she isn't. Look, this isn't easy for me to say, but I think I was dead wrong about the Akorans. They don't seem to have had anythin' to do with what happened to the *Defiant*."

"You really believe that?"

"Yeah, I do. Your idea about Hawley schemin' for a naval base makes sense. And there's no gettin' around that he was a real bastard."

" 'Was' appears to be the operative word," Benjamin Sherensky said as he came into the room. Looking from one brother to the other, he affected an expression of dismay. "Shocking news."

"What would that be?" Shadow asked.

"About Hawley, of course. Lord Simon Hawley found murdered in one of our fair city's less savory venues. Victim of footpads, apparently."

"Is that what the authorities think?" Niels inquired.

"So I gather. What else are they to think, after all?"

"Could be worse," Shadow offered philosophically. "They could have just dumped him into the river."

"They?" Benjamin inquired with a small smile.

"The footpads."

"Yes, of course. Niels, my friend, how are you?"

"Grateful to see my brother so well. Thank you, Benjamin."

"Not at all, glad to do it. Shadow is welcome to convalesce here. I perceive he will need some time yet to recover, as is only to be expected, and his continued company would be much appreciated."

"That is very good of you," Shadow said.

Niels walked over to the window and looked out. He saw not the busy London street, but his last sight of the woman he loved, lying so pale and still in a rented bed.

"Amelia has gone back to Akora," he said. Away from him.

Reflected in the windowpane, he saw his brother and Sherensky exchange a glance.

"Why would she do that?" Shadow asked.

"Hawley hurt her, but it was still my fault. I should have taken better care of her, protected her better."

There was silence for a moment until Sherensky said, "I have the utmost admiration for the princess, but to be frank, I doubt she would be pleased to hear you say that."

Niels turned back to the room. "Why not?"

"The Akorans strike me as a people who have a very clear-cut concept of good and evil. It is part of what has sustained them for so long. Hawley's guilt is his own, not yours."

"I doubt either Amelia or her family can hold me blameless." To the contrary, they had every reason to condemn him.

Shadow sat up straighter in the bed. "Just what are you goin' to do?"

Niels crossed the room to stand beside his brother. Softly, he said, "I have to go after her."

"To Akora?" It was Sherensky who spoke, voicing the question that was clearly also uppermost in Shadow's mind. "Akora is closed to *xenos*," the arms merchant said. "Outsiders are not permitted, with rare exceptions."

"I still have to go."

"Fine, then," Shadow said after a moment. "I'll go with you."

Niels shook his head. "You're not in any shape for that. Besides, this is something I have to do alone."

"What makes you think they'll let you get anywhere near her?"

As opposed to simply killing him, which they might feel entirely justified in doing if he arrived uninvited on their doorstep. Andreas had looked to have an itchy hand on the sword hilt and he wasn't likely to be the only one. Not that it mattered.

He could have said something about needing to hear from her own lips if there was no future for the two of them. He might even have said that he loved her enough to walk away and leave her to the safety of her Fortress Kingdom, if that was what she wanted.

But he didn't say any of that, mainly because none of it would have been true. Instead, he spoke a truth so great as to banish all disagreement.

"She is mine," the Wolf said, and with the mere uttering of those words, he felt a sudden lightening of his spirit, so great as to seem a benediction.

# Chapter Nineteen

"It's a beautiful day." The young woman seated opposite Amelia on the wide stone terrace smiled as she spoke. "Perhaps you'd like to go for a ride."

Amelia looked up from the book that failed to hold her attention despite being written by her favorite novelist, Jane Austen. Her cousin, Clio, was right; it was a beautiful day. The sky was a particular shade of teal-blue she associated only with Akora. Below, in the broad swath of the harbor that served the royal city of Ilius, dozens of proud, bull-headed vessels came and went, some setting out only to cross the Inland Sea, others venturing much farther. Their billowing white sails stood out brightly against the indigo water.

The air smelled of the sea mingled with the perfume of the lemon tree groves that were in bloom. Birds flitted among the vines, sipping nectar from vivid scarlet flowers. Off in the distance, someone was singing. Akora was blessed with a generally benign climate, but not even those long accustomed to such days could take them for granted.

Even so, the sheer beauty of her surroundings did not raise Amelia's spirits. "I don't think so," she said. When Clio looked at her gently, she added, "I fear I am not very good company right now."

"Nonsense," her cousin said loyally. She brushed back a strand of the brilliant red hair that was her legacy from her mother and which set her so apart from her twin, Andreas. Twins they were, and deeply loving brother and sister, but the children of the Vanax Atreus and his consort, Brianna, could scarcely have been more dissimilar.

Clio was, as she herself said, the quiet one in a family she cheerfully acknowledged was anything but. Shy as a child, and still inclined to seek the background rather than put herself forward, she was nonetheless a kind and caring friend. Amelia found her mere presence soothing.

"It's just that you've had a difficult time," Clio said gently. "Is your throat paining you?"

Instinctively, Amelia put a hand to the pale scar, less visible with each passing day. The healer who cared for her on the voyage home had done an exemplary job. Physically, she was almost entirely well. Emotionally was another matter altogether. "I'm fine," she insisted.

"Then you need diversion," her cousin said, putting down her own book. "And so do I. If you don't want to ride, we could swim."

"We could, or" — thinking of what her cousin would truly prefer, Amelia mustered a smile — "we could go play in the dirt."

Clio laughed in perfect understanding.

"Would you really like to do that?"

"Nothing would suit me more." Certainly it was better than sitting about feeling sorry for herself, which she had shown a distressing tendency to do of late. And it would delight Clio, who showered her with such patient kindness. Definitely, some serious dirt-digging was called for.

"Do you remember," Clio asked as they rose and walked from the terrace, their white tunics fluttering in the breeze, "what terrible messes we used to get into as children, flailing about in the dirt, making mud castles and the like?"

"I remember what terrible messes I and most of the others got into. We weren't allowed back into the palace without a swim first. You always stayed more or less tidy."

This was mainly because Clio invariably managed to find stray bits of things — small rocks, broken bits of pottery, seeds and the like — which would then fascinate her for hours. She would pore over them, sorting them into categories, sketching them meticulously, wondering aloud how they had been formed or what their use might have been.

Initially, such behavior had concerned her elders. It seemed too serious and even somewhat obsessive for a young child. But Atreus and Brianna were wise parents; they watched their daughter carefully even as they allowed her to be herself.

In the years since, Clio had amassed a vast

collection of bits and pieces belonging to Akora's past. She continued to catalog, sort, and sketch them, and, from time to time, she managed to actually reassemble an object. So great was the Akorans' respect for their history that her activities were no longer looked at askance. But neither were they afforded any particular seriousness. The palace's vast libraries held a treasure trove of thousands of years of their ancestors' written words. Surely, the pieces of their broken pottery were of no particular importance when compared to all that. Even so, Clio persisted, insisting in her own quiet way that the most ordinary objects had stories to tell.

For several months, she had been digging in the cellar of one of the oldest houses in Ilius, allowed to do so by the gracious owners who had moved elsewhere. Amelia had not seen the site since her arrival from England and she was startled when she did so.

The house was near the top of one of the winding, climbing roads that led up from the harbor and all the way to the hill where the royal palace stood. Even to the untutored eye, it looked very old, although well maintained. But the cellar —

"Good Lord," Amelia exclaimed when they had clambered down the ladder from what had been the ground floor into the now much deeper basement. As Clio lit the lamps set around the chamber, Amelia said, "I had no idea you meant to go so far."

"Neither did I," Clio admitted cheerfully. "At least not when I started. But the farther I dig, the more of interest I find." She pointed to shallow baskets set up on a wooden table near the far wall of the basement. "Here, look at these."

Amelia took the half-dozen tiny carved animals that Clio handed to her and studied them carefully. "I've never seen anything like these. This one looks like a mongoose, but different somehow."

"I think it is a mongoose," Clio said, "but not the kind we have here now."

"You mean, someone carved these to represent animals from other parts of the world?"

"Possibly. Look at this one, what does it remind you of?"

Amelia turned the meticulously detailed statue over, examining it. The animal was standing upright on its back legs, its front paws extended as though to grasp something. It had a long, thick body, a pointed snout, and small ears pinned close to its head. "I have no idea what this is."

"I think it's a sloth," Clio said, returning the statues to the basket.

"What's that?"

"An animal I've read about, although I can't find any descriptions that precisely match that carving. It may be that this particular sloth no longer exists anywhere. I think these statues might be of animals that lived on Akora before the volcano exploded."

Amelia absorbed this slowly, well aware that it could be of tremendous importance. "But that would mean —"

Clio nodded happily. "That they were preserved by one of the survivors. That would mean that in finding them again, I've reached a very old level from a time when this place was occupied shortly after the explosion."

"But Clio, that's incredible. Almost nothing survived from before."

"I may not be right," her cousin cautioned. "But at the moment, it seems the most plausible explanation."

It did to Amelia as well, so much so that she got to work with unfettered eagerness, helping Clio to clear several more square feet of dirt, all of it carefully sifted for even the smallest remains. They did not find another of the statues but they did find several shards of pottery, which Clio seized on gleefully.

For a precious time, Amelia felt taken out of herself, distracted from the burden of hurt and longing that had dogged her since leaving England. But only for a time. Too soon, her mind turned, straight as a compass needle homing north, to the matter of Mister Niels Wolfson.

She had last glimpsed him for a scant moment as he laid her on the bed at the Three Swans, just before treacherous sleep enveloped her. Beyond that, she had only a faint memory of men's voices. One of them might have been Niels's, but she truly couldn't be sure.

She had awakened to the gentle touch of an Akoran healer and the sight of her father, sitting beside the bed, holding her hand. The proud, indomitable man she had always known as a beacon of strength looked unutterably stricken, so much so that she reached out to him in mingled comfort and apology.

He had held her tightly, his embrace the assurance that his love was unwavering. Such love, however, did not extend to providing her with any information about Niels. His only response to the questions she managed to croak out was to tell her grudgingly that Wolfson lived. Now there was comfort! She had scarcely begun to gather her thoughts before she found herself on a fast ship bound for Akora.

Her mother was no more forthcoming, making it clear that she, too, had nothing to say on the subject. As the days and the miles flew by, England growing ever more distant, Amelia had to confront the likelihood that she would never see Niels Wolfson again.

If she put his welfare above her own longings, she had to acknowledge that distance from her might be his best protection. That he still lived was proof that her father could stay his hand, but that might not remain the case forever.

" 'A rose by any other name,' " Niels's note had said. Staring out at the empty sea, she had entertained the treacherous wish that she might be someone, anyone else. Not Amelia Atreides. Not an Akoran princess. A woman free to be with the man she loved.

But now, digging into the dirt of her native land, that wish seemed so alien as to belong to another. She was who she was. By any other name, she would be no different. No future that denied that was worth having.

"I think we have done enough," Clio said as she dusted off her hands. "It will be time for dinner soon and we both need to clean up."

Amelia stood slowly and looked around. "I wonder who used to live here, and under what circumstances."

Clio hesitated. Her cheeks were flushed. She looked uncharacteristically suffused with excitement that could barely be contained. "I did find something a few weeks ago —"

"What?"

"I'm not sure . . . it was in pieces but I think I've put it back together accurately. It appears to be an emblem of some sort. The image on it is a tree with branches heavy with fruit."

"An emblem like that is used for the priestesses of Akora."

"Yes, and I suspect it has been for a very long time. I think there's a chance a priestess lived here."

"Shortly after the explosion?" When Clio nodded, Amelia said, "The only priestess among the survivors was Lyra." If her cousin truly had found the home of their fabled ancestress, the home she had shared with the equally fabled Atreides, it would stun all Akora.

"I'm not sure," her cousin cautioned firmly, "and it will be quite some time before I am ready to say anything publicly, if ever. But I think it's possible that Lyra and Atreides lived here while construction began on the palace. They probably weren't here all that long, but it would have been at the beginning of their life together."

"Then why did Lyra leave things here, if she did?"

"I don't know. That's a mystery I may never be able to solve, although I doubt I will ever give up trying."

When they had climbed back up the ladder, Amelia turned to her cousin. "Thank you for sharing this with me."

"It was your idea to come digging."

"Yes, but you didn't have to tell me about what you've found." She looked down into the excavation, dark now that the lamps had been extinguished. Within her lay the conviction that Clio was right. A woman to whom they had the most profound and enduring connection had lived out a vital part of her life almost directly where they stood.

Lyra, who had seen her world destroyed, and who had responded by building it anew.

Beside her memory, Amelia suddenly felt very small. It had been five weeks since she had left England. Five weeks feeling helpless and lost.

It really was quite enough.

"What do you mean, you want to return to England?" Her Uncle Atreus, Vanax of Akora, looked at her across the width of the large, plain table that served him as a desk. The room he used as an office was one of the oldest in the palace. Wide windows looked out to the city and harbor below. It was the morning of the day after Amelia had come to her decision. She had spent a restless night before approaching her uncle.

Now in his mid-fifties, Atreus had emerged from the caves beneath the palace more than thirty years before as his people's chosen leader. To attain that position, he had risked his life in a ritual shrouded in mystery and legend. Much of both clung to him, yet he was also a very real and caring man, and someone who Amelia trusted implicitly.

Therefore, she believed he would see the rightness of her decision, if only she could find the right way to explain it to him.

"I don't know if anyone has told you of a man named Niels Wolfson —"

"Your father sent along a letter, and I have spoken with your mother. I believe I understand the situation." His dark eyes settled on her unrelentingly. Supremely fit, thanks to long hours on the training field and even longer hours in his studio carving stone from which he drew such beauty, Atreus was himself no stranger to passion. On the contrary, he and her Aunt Brianna were among the most loving of couples. But he was also a man of wisdom and authority, accustomed to being obeyed.

Accustomed, as well, to speaking bluntly.

"Niels Wolfson endangered you. Moreover, he did it for his own ends. He used you to insinuate himself into the circle of our family, the better to discover if we were responsible for a heinous crime. Had he judged us guilty, do you really believe he would have hesitated to exact the most terrible vengeance?"

Quietly, Amelia said, "Niels sought justice, not vengeance. There is a difference, as you well know. If he had thought us guilty, he would have gone back to America and told President Van Buren that. The most likely result would have been war between our countries."

Atreus ran a hand through thick black hair lightly sprinkled with silver, and sighed. "What makes you think that isn't still the likely result?"

The question brought her up short. She had not considered it. "What are you saying?"

"Your father wrote that shortly before he died, Simon Hawley accused us of hiring him to destroy the *Defiant*. That is, of course, a lie, but what makes you so certain that Mister Niels Wolfson didn't believe him?"

"Niels would never believe Hawley," Amelia said at once. "He knew I was willing to die for the truth."

"He came very close to letting you do just that."

"He did what he had to do. Moreover, I pleaded with him to kill Hawley. If he hadn't, I wouldn't have lived anyway. Hawley would have killed me. Niels is blameless for what happened to me and he knows we are blameless in the matter of the *Defiant*."

"What about the matter of his brother stabbed by an Akoran knife?"

"Hawley, again, as I am certain Niels realizes. He is not our enemy. You are wrong about him, completely wrong."

"If I am not, we can expect the arrival of American warships in these waters very shortly. I am sorry, Amelia, but under the circumstances, there is no possibility of your leaving here."

And that, it seemed, was that. Though she was tempted to plead further, Amelia realized the effort would be futile. Atreus took council from many, but his decisions, once made, were rarely altered.

That left her with a terrible quandary. Under ordinary circumstances, the mere fact that she was on an island several thousand miles from England would have settled the matter. But she was desperate enough to wonder if there was any possibility of finding someone, perhaps among the few *xenos* ships allowed these days to call at Akora, who could be persuaded to take her on board. With the possibility of a crisis looming, any such ships would likely be departing forthwith for safer waters.

But if she did any such thing, she would be going against the direct orders of the man who was not only the head of her family but also of her people. A man to whom she owed absolute loyalty.

The alternative was to accept that Niels was no longer part of her life. If her family had been no more forthcoming with him than they had been with her, he might think she had left England of her own volition. How could she possibly let him believe that? How could she do otherwise?

Mulling all this over, she wandered down to the harbor, where she took note of what had eluded her in the weeks since her return to Akora. While the port of Ilius seemed as busy as ever, it was business of a different sort than what she was accustomed to. Many merchant ships were in port, not unloading and preparing to go out again, but riding empty at berth. By contrast, the highly agile warships seemed to be everywhere, loading men and supplies before setting out through the twin straits — one to the north and the other to the south — that were the only entrances to Akora from the open sea.

Moreover, she saw white-kilted warriors in

far greater number than usual, moving through the city streets, going out to man the guard towers all along the headlands. Even as she watched, a man of perhaps thirty appeared in the door of a tidy bakery followed by a slightly younger woman who held a baby in her arms. The man leaned the spear he carried against the wall, embraced his wife, and spoke to her gently. She nodded and offered a smile, although it was clear she was fighting tears. He kissed her and went down the street, looking over his shoulder several times before his path took him out of sight.

How often was that scene being repeated in homes all over Akora? With the possibility of an American fleet appearing suddenly, Atreus would take all sensible precautions. Since virtually every Akoran man was a trained warrior, the Vanax had a large reserve of soldiers to call upon in a crisis. The danger was that such a force, once put in place, took on its own momentum. There was a real possibility that if Americans approached Akora peacefully, their intent would be misunderstood and war would be the result anyway.

With such dire thoughts swirling in her head, Amelia went back to the palace and sought the privacy of her own quarters in the spacious family wing. There she struggled to try to decide what to do as the day aged. She deliberately avoided both her mother and Clio, guessing those two very insightful ladies would sense her disquiet all too easily.

At dinnertime, she pleaded a headache and remained in her quarters. When Joanna came to check on her, as Amelia knew her mother would, she feigned sleep. The deceit troubled her, but she thought it necessary.

Awake, staring at the ceiling above her bed where painted stars gleamed, she struggled to decide what to do. When no ready solution presented itself, she gave up the effort to court sleep and got up. By long habit, she opened the carved chest on the table near her bed. It held her most beloved possessions: a doll she had received when she was very small, several well-thumbed books, and, nestled in a covering of velvet, a golden ball that was her Aunt Kassandra's gift to her on the day of her birth.

The ball was one of only a handful of its like ever made. It was the product of a master craftsman whose skill was long lost. Seated on the side of her bed, Amelia lightly tossed the ball from one hand to another. As she did, air passed through cuts incised in the gold. Very quickly, a haunting melody filled the room. The music and its familiarity both soothed her. Her eyelids grew heavy and soon enough she thought it prudent to put the ball safely away.

Sleep did come and brought with it troubling dreams. Twice she surfaced from them with Niels's name on her lips.

It was very late in the night when she noticed that the wind had changed. Rising, she went to close the shutters. A splash of rain in her face caught her by surprise.

A sliver of the moon still showed between clouds. Its light was enough to reveal the dark wall moving quickly eastward across the sky. A mighty storm was descending on Akora. They had weathered the same and worse often enough. But all thought of sailing off on her own had to be put aside. Daring she might be, but not foolish. Moreover, if there was an American fleet approaching their shores, its sailors were about to face serious challenge not from Akora's own formidable navy, but from nature itself.

She returned to bed and pulled the covers up over herself. Her last thought before drifting back to sleep was the hope that all those on the sea would be safe this night.

# Chapter Twenty

It was going to be damn ironic if he got almost all the way to Akora only to be pounded to a pulp on its shores by the storm whose approach he'd been watching for hours.

Bailing with one hand while he gripped the rudder with the other, Niels gauged the wall of water about to descend on him and decided he had a pretty good chance of getting up and over it. That was thanks not only to his own skill as a sailor, but also to the fine little boat he'd acquired in London. It was a Cornish pilot gig, eighteen feet from stem to stern, rigged for sail but rowable as well. Ordinarily, it would have been used to take ship pilots to and from larger vessels coming into port, but it had done very well on the open ocean. At least until now.

Up and over the wall of dark water, he had a moment's respite before the sea swelled again. The storm seemed to be getting worse. He hadn't taken a bearing in several hours, but he was reasonably sure he was close to Akora. Night and the weather eliminated any chance of a sighting. Worse yet, he had limited information about the approaches to the Fortress Kingdom except that they were rumored to be treacherous. So he'd been told all along the coast, every time he'd put in for food and water. He'd done that as rarely as possible, grudging every moment spent on land, although truth be told, he'd been kindly received everywhere he stopped. Under other circumstances — namely, if Amelia had been along — the voyage would have been sheer pleasure. At least until the storm hit.

As it was, his clothes — what was left of them after more than a month at sea — were plastered to him, he was chilled to the bone, and he could no longer really feel his hand holding the rudder.

All in all, not good.

But he'd been in tougher spots and still managed to —

No, actually he hadn't been, not judging by what was about to hit him. Though he craned his neck back, he couldn't see the top of the monster wave coming straight at the bold little gig. He took a breath, well aware it might be his last, and locked both hands on the rudder.

Up and over . . . that was all he had to do . . . up and over —

It didn't work. The brave little ship tried, and Niels bent all his strength to help, but it wasn't enough.

One more breath, drawn deep before he heard the rending shriek of wood coming apart.

Once before in his life, Niels had cried out from the edge of death. That time he had called to Shadow, who miraculously heard him. This time it was Amelia's name he uttered — not in any hope that she could help him, for he was profoundly grateful she was not there to share his fate. No, he cried out in desperate need that somehow she would know that he had come, that he had tried.

He had wanted them to be together.

Her name was caught on the wind, blown high even as all other sound and, with it, all awareness of the world was drowned in the roar of the hungry sea.

Amelia was awake before dawn. She had slept, but fitfully. Rising in darkness, she threw on a tunic, left her hair in the braid she had slept in, and went down to the palace stables.

She chose one of her favorite mounts, a sprightly young mare who looked ready and more for a good run. Talking to the horse gently, she tacked up and swung lightly into the saddle.

One of her earliest memories involved riding perched in the saddle in front of her father, as she shrieked with unbridled glee.

That was the same night she crept from her bed and snuck down to the stables, where she crooned to a sleepy horse before clambering up on his back and trotting out into the palace yard, utterly delighted with herself. That, too, she remembered.

Along with the swift reaction of the palace guards who had wasted no time summoning her startled parents.

Joanna had cried out and hugged her tightly when she was taken, protesting, from atop the horse.

Alex had declared it was time for her to learn to ride.

And ride she did now, out of the stable yard and through the vast expanse in front of the palace. It was said to be large enough to hold the entire population of Akora, more than three hundred thousand people, and she did not doubt it. She went out through the immense gates framed by statues of lionesses standing erect. The first faint rim of light shone against the eastern horizon when she trotted down the lane toward the coastal road.

Such were the winds and tides around Akora that there were only a handful of places where the victims of shipwrecks — or their remains — were likely to come ashore. These were well-known and were always patrolled in the aftermath of any storm.

Instinctively, Amelia headed toward one of them, a small bay north of the port of Ilius. Decades before, not far from there, her Akoran grandmother had discovered the man who was to be Amelia's English grandfather. It was a favorite family story — the stranger taken from the sea by the princess with whom he found his life's love. Phaedra and Andrew themselves still spoke of it from time to time.

Wistful yearning stirred in Amelia as she neared the place, down past the dunes where fragrant scrub grass grew and the wild roses, battered by the wind, were beginning to revive. There she dismounted, threw the reins over a bush near a likely grazing spot, and stared out over the Inland Sea.

White-capped waves still splashed along the crescent curve of the beach, but she had no doubt the water was far calmer than it had been during the night. It was only when she looked toward the northern strait, the small opening through the headlands, that she saw the ocean pushing its way in, still smashing against rocks the size of houses.

Kicking off her sandals, she began walking along the beach. She had gone perhaps a quarter-mile when something caught her attention. Shading her eyes from the rising sun, she stared at the dark heap on the sand.

A trick of the light? A seal basking? Or —

She was running, her heels kicking up golden sprays of sand. Her tunic clung to her long, flashing legs. Getting closer, she gasped when she realized what she saw.

A body. Please, God, a survivor. She had heard tales about those who found the *xenos* washed ashore, how they always felt a personal responsibility for the people they discovered. As a child, she had imagined how dramatic and wondrous it would be to find someone. The most she had ever discovered in the aftermath of a storm was a stray bit of driftwood.

That was changed now suddenly, utterly changed.

She skittered to a stop, dropping to her knees beside the still form. A man, bare from the waist up, his shirt having been ripped to shreds. He still wore trousers, though, and boots. He was very tall, dark-haired, turned on his side away from her so that she could not see his features . . .

And yet she knew him. All in an instant. Knew the curve of his back, the broad sweep of his shoulders, the faint white scar near his spine, the powerful length of his thighs.

Trembling, she reached out a hand and touched her fingers lightly to the side of his throat where his life's blood should beat.

A moment . . . then another before the steady rhythm of his heart coursed through her.

*"Niels!"*

He lived; he was there. With her.

And at any time, the patrol looking for shipwreck victims would come by.

"Niels, Niels, can you hear me?" Desperately, she turned him over, staring into his beloved face. He was unshaven, his thick black hair unkempt. More than ever he looked like the Wolf.

Her own beloved wolf.

"Niels, you have to get up. There's a patrol coming. Please!"

He stirred, but slightly. She dug her knees into the sand and got an arm around his shoulders, trying to tug him upright. She was strong for a woman, but she couldn't budge him.

Finally, desperation growing by the minute, she did the only thing she could think of doing.

Crouched on the golden sand, her hands cupping his face, the Princess of Akora kissed her prince awake.

His lips were cold and tasted of salt. She did not care. Passionately, she deepened the kiss, breathing her own life into him.

He stirred again, still faintly. She kissed his eyelids, the hard line of his cheek, the pulse of life in his throat, and his lips again . . . warm, demanding lips that took hers fiercely even as his arms closed round her.

*"Amelia."*

If this was heaven, and it sure felt like it, he'd been a whole lot better in his life than he thought he'd been. Either that, or God really was forgiving.

Either way, it suited him just fine. He could go on doing what he was doing for the better part of eternity.

Except that she tore her mouth from his and, looking down at him, said, "We have to go. The patrol is coming."

He was not yet sufficiently recovered to really understand what she meant, but something of her urgency reached him. Holding on to her, Niels stumbled to his feet. The world wavered, and for a moment he thought his legs wouldn't hold, but he willed himself to stay upright as he looked around.

The nightmare world he remembered, of howling wind and surging sea, was gone. In its place was . . . paradise?

He was on a beach beside a sparkling sea. The woman he loved was with him.

But he was definitely breathing, and the more he thought about it, improbable though it seemed, it appeared as though he were still alive.

Which would have to mean that he'd reached Akora. The Fortress Kingdom beyond the Pillars of Hercules. The realm of myth and mystery.

If Akora was real, so was Amelia. She was there with him and she'd said something about . . . a patrol?

"Come on," she said urgently and began tugging him up the beach toward an outcropping of rocks. He stumbled, but his strength was returning quickly and he managed to keep up with her. Fifty yards or so from the water, there was a large boulder that formed a natural screen. The sand behind the boulder was cool and damp. Niels flopped down on it and stared at Amelia.

"I can't believe you're here," he said.

"I was about to say the same. That storm —" She broke off, interrupted by the sudden sound of hoofbeats. "Don't move," she said and quickly stepped out from behind the boulder.

He heard words exchanged in a language he did not know. Akoran, by the sound of it. The patrol consisted of three men who seemed to know Amelia and spoke to her with friendly respect.

Just as well for them.

When they were gone, she came back behind the boulder and knelt beside him. "They will see my horse. If I hadn't greeted them, they would have searched for me."

"Why are they here?"

"Looking for anyone shipwrecked by the storm. This is one of the places such people are most likely to be washed ashore."

"And what happens when they're found?" He was thinking of the old stories that strangers who landed themselves on Akora were likely to be executed.

"Nothing terrible," Amelia assured him. "Usually," she added.

He grinned even though it hurt. It felt so good to be there with her. Hell, it felt good just to be alive. She was the bonus to end all bonuses. "You don't think the authorities would be thrilled to see me?"

"Let's just say I have concerns. Niels, did you come alone?"

She was asking about Shadow. He nodded. "My brother's doing well, but I convinced him to stay in London. He needs more time to recuperate, or at least he did. He ought to be fully recovered by now."

"That is good to know, but I meant anyone else. The American fleet, for instance?"

"Why the hell would I —"

"My uncle, the Vanax, thinks you may have believed what Hawley said about us being ultimately responsible for what happened to the *Defiant*. He thinks that, as a result, we may be on the verge of war with America."

"Your uncle, the Vanax, couldn't be more wrong."

She laughed, though he couldn't tell whether it was with relief or shock at his blunt speech. "Then you didn't believe him?"

"The day I believe a piece of slime like Hawley is the day I —" He broke off, staring at her. His sudden silence raised a question in her eyes. Grinning, he answered it.

"My God, you're beautiful."

"No, I'm not," she said automatically. "My mother and aunt are beautiful."

"Fine women, I'm sure, but you, *Princess*, are beautiful." Matching deeds to words, he ran a hard hand down her length, savoring every inch of her. "Is that patrol likely to come back anytime soon?" His touch communicated his meaning more clearly than any words.

"Niels!" She affected shock, but she was really devilishly pleased. As she made quite clear a moment later when she stretched out beside him. "I've missed you," she said, her finger stroking his chest. "I was thinking of setting out for England even though Atreus said I couldn't, but then the storm came up and —"

"You were thinking of what?" He rolled over

on his side, moving her under him. That took just about all the strength he had at the moment, but he wasn't about to let her know that.

"Going to England. We were separated so suddenly and —"

"Going with whom?"

"I thought perhaps I could persuade the captain of a *xenos* ship to —"

"You were prepared to go off like that, trusting your life to strangers? My God, Amelia, what were you thinking of?"

"You," she said and kissed him again.

He'd grow old trying to protect her properly, he realized, but that was all right. He accepted it as part of the price of loving a princess.

Speaking of loving . . .

There on the cool, wet sand, in the shadow of the ancient boulder, hard by the crescent beach, he drew her to him. Every inch of his body hurt from the pounding of the storm and he felt weak as a newborn kitten, but it didn't matter.

Amelia smiled as she rose above him, her smile deepening when she drew off her tunic. The sight of her body, perfect in his eyes, stole his breath. He cupped her breasts as she reached for the waistband of his trousers.

Soaking wet and encrusted with salt, it gave her a little trouble, but she persevered. Release from the confines of his clothes brought him some relief but not much. He was rock hard, ravenous for her. When she bent her head and stroked him delicately with the tip of her tongue, he damn near came undone.

Again she teased him, easing him into her mouth, her body moving over his tantalizingly.

No doubt about it, this was a hell of a lot better way to die than in the storm. All the same, he'd prefer not to disgrace himself. Gently, he raised her head and drew her upward, kissing her long and deeply. Their tongues played as she fitted herself carefully to him.

At length, Amelia raised herself, lifting the heavy weight of her braid, and stretched luxuriously. "Do you have any idea how you feel inside me, Niels? So powerful, so wonderful —" She moved again and he gasped, his hands clasping her hips.

"So very good," she continued and slid down him, riding him slowly and smoothly. Waves of pleasure undulated through his battered body. He held on, truly he did, until she cried out softly and he felt the powerful, inner clenching of her muscles that signaled her release. Only then did the Wolf surrender himself to a storm of an entirely different sort, bringer not of death, but of life.

They slept, though not for long, he judged, when he slipped from Amelia and, righting his clothes, stepped back onto the beach. Shading his eyes, he looked out over the curve of the beach and the sparkling sea beyond. My God, it was lovely here. He couldn't remember ever seeing a place more beautiful. No wonder people had thought Akora more legend than reality.

It was also Amelia's home, which he did not doubt she loved just as dearly as she loved her family. The family, or at least more members of it, he could expect to meet before too much longer.

There were bound to be certain issues among people who regarded him as a potential enemy, possibly also as the despoiler of their beloved princess, a rude American of no lineage, and all-around not someone they would welcome with open arms.

Good thing he was a man who appreciated a challenge.

He woke her gently and grinned when she stirred, smiling even before she opened her eyes.

As her arms reached for him, she murmured, "Niels, you're really here."

"I am, Princess, but I shouldn't be. At least, not like this, with you."

She didn't deny it. He had known when she misled the patrol that she was deeply concerned about the reception he would receive. Tentatively, she said, "We could return to England."

"On what? The boat I came in is in splinters now, and besides, that's no way to convince your family to accept me."

"You're right, I know." She stood and shook the sand from her tunic before putting it on. Her head lifted. She looked at him proudly. "Let's go, then."

She looked so good standing there in the midday sun that he had trouble concentrating on what she was saying, much less on the problem confronting them. With an effort, he wrenched his mind back. "Where?"

"To the palace."

The palace. Oh, yes, a princess would live in a palace.

"You go. I'll come along." When she looked surprised, he added, "Don't laugh, but I'm trying to be discreet."

She did laugh, but only a little. "Niels Wolfson, diplomat."

"I'm new to it, I admit, but I think it's time to give it a try."

Amelia hesitated a moment before her hand gently touched his. "All right, just don't get lost."

"I won't." She was walking up the beach, away from him, when he had a sudden thought and called after her. "Amelia, just where is the palace?"

She turned back, her gaze lingering on him. "Follow the road. You can't miss it."

A short time later, he saw a horse and rider pause on the highland above the beach, face toward him for a moment, and then ride away.

# Chapter Twenty-One

Niels walked, slowly at first because he was still weak, but with growing strength and just plain enjoyment. He might be going to the most important meeting of his life — upon which his entire future hung — but that didn't make him impervious to his surroundings.

So this was Akora. For a place in which he'd had no interest other than a desire not to encounter it in war, it was proving entrancing. That had a lot to do with Amelia, of course. Still, there was no denying Akora was as pretty a place as a man could hope to find.

He walked a mile or so from the beach before he saw the first signs of habitation. A small white house was nestled up on the side of a hill, a flock of sheep spread out over the nearby pasture.

A woman was in the garden in front of the house. As he neared, she straightened and he got a clearer look at her. Her skin was the hue of caramel. She wore her ebony hair twined in a neat braid. She frowned slightly when she saw him and hurried to the garden gate, opening it.

"You've just arrived, haven't you?" she asked tentatively, as though unsure he would understand.

But he did, because the lady spoke in English

— clear, unmistakable American English. So much for the rumor, which Amelia had put to rest anyway, that the Akorans killed *xenos* unfortunate enough to wash up on their shores. The woman he saw looked as far from unfortunate as it was possible to get and she was obviously, vibrantly alive.

"Sit down," she said, guiding him to a bench near the front door. "I'll get you some water. Are you hurt? Do you need a healer?"

"I'm fine, ma'am, but I will be grateful for a drink."

When she returned, he drank appreciatively and handed the goblet back to her for a refill. His thirst slaked, he looked around thoughtfully. "Nice place you've got here."

Her golden-brown eyes crinkled as she smiled. "I like it. I'm Elizabeth Johnson, by the way. And you're — ?"

"Niels Wolfson, ma'am. Do you mind my asking how long you've been here?"

"Five years next month. Ever hear of the *Northern Star*?"

The name stirred a memory. A passenger ship sailing for England, never reaching port, its fate unknown.

"What happened?" he asked.

"Same as must have happened to you last night. We got caught in a terrible storm. I thought I wouldn't live to see another day, and there were some who didn't, God rest their souls. I was lucky, though, along with all the

357

rest who washed up here." Reassuringly, she added, "You will be, too."

He thought of what awaited him in the royal city of Ilius. "I hope so. What do people do when they arrive?"

"Go to the palace. It's quite a place, and it's where everything happens. You're welcome to use my horse and wagon, if you'd like."

When he looked at her with surprise, she smiled again. "You'll find people here are generous, Mister Wolfson, and trusting. They've worked things out better than folks elsewhere. That's a big part of why I decided to stay. This is a rare place, worth being a part of, worth protecting."

They spoke a little longer before he stood, thanking her for her hospitality. Elizabeth Johnson walked with him to the road and saw him set in the right direction. He looked back over his shoulder and returned her cheerful wave.

A little farther on he came to another house, and then a small cluster of them. No one was about, likely because they were off working in the fertile fields and orchards he saw in all directions.

Around a bend in the road, Niels came upon a man. He was young, tall, and broad-shouldered, with dark blonde hair. He was doing something with a stick, trying to get it to stand upright while he consulted an instrument attached to it. The man looked up as

Niels neared, and spoke.

"Sorry," Niels replied, "I don't speak Akoran."

"No problem," the man said, switching to perfect English. "Could you give me a hand?"

"Certainly." Leaving the road, he joined the man on the side of the hill.

"Just hold that, will you?" The man indicated the stick.

Niels did as he asked, holding the stick steady while the man completed his measurements. When he was done, he straightened and nodded. "Thanks. It usually works fine for one person, but the ground here slants too much. I'm having difficulty getting reliable readings."

"Of what?"

The man hesitated. There was something familiar about him that Niels couldn't quite place. He was here on Akora, but he sounded like an English aristocrat Niels might have encountered in London. Yet he was quite sure he had not met the man before.

"Just the ground." He looked disinclined to discuss the subject further, but he did offer his hand. "Gavin Hawkforte. Have you just arrived, by any chance?"

"Yes, I have. Hawkforte?" He saw it then, the resemblance to the man he had met at Boswick: Royce, Earl of Hawkforte, the Shield of England. The younger man had the same deepset, hazel eyes and blade-straight nose, but his mouth was different, closer to that of his

Akoran mother's, Princess Kassandra. He wore a simple tunic and sandals that revealed limbs rippling with muscle. His skin was well-tanned, indicating that he spent a great deal of time outdoors.

"You're the heir to Hawkforte, aren't you?"

Was he mistaken or did Gavin frown slightly? Even so, he said, "Yes, I suppose. And you would be — ?"

Now or never. "Niels Wolfson. I'm going to marry your cousin, Amelia."

Gavin looked him up and down with frank interest. "Are you? Does Melly know that?"

"Let's just say she has strong reason to suspect it."

"I see . . . did you come in last night, in that storm?" When Niels nodded, Gavin whistled softly. "You must be a hell of a sailor."

"Why do you say that?"

"You're alive. Look, I can be finished here. You could use some clean clothes and probably something to eat before you meet the elders."

"Thank you." As they began walking along the road, Niels said, "I have met some of them in London, including your parents."

"What took you to London?"

"I was looking for someone."

"Did you find him?"

"Yes, I did. I'm finished with what I went there to do."

Gavin grinned. He looked suddenly a younger man, more relaxed and carefree, which in turn made Niels realize how preoccupied and even concerned he had been while taking the measurements he would not discuss.

"That's just as well," Gavin said. "I imagine Melly doesn't leave room for too many distractions."

Surrendering to the temptation to talk about the woman he loved, Niels asked, "You all grew up together, didn't you?"

Gavin nodded. "At Hawkforte and Boswick, in London and, of course, here on Akora. We were all born within a few years of one another, so we've always been close."

"Are there others in your immediate family?"

"I have a younger brother and two sisters. What about you?"

"A brother. I have to admit, your family is a little . . ."

He was searching for a diplomatic word when Gavin said, "Overwhelming? You'll get used to it."

Niels was considering how likely that might be when they rounded a corner in the road and he stopped suddenly. Ahead lay a harbor shimmering in the sun, with a city unlike any he had ever seen, rising above it. Flower-bordered roads were lined with trim houses painted in a rich palette of creams, reds, blues, and greens. Carts and wagons came and went along the roads, but as he watched, a vehicle of another sort appeared. He felt suddenly as though he were watching a scene from another time, or perhaps one that had simply been preserved so well that past and present blended seamlessly.

"Is that a chariot?"

"It is. Racing them is a popular sport hereabouts."

"I wouldn't mind trying that myself." He was thinking of what it would feel like to fly over the ground so unfettered, as he watched the chariot's progress along the road. It moved upward to what appeared to be broad stone gates, beyond which lay —

A long, low whistle escaped him.

Gavin laughed. "That sums it up fairly well."

With difficulty, Niels dragged his gaze away from the vast expanse of buildings that dominated what appeared to be the sheared-off top of the hill. "That's the palace?"

"The one and only. Three thousand years in the building, nothing ever actually torn down, just additions made. Some say it's a labyrinth, and they do have a point, but you can find your way around with a little help."

"And a trail of breadcrumbs? Do you know there are still people who think Akora is a primitive society?"

"Sometimes it's useful to be underestimated."

Niels had no argument with that. He'd played the Kentucky card a time or two when he wanted to gull an opponent into thinking him less than he was.

As they passed between the twin stone lionesses guarding the broad gates, each easily the height of half a dozen men standing foot to shoulder, Gavin reached out and touched a rear paw of one of the statues. "An Akoran tradition," he explained, "for luck."

"Maybe I ought to try a swipe myself."

They continued on through a vast courtyard where thousands of people appeared to have gathered for no particular purpose. Men and women, both, were standing around talking, or hurrying to and fro.

"Is there some special event here today?" Niels asked.

"Not at all. The palace is the place where everyone meets. Nobles come to see and be seen, keep an eye on the Vanax, and so on. Merchants come to trade with the palace and with one another. Investors and those seeking capital come as well. The mint is located here, and many business deals are made in side rooms around it. There always seem to be Council meetings of one sort or another going on, and anyone with an interest attends those. The scholars come for the libraries, and the astronomers — they're asleep right now — come because of the observatories on the roof. Artists come because the Vanax is one himself, and he encourages them with regular exhibitions of their work."

"And his work as well?" Niels asked, trying to absorb it all.

"Actually not. Uncle Atreus is very reticent

about his own art, although I have to say, it's magnificent. At any rate, this looks like a fairly quiet day here."

Niels would have to take his word for that. He couldn't remember ever seeing so many people gathered for anything that didn't involve a parade, fireworks, and plenty of whiskey.

The courtyard was framed on three sides by the palace. Columns in brilliant red, yellow, and orange rose three stories to a blue-tiled roof. The outer walls were a bright white except where they were decorated with geometric patterns. Beneath the eaves of the roof, carved stone horns jutted out. Broad stairs rose upward to immense double doors that stood open.

"This way," Gavin said and led Niels not through what was certainly the main palace entrance, but down the colonnade to another staircase, and then up those stairs to a wing where quiet reigned.

"The family quarters," Gavin explained. "The palace itself is regarded as belonging to the people of Akora, but no one intrudes here."

He opened a carved door and stood aside for Niels to enter. The apartment they entered was spacious and sparsely, though elegantly, furnished. A collection of scientific instruments, surrounded by strewn papers, stood on a long table near the windows that overlooked the harbor.

"You can bathe in there," Gavin said,

pointing to another door. "I'll get you some clothes."

Half an hour or so later, Gavin called, "Everything all right?"

Standing under a rush of steaming hot water, which he'd started by fooling with a valve in a tiled enclosure, Niels opened his eyes.

"Fine," he called, "just enjoying how you primitive folks keep clean."

Gavin chuckled as he opened the door and set the clothes on a wooden chest. "There's shaving gear by the sink."

A short time later, Niels emerged, clean-shaven and freshly garbed in trousers and a shirt that fit well, which was not surprising since he and Gavin appeared to be about the same size. He'd towel-dried his hair and combed his fingers through it, but he knew he could do with a trim. That would have to wait. He'd delayed as long as he could.

Even so, he took a few more minutes to tuck into the lemonade, fresh bread, slices of ham, and round of cheese that Gavin had rustled up. Thus fortified, he steeled himself.

"Best to get on with it."

Gavin nodded. He looked amused yet sympathetic. "This way," he said, as he led Niels down a wide corridor and a flight of curving stairs, along more hallways, and through half a dozen antechambers into what had to be a throne room. The giveaway was the immense throne carved from black granite that dominated the far end of the room. It suited the man sitting in it, his hands resting on the stone arms carved to resemble a lion's paws.

Several men were standing near the throne. When Niels and Gavin entered, the Vanax spoke a few words. With quick glances in their direction, the men departed through a side door.

"Just remember," Gavin said cheerfully. "Atreus loves Amelia just as though she were his own daughter." With a friendly pat on the back that would have knocked a lesser man over, he left.

Alone, Niels walked across the wide expanse of the throne room toward the ruler who awaited him. Atreus might be an artist, but he looked all warrior — dangerous, alert, and not exactly brimming with patience.

Without preamble, the Vanax of Akora said, "The patrol saw two sets of footprints on the beach."

That was damned impressive. Even as he gave credit where it was due, Niels said, "I'm entirely responsible, sir. Amelia shouldn't be blamed."

"Protecting her, Mister Wolfson?"

"Yes, I am. I intend to go right on doing that for the rest of my life."

Instead of replying, Atreus looked over Niels's shoulder in the direction of the door. "I'm curious as to what my niece has to say about that."

Niels turned to see Amelia, slightly flushed, striding into the throne room. Instead of the white tunic she'd been wearing — some of the time — on the beach, she wore a deep blue tunic that he thought suited her very well.

Her appearance caused her royal uncle to raise an eyebrow. "Making an announcement, my dear?"

Coming to a stop beside Niels, Amelia reached out and took his hand. Head high, she said, "Yes, I am."

At Niels's quizzical look, the Vanax kindly explained, "On Akora, virgins wear white."

"Didn't we talk about diplomacy, sweetheart?" Niels murmured.

"Mister Wolfson," the Vanax said, "you kidnapped my niece and feigned her rescue in order to insinuate yourself into our family circle."

It wasn't a question, but Niels answered all the same. "Yes, sir, I did."

"You seriously entertained the notion that we were guilty of an act of war against your country."

"That is so."

"You involved Amelia in your conflict with Lord Simon Hawley, almost resulting in her death."

"It was my own stubbornness that put me in Hawley's path," Amelia interjected.

"Even so," her uncle said, "you want this man, despite everything he has done?"

367

Her hand tightened on Niels's. Quietly but firmly, the Princess of Akora said, "No, Uncle, I want him *because* of everything he has done. Niels is a man of courage and honor. He has never failed to uphold the values we ourselves hold dear."

In his hard life, Niels had received many accolades, some from men genuinely grateful for his work, many from those merely wishing to curry favor. But never had anyone said anything that struck him so deeply. The man others called Wolf, the man who had heard the winter wind blow through his soul, knew himself to no longer be alone.

Without taking his eyes from them, Atreus said, "You have a rare gift, my niece, to know what is in the heart of another."

"That is true, but I need no gift to know what is in Niels's heart, or mine."

The Vanax of Akora stood. He left his throne and came across the wide floor to them. His hard face gentled as he looked at his niece. To Niels he said, "Take care of her, Mister Wolfson. Take very good care."

Amelia gave a little whoop of delight and threw her arms around her uncle. Niels was fighting the extraordinary urge to do the same when he happened to glance in the direction of the side door.

Shadow grinned back at him. A Shadow who looked entirely fit and recovered.

"The Akoran ships are marvelous," his

brother informed him when he had walked over to join them. "Fast and comfortable." As though on an afterthought, he asked, "How was your trip down?"

Swallowing his astonishment, Niels said, "Fine. It was fine."

"Good. What about that blow last night? We were on the edge of it, but I thought you might get clipped."

"It was fine. What the hell are you doing here, Shadow?"

"I suggested he accompany us," Prince Alexandros said as he came forward to embrace his daughter. "Once we knew you were on the way here, Mister Wolfson, there wasn't any reason for us to tarry in England."

"You expected when you let me go that I would follow Amelia." The idea stunned him, but their sudden appearance made such a conclusion inescapable.

Alex shrugged as though it was all rather obvious. "If you deserved her, you would."

And that, it seemed, was that.

Except later that evening, as the family sat at dinner in a cheerfully informal room lit both by tapered candles and by moonlight, the soon-to-be father of the bride did raise a further matter.

"By the way, Niels," Alex said, "there is something I've been meaning to ask you. It is evident that you are a man of means, yet the source of your wealth remains unclear."

It seemed a reasonable line of inquiry from a

man who had agreed to give him his daughter. Niels said, "I fell into a gold mine."

"Is that an American expression?" Amelia asked. As a fan of penny novels, she brightened at the thought. "Perhaps you won it in a card game?"

Shadow chuckled as Niels shook his head. "No, I fell into it through a hole in the ground, probably a mining shaft, hundreds, maybe thousands of years old. While I was waiting for Shadow to get around to rescuing me, I struck a light and found myself staring at a vein of gold thicker than I was tall."

"How old were you then?" Joanna asked.

"I was fifteen."

"And you managed to hold on to a gold mine at that age," Gavin said. "There must have been more than a few who tried to take it from you."

"They tried," Shadow said quietly. "But they got discouraged real quick."

The Akorans seemed to approve of this. They were all smiles until Joanna said, "We will miss you, Amelia."

Atreus cleared his throat. "Yes, well, as to that, Alex and I have been talking. Perhaps it is time for Akora to establish diplomatic relations with a select number of countries — not too many, just a few. The United States would, of course, be among those. That would require an exchange of ambassadors. Andreas has indicated an interest in being posted to Washington, and I am in agreement with that. With your permission, Niels, I will suggest to your president that you are the appropriate man to represent the United States here."

"Thank you, sir," Niels replied, even as his mind opened to the extraordinary opportunity suddenly laid before him. He might not be what anyone would call a natural diplomat, but he'd work at it and he'd learn.

So he said to Amelia when they walked alone later on the terrace overlooking the sea. "We'll have to spend some time in Washington," he told her, "and I've got property in New York I'd like to look in on occasionally. But we'll be here most of the year. This will still be home for you, sweetheart."

The woman born a princess turned in the arms of the man she loved. She set her back to the sea and the moon-draped islands gleaming within it, and looked instead into his eyes.

"Your home as well, here and wherever we both shall be."

The Wolf nodded. He gathered her to him, holding her with tender care. Above them, the stars turned and a new day waited to be born.

*On the shore beneath the palace, a man walked along the curve of the Inland Sea. Gavin was tired, happy for his cousin, of course, but unable to shake the apprehension that had been growing in him for months. If his calculations were correct —*

*The answer to whether they were or not lay out*

there, in the trio of small islands that were the sole visible remains of the volcano that had ripped apart Akora three thousand years before. He needed to get out to them, to take more measurements, to discover — he hoped — that he was wrong.

The islands seemed to call to him, one of them in particular — Deimatos, whose name signified a place of fear.

He had never been there. No one went, although there were ample stories about the island. In recent months, it had grown in his mind into an object of fascination, appearing even in his dreams as though something — someone? — called to him. He would go there soon, though, and he would find . . .

. . . moonlight gleaming on the beach as it always did on such nights when her loneliness seemed to swell inside her. She should be used to it by now, she who lived apart by choice and by necessity. But not for much longer. Soon she would have to go across the ribbon of the moon road to the city she shunned, to tell the people she feared what she knew.

The thought filled her with dread and yet there was something more, a strange sense of being drawn toward a destiny she could not glimpse. She stood, slim and tall, her bare toes curling into the gently lapping waves, and looked across the dark sea. For just a moment, inexplicably, it seemed as though her gaze brushed another's. The sensation was gone the instant she looked away, but the memory of it lingered, a disturbance of her solitude.

And a promise.

# About the Author

Josie Litton lives in New England with her husband, children, and menagerie . . . mostly. Her imagination may find her in nineteenth-century London or ninth-century Norway or who knows where next. She is happily at work on a new trilogy and loves to hear from readers.

Visit Josie at www.josielitton.com.